Family Fun

ALSO BY DAVID OLLIER WEBER

FICTION

Vanity

Baja

Catch/Release

My Life in

Sports CHUN

Bad Trips: Stories

Still Life with Colostomy (Book One) Not Me

Still Life with Colostomy (Book Two) Yes, You

The Crocodiles of Chibembe: A Natural History

NONFICTION

Oakland: Hub of the West

Accustomed to Hope: The Episcopal Church on the Mendocino Coast

Family Fun

Stories

David Ollier Weber

Kila Springs Press is an imprint of the Kila Springs Group, Placerville, CA.
E-mail: press@kilasprings.net

"California Standard" first appeared in *The Antioch Review* (Winter 1977).

Second Edition

ISBN-13: 978-0-9716481-3-5
ISBN-10: 0-9716481-3-1
Library of Congress Control Number: 2005911218

For Peter and Erec-Michael

Contents

Boy with Dog

M ark?"
His mother had gone straight upstairs.
Now her voice seeped down to him. "Has
Peppy been outside yet?"
Mark slouched in the big armchair in the family
room across from the TV set, the chair that used to be
his Dad's in the evenings. His backpack lay unzipped
on the rug under his outstretched right leg. A
schoolbook was splayed open on top of the lined
paper in his three-ring binder, with a stick ballpoint
carelessly slotted in its gutter. He was watching a
cartoon.

"Mark?" she called again.

He became aware of her footsteps thumping from
the bathroom across the bridge toward the top
landing.

His eyes flickered reflexively from the screen
in search of the little dog. Which wasn't on the
frayed old sofa pillow his mother had given it to
nest on, between the end-table next to the hide-a-
bed couch and the corner. Pepe had been there
when he'd come in, Mark thought.

"I don't know," he replied.

"Well if you didn't take him out, who would've?"

"I don't know," he said. He wished she'd be
quiet.

"Would you do it now, please? I'd appreciate
it. He needs a walk."

"Okay," Mark muttered.

"Mark? You hear me?"

"Yes, Mother!" he roused himself to yell louder.

"What are you doing?"

"Homework," he answered, which was categorically
true.

"You have the TV going?"

"Mm-hm," he acknowledged, dutifully humming up-register, in his sinuses, though not necessarily with enough force to carry to her.

"Well turn it off," she commanded. "If you can watch TV, you can give Peppy his walkies."

"Okay," he repeated.

He was trying not to let her intrusive voice distract him from hearing details of the plot the evil scientist was describing to his thuggish minions in the underground control room.

"Mark!"

"I said 'All right,' Mother."

Her footsteps receded toward her bedroom. He heard the door close.

The crew of fresh-faced young crime-fighters with their callow voices and limpid, enormous Japanese-style Caucasian eyes were parceling out assignments to deal with the widespread depredations visited upon the world by the criminal genius when his mother's footfalls again purposefully thudded overhead. He tensed. He'd watched through the cereal commercials. He knew there'd be at least one more break before the episode climaxed. He'd seen it already.

Her bedroom door creaked open. "Mark!" his mother called.

"I am! Just a minute!" he implored.

"It's gonna be dark before long."

"No it's not. I just want to finish this one thing, okay?"

"I told you to turn it off."

"I know. I'm going to."

"Do it now."

"Just till this one's over? It won't be long."

With all the conversation, he was having a hard time concentrating on the cartoon dialogue. He'd turned the sound low as soon as he'd heard her key scritch in the cylinder in the front door. He scooted his rump forward and wormed sideways, patting for the remote on the rug under his knee. It came to hand immediately. He aimed from the hip, as it were, up and under without sighting. Skillfully he tapped the volume-plus button twice with the pad of his forefinger.

"There's at least twenty minutes to go," his mother was objecting.

"No there's not. It's almost over," he countered.

"Things end on the hour," she noted. "Or the half-hour."

He wondered incuriously what time it was.

"Not these ones," he argued.

"It doesn't matter. I want you to turn it off right this minute and give Peppy his walkies. I'm tired of yelling at you from upstairs. You need to do something more yourself than just plop in front of the TV all the time."

"I had soccer practice!" he pointed out.

"Good. Nevertheless. Come on, Mark."

Now his mother was pleading. Trying to make him see reason with her. He hated that. It was so bogus. So weak.

He sighed in annoyance, planted his cross-trainer soles, braced his knees and, using his head and the muscles in his neck, shoved himself forward until his butt-weight could tip him off the edge of the chair cushion. He folded at the waist and dropped heavily onto the plaited rug. Still eyeing the screen, he slammed the heel of his palm down where the remote should be. The off button was among those he mashed.

The stupid little heroes were sucked into a black hole.

He rolled sideways across his lumpy backpack and books and, once free of the chair, kept his elbows tucked and unjackknifed into another full revolution across the rug and onto the wood floor before scrambling upright. Embracing disorientation, he lurched forward a couple of steps and lowered his left shoulder into the jamb of the hallway portico. He let the impact spin him counterclockwise, like a running back who's just taken a glancing hit. He staggered backwards— "Lift those knees! Keep 'em workin'! Drive, drive!" his Dad used to exhort when they played mock tackle football in the park, a huge arm around his stomach, a massive hand grasping at his hip, his Dad waltzing spraddle-legged behind him, laughing, pretending to be trying to drag him down but actually helping him struggle forward for another five or six yards before they tumbled together onto the slippery, pungent grass.

Already Mark wore a size-ten shoe; he had every confidence he was going to add pounds and inches to catch up with his feet during the coming summer. His Dad was tall and muscular. Therefore, Mark knew, he would be too. Next year he planned to go out for freshman football.

Exercising his peripheral vision, Mark gauged the distance to the far wall so that he could flatten his shoulderblades against it before he pitched too far off balance. He let it brace him to a jarring halt. The plaster reverberated satisfyingly. The ceiling light jangled on its chain and the key rings and sunglasses and ceramic knick-knacks lining the narrow shelves of the hall table leaped and chattered.

"Mark!" his mother howled distantly. "What in the world! Stop that!"

"Sorry," he called, grinning.

"I've told you! No jumping! You're gonna bring the house down!"

"I'm not jumping."

"What are you doing?"

"I stood up too fast," he explained. "I got dizzy. I banged into the wall."

Maybe, he realized, she'd take a hint that it was her fault, that if she hadn't asked him to take the dumb dog for a walk he wouldn't have suffered this potentially grave semi-blackout. Which was what it had been, more or less. He could have hurt himself. Broken an arm, got a concussion. He was lucky to have escaped unscathed. Although his collarbone was a little sore. Maybe she'd appreciate better the effort he was putting out. His obedient, conscientious sacrifice.

"You're okay?" she called. She didn't sound unduly anxious.

"Yeah, I'm okay," he allowed stoically.

"You didn't knock anything over, did you? You didn't break anything."

"No."

"Better not have. Listen, I'm just going to lie down for a minute. Then I'll start dinner. Okay? So go take Peppy while there's still time."

"I'm going now," he called.

"Thank you."

He pushed off from the wall and headed for

the kitchen. "

"Peepee. Peepee le Pew!" he announced in a teasing singsong. "Ready for your walk, boy?"

As he'd anticipated, the dog crouched far back under the table in the breakfast alcove, between the rear legs and the baseboard. Its muzzle rested on its out-thrust forepaws. Its beady onyx eyes were fixed on Mark, but from askance. Pepe had not deigned to stir at his approach.

"Come on, boy," Mark said. He stepped forward so the heavy swinging door could flap shut behind him. He stooped and clapped his hands in front of his knees three times.

"Come on," he urged the dog in the high, mincing voice of invitation. "Let's go. Don't you want your walkies, buddy? Walkies!"

He gave the word a cheery, enthusiastic emphasis on the assumption that Pepe recognized it. And somewhere in that walnut-sized canine brain still associated it with pleasurable activity.

His grandmother always conversed with the little dog in babytalk; his mother had accommodatingly followed suit. After some initial discomfort, Mark had absorbed the vocabulary too.

Abuelita Jeanne lived down south in an old, pink, funny-smelling Spanish-style house surrounded by a garden thick with flowers and citrus trees on a steep curvy street lined with others just like it below the Griffith Park Observatory. They used to stay there every so often when he was a small child—Mark, his mother and father, and his sister Paige, who was away now in her first year at Bryn Mawr.

His grandmother had had another toy poodle then, M'sieu Maurice. He'd overheard his Dad telling his mother one day that he was embarrassed to be seen within a hundred yards of the poufed and ribboned and perfumed Maurice. And it was his Dad who'd first affixed the obvious nickname "Le Pew" to the successor poodle – though not in Abuelita Jeanne's presence.

(He'd also heard his Dad scoff at her insistence the children use her first name, jarringly paired with a pretentious tongue-twister, he said, from a language she could barely speak except for a few words she'd learned from maids and gardeners. Less ill at ease with the age implications, his father's own mother had settled for "Grandma.")

Pepe's full name, his formal name, was "M'sieu Pépé le Moko du Casbah d'Algiers." Abuelita Jeanne reminded them of that each time she brought him. She always used French pronunciations: "Pay-pay" and "Ahlzhay." She said it came from a movie with Sharl Bwahyay or somebody, that his grandfather Dick, whom Mark couldn't remember having met, had worked on when he was just starting out at United Artists. He'd been a studio sound technician. He'd known all the stars. (Hardly any of whose names meant anything to Mark when she recited them.) He'd died of a heart attack when Mark was still a toddler.

Abuelita Jeanne was a travel agent now in West Hollywood. This was the second time she'd left Pepe with them while she went away on a fam trip; her maid, Consuela, was taking the opportunity to go home to Culiacán for a visit. Abuelita Jeanne had driven up to deliver Pepe in her seven-year-old Lincoln Town Car. (His Dad said it had the style and handling of an oil tanker.) She left it parked in their driveway while she flew out of SFO to connect with a cruise through the Greek Isles. ("'Isles,' his father repeated sarcastically on the telephone. "Is that spelled A-I-S-L-E-S?" Mark thought it was hilarious because he got it immediately. His mother had only made a face, however, when Mark quoted the joke.) Pepe had been with them for almost two weeks. Mark wasn't exactly sure how much longer the dog was supposed to be staying.

"Walkies!" Mark said again, more sternly.

It was pretty obvious the word offered no excitements to Pepe.

Mark strode to the table and hunkered. Pepe eyed him inscrutably. There were times when Pepe was lively and fun, but he seemed a lot more subdued on this visit. Mark dated the change in attitude to the time stupid Paige had slammed the car door on his paw.

It happened the first time they'd dogsat. He and Paige had just come back from the mall. They'd taken Pepe along for the ride but left him to hurl himself from window to window in the back seat yapping territorially at passersby and dogs in other cars in the parking lot while they were inside trying on cleats. Paige played soccer too. She was a sweeper.

On the way home Mark had been ragging on her about how many more goals he scored and how much better a driver he was going to be when he got his own license. In the driveway she'd snapped some parting four-letter advice – Paige had a hilariously filthy mouth – and slid her fat ass out from behind the wheel. She gave the door a backwards kick, like a mule.

Unfortunately, Pepe had scampered through the gap between the two bucket seats, over the center console, impatiently bounding for the momentary opening rather than waiting for Mark to quit cackling and uncoil himself on the passenger side. There was a sudden piercing shriek. Paige whirled. Mark jerked upright in his seatbelt and recognized that the dog's left paw was vised in the jamb. (Just as his own thumb had once been when he was very little.) He fumbled for the belt release and shrugged himself out of the harness.

"Jeez! You caught his leg!" Mark yelled accusingly, craning for the door lever.

Pepe bucked and bleated piteously. When Mark's hand neared, Pepe bit at it. Mark flinched away. Paige's guilt-stricken face loomed in the window; she jerked the door open. Pepe spilled to the ground and scuttled on his three good legs underneath the car, mewling in fear and fury and pain, to cower in the safe lee of the left rear tire.

It took them about ten minutes to extricate him. Mark had to wriggle on his belly, coo blandishments, feint cautiously as Pepe snarled and snapped. Paige scrambled back and forth on her knees and elbows on the other side to distract the terrified dog and head off his hobbled attempts at escape.

Finally Mark succeeded in grabbing Pepe's rhinestone-studded collar at the scruff. Inching backwards, he hauled Pepe gawping and screaming along with him, out from under the differential housing and into the open. He pinned the writhing dog's head and tufted body to the gravel so they could examine his bloody paw. Paige moaned apologies. Pepe showed the whites of his eyes. Mark wrapped the mangled paw in the tail of his shirt while Paige sprinted into the house. Then he warily cradled the quivering dog on his lap and stroked and comforted him while Paige ran stop signs to the pet hospital she'd looked up in the phone book.

Pepe was still peg-legging around forlornly in his cast when Abuelita Jeanne returned. Paige shouldered responsibility for the inexcusable carelessness and its consequences. Abuelita Jeanne somberly excused her. Mark made it clear in his accounts that he'd been no more than a horrified witness and alacritous emergency medical technician.

Pepe, meanwhile, slunk out of rooms soon after Mark entered and cringed whenever Mark stretched out a hand to pet him. Since Mark had been the closest human being and had tormented him in his misery – never mind out of solicitude – the dog seemed to blame Mark, to regard him, not Paige, as the agent of his trauma.

But a year had passed. Pepe's leg and paw were fully healed. And he hadn't bolted or growled at Mark when they'd been reintroduced. Still, their relationship was no longer uncomplicated. When his mother came home tired from work, which was usually, Mark clipped the matching jewel-studded pink leather leash to Pepe's collar and led him from bush to bush in one or another direction along their block so Pepe could sniff disdainfully and squat every so often to piddle like a bitch. (It was great, Mark thought, that you could say that word with impunity whenever you were talking about dogs. Not so Paige.)

Mark carried a clear plastic produce bag stuffed in his pocket. He'd learned to slide it over his hand like a glove to pinch Pepe's mushy poops up off the sidewalk or the neighbors' grass if he thought anybody might be watching. Then, nose wrinkled (at first he'd gagged), he would gingerly turn the bag inside out to create a nasty parcel he'd have to dangle all the way home unless he found somebody's garbage can accessible enough to ditch it in. An added embarrassment. As if the company of the effeminate mini-dog on the pink leash weren't bad enough. Fortunately, none of the friends who might make him exert his dignity perversely defending Pepe if they spotted him carrying the little dog's shit lived in the immediate vicinity.

Then there was feeding. With Paige gone, Mark was not only the primary walker, he had to dial the lids off cans and spoon the gelatinous brown glop into Pepe's flowered dish twice a day according to Abuelita Jeanne's instructions. ("I have to buy the stuff," his mother explained the division of responsibilities. "And of course dry food isn't good enough for him. You don't suppose she called him 'Pay-pay' for nothing.")

Pepe was developing the same weight problem that had contributed to Maurice's premature passing. (Abuelita Jeanne always said Maurice and Grandfather Dick had "passed away." His mother's word was "died." He'd overheard his Dad greet the news of Maurice's demise thus: "poor little dipshit croaked, huh?") It was necessary to save Pepe from his gluttonous instincts, Abuelita Jeanne said. She herself was too soft-hearted to be consistent at it, she admitted. But Mark could be counted on. And he suspected Pepe resented *him* for that too.

It was Mark, after all, who doled out the insufficient portions. It was Mark who was oblivious to canine hypnotism – the steady stare aimed to induce by force of telepathic suggestion, it would seem, a second helping – and unmoved by Pepe's fallback tactic, poodle coquetry.

At Mark's least twitch once the meal had been gulped down Pepe would pop up off his powder-puff haunches, tilt his saucy topknot expectantly, curl his pink lips into a grin, unfurl his tiny, slavering pink tongue, give the pompom on his stubby tail a couple of shakes while shuffling his anklets... only to find the terpsichore wasted. Even when Pepe pointedly nuzzled his empty dish back and forth across the varnished red Mexican clay pavers Mark remained bowed over the comics or the sports page or the crossword puzzle, which he labored at because his Dad liked them. (The much harder Sunday ones that Mark found completely opaque.)

So until harried out for yet another forced march to void bowels and bladder – you'd think he'd be anxious for it – Pepe now spent most of his time napping away his exile sentence or, when it was too much effort to leave the room, balefully keeping watch on the mean-spirited and potentially vicious warder into whose custody ill luck had remanded him.

Anyway, that's what Mark sensed – in all those nuances if not in precisely those terms. He wasn't surprised at Pepe's present reluctance. "Hey! You hear me? Walk time! Pee-pee time, huh? Peepee Le Pew? I'm talkin' to you!"

The rhyme had been inadvertent the first time he'd recognized it. Now that sequence was a part of his standard I-mean-business repertoire. Calling Pepe "Peepee" was another inspiration that had been Mark's own, as obvious and irresistible as "Le Pew" had been to his Dad. (Of course, he and Paige had seen the cartoon skunk on television many times too and surely would have come to it themselves.)

Pepe was not amused. He answered to Peepee readily enough when food might be involved. But he was perfectly well aware of the difference between "walkies" and "din-din." He was contemplating Mark with a sulky expression that was the equivalent of Mark's slack resistance when his mother had been badgering him. Having rustled his own bootie, Mark wasn't sympathetic.

He reached his hands forward under the table to get them nearer Pepe's muzzle – not all that near, three or four feet – and brought his cupped palms together as sharply as he could.

At the sudden noise in the relatively confined space, Pepe heaved up onto his braceleted forelegs as if he'd been jerked off the floor at the shoulders by a puppetmaster's strings. His claws scritched on the clay tile as he scrabbled sideways to press his woolly shoulder into the wall.

"Oh, come on," Mark chided apologetically. He patty-caked his outstretched fingertips softly to mitigate the previous clap, which had been a good one, right up there at the top of his decibel-production capability. "Don't be a scaredy-cat. You can handle it. You're a big brave boy. Anyway, you brought it on yourself. You gotta come when I say."

Pepe regarded him mistrustfully.

"What's the matter? We're goin' for a walk, that's all. You can pee and poop. Won't that feel nice? Walkies! You're a *good* boy! I'm not mad at you."

Pepe was trembling dramatically.

Mark splayed his fingers alongside his toes for support and kicked out of his squat onto his knees. Now he was down on all fours like a dog himself. He thrust his head under the tabletop, chin jutted, beetled his brow and scowled deep into Pepe's eyes. Paige always said dogs don't like that. Pepe quickly turned in profile, as if some motion in the corner had just caught his attention.

Mark considered him for a moment as he awaited compliance. Pepe hadn't been to a groomer since at least as long as he'd been at their house, and probably not for a couple of weeks before that. The variant of the "Continental" clip Abuelita Jeanne kept him in was no longer symmetrical. His frizzy crest had loosened and flattened on one side; it seemed slightly wobbly and off kilter. His mane and chest had grown out too; they were kind of squashed down in places, like a slept-in permanent. Where his coat had been buzzed to the porcine skin – along the muzzle below the eyes, the underjaw, the whole midsection, his haunches, the base of his tail, his legs and toes – fuzz had now sprouted.

Mark had tried using the wire-brush Abuelita Jeanne had provided among Pepe's supplies, but Pepe had quavered and yipped and squirmed as if it were another assault. That had only made matters worse in the shape department. Carpet lint, crumbs, twigs and leaf fragments from the curbside planter strips had worked their way here and there into Pepe's curls.

Abuelita Jeanne described his color as "champagne." Without benefit of shampoo and a blow-drier it had darkened, the way unwashed hair does. From walks in the outside world and flops on the floor Pepe had acquired a dingier, greasier tinge. The tips of the squared-off feathering that hung from his droopy ears had congealed in dark points, like a bunch of little water-color brushes. One loop of the red bow behind his right ear had come untied. Not that he looked totally bedraggled or gross from neglect. Just lived-in. More like an everyday dog – although there was still a long way to go with all the weird puffs and ruffles.

Because Pepe was a toy, he had that dwarf disproportionality – the foreshortened snout, the popeyes – that had made the corpulent Maurice's haughty airs so hard for his Dad to stomach.

Toy poodles could never aspire to anything more than a puppy cuteness, Mark had decided. That was after he'd met a standard poodle. He'd been amazed at the contrast. It was about the most elegant dog Mark had ever seen – loose-limbed and self-assured like a warrior king, not petulant like a spoiled baby princeling. Of course, that animal had been tall and rangy and tweedy-black, like one of those Persian caps – sensibly clad, in what Abuelita Jeanne identified when he described it as a "sporting" clip. Another revelation: that poodles could be allowed to wear a more or less ordinary coat. The bare paws and long snout even looked aristocratic and athletic, like Scottie Pippin.

Mark asked her hopefully why she didn't groom Pepe that way. She said it wouldn't fit his personality.

Mark didn't know all that much about breeds. His friend Damian's dog Sam was a golden retriever, burly and friendly and slow, with rheumy eyes and lank orange fur that stank like sweatsocks. It waddled after Frisbees and tennis balls and brought them back all covered with slimy slobber. Sam couldn't catch them until they'd basically rolled to rest, though. On TV Mark had seen wiry little leapers – terriers or something, he thought, make amazingly acrobatic Frisbee snatches twisting high in mid-air. A dog like that would be fun.

Mark had tested Pepe before Paige had messed up his leg. Pepe disdained balls. Well, he would dodge and snarfle in mock rage at the soccer ball Mark and Paige sometimes instepped back and forth slowly with Pepe in the middle, until the little poodle got bored and irked for real. Before he got his cast, Pepe had trotted alongside them when they'd jazzed up his walks by jogging around the baseball field. Mark had to concede he probably wasn't playing with Pepe enough anymore. Part of the problem was that Pepe always had to be on the leash. Ever since the incident with the sled dog.

It had happened on the afternoon of Pepe's arrival this time. Mark had taken him into the park and let him loose to reacquaint himself with the surroundings. Pepe had just finished wizzing on a clump of juniper when a large husky loped up behind them to parse the aromas.

Perhaps the strange dog had trespassed into some megalomaniacally extended field of what Pepe considered his personal space. Maybe Pepe had become proprietary about his precious bodily fluids. Whatever, the diminutive poodle suddenly veered from Mark's ankles to hurtle back at the huge husky with berserk vengeance.

The sled dog looked up and cocked its handsome black-and-white face quizzically, bemusement in the deadly blue wolfish eyes, as if it wasn't quite sure what species this tiny, bizarrely tufted kamikaze was. Certainly not its own. A rabid mongoose? A Tasmanian devil?

Pepe skidded to halt before the unmoving object of his wrath, still gnarring and slavering truculently. The bigger dog lifted a forepaw and calmly tromped Pepe into the dirt.

Almost daintily, but with lips peeled back menacingly from its long side fangs, the husky lowered its nose and toed Pepe onto his back, supine like a capsized beetle – or maybe Pepe, dumfounded into contrition and a recognition that discretion was the better part of valor, was petitioning for mercy.

Mark was sure he was about to watch Abuelita Jeanne's beloved pet disappear in one gulp down the lupine maw. But just then a woman's voice shouted urgently "Kolyma! Heel!"

The husky hopped sideways, releasing Pepe, and blithely galloped off to her.

Mark, heart pounding, scooped up Pepe before he could act on his abruptly rekindled belligerence. Pepe was scolded the departing antagonist as if he'd taught it a lesson it had damn well better never forget.

The woman ran to the husky and snapped a leash on its collar. Then she hastened over to make sure Pepe was okay.

"He started it," Mark acknowledged ruefully.

"Kolyma's pretty mellow," she said. "I'm amazed, though, that he actually came to me that way. It's like the first time. Siberians aren't the most obedient dogs in the world."

Firmly restrained in the crook of Mark's arm, Pepe was continuing to belabor the husky, who no longer displayed the least interest. It had its nose shoved into an old gopher hole.

"Your guy's a little scrapper, isn't he?" the woman smiled.

"He's a wimp," Mark muttered.

From then on he kept Pepe tethered whenever they were outside.

Pressed against the wall, Pepe was still shivering in misery. Actually, he shivered quite a lot. It was colder up here than in L.A. And Abuelita Jeanne explained that he was "high-strung." Alternatively she termed it "sensitive."

When Pepe ventured another glance, Mark said to him, in a not unkindly tone, "Woof."

Pepe averted his eyes. He seemed offended. Abuelita Jeanne always said that he didn't consider himself a dog.

"This is your last chance," Mark added. "You don't want to make me have to crawl back in there and get you."

Pepe rose off his haunches. He shook himself. Then he paced in a tight clockwise circle, sniffing the floor where he'd lain before plumping down again.

It occurred to Mark that whatever suspicions or misgivings Pepe might be harboring would have been quelled, perhaps, if he'd seen the leash. An earnest of intent.

Mark rocked back onto the balls of his feet, humped his back and ducked out from under the table. But he misjudged slightly. The back of his head clacked against the table-edge as he bounced erect.

"Owwww!" he bawled at full lung, more in protest at the surprise and the insult than the mild pain. He winced and rubbed his scalp. He'd knocked the table askew and frightened Pepe up *en pointe*. Mark couldn't feel any damage. No blood came away on his fingertips. Not that he'd expected any, of course. He'd been spared martyrdom once again.

Peevishly he joggled the table back square with the wall. Then he wheeled and banged out through the door into the hall.

"Pepe doesn't want to go for a walk!" he bellowed.

There was no response. He pictured his mother supine on her quilted bedspread, a pillow over her eyes. Stockinged toes splayed. He regretted having disturbed the twilit peace.

"Mark, he needs to," her voice drifted down to him, muffled and plaintive. "Otherwise we'll have an accident later. Go on, honey, do it. Convince him. I have a headache. Can I have a little quiet for just a few minutes?"

He figured no answer would be the best acknowledgment. He walked to the coat-pegs by the front door and grabbed the leash. He returned to the kitchen. He pulled open the second drawer down, directly to the left of the sink, and separated out a crumpled produce bag. He stuffed it into his back pocket. He went to the table, hunkered, patted his thigh with his left hand and dandled the leash ostentatiously in his right. "C'mon, Peepee. No more futzing around. Walk-time. Okay? Poopootime? Let's get it over with."

Pepe had repositioned himself in the corner of the dining alcove behind the legs of the rearmost chair. The light coming in through the kitchen windows was fading fast. Their back yard faced east. They'd lived here since Mark was in the second grade. Now that his mother and Dad were divorced, and Paige was going to be away most of the year in college, his mother was talking about selling the place and getting something smaller.

Mark didn't want to think about it. His mother told him his Dad was being nice by letting them keep the house, but that he really needed the money. He had the right to "half the equity," she explained. She believed kids should be fully informed about these important matters, she said. His Dad was living in Seattle, now, on a houseboat, with his new girlfriend. Mark called her by her first name, Karen. She was okay. They'd curtained off a corner of the loft for him for when he came up to stay with them, in the summer, and for part of Christmas vacation. He might have gone during spring break too if he hadn't been coaxed to stay and take care of Pepe.

He'd accompanied his Dad to a bunch of Mariners games – he'd gotten a baseball with the team's autographs. He'd seen the Seahawks and Sonics play. They'd gone skiing at Snoqualmie once. And to the top of the Space Needle. Seattle was pretty boring, though. He had a bunkbed, and you got rocked to sleep at night, and gulls squawked you awake in the morning, and there was a great view across the water to the mountains when it wasn't raining and misty. So that was cool enough. Although he preferred it here. Unless his mother was freaked, or was on his case. Now that Paige wasn't around, her attention was undivided.

Pepe's oval eyes glittered in the gloom. He looked like some ancestral predator hiding in a thicket. His bushy overhanging brow gave a tentative cast to his expression, though: he seemed less predatory than nervously calculating. Carefully gauging the limits of defiance. Poodles are very intelligent, Abuelita Jeanne was fond of reminding them.

"You are being... a very... bad... doggy," Mark told him. He riveted his eyes on Pepe's while enunciating each word for maximum comprehension. " A *bad* doggy! You know that?"

Pepe didn't avoid the stare this time. He shuffled his extended forepaws as if he were about to haul himself upright. But he didn't. He opened his mouth wide and began ostentatiously panting.

"Aren't I too cute for words?" Mark read the ploy. An attempt at distraction. Pepe was manipulative, no doubt about it. Abuelita Jeanne said that. And, she added indulgently, he was used to getting his way.

But this was Mark he was dealing with. Mark's patience had run out.

"Sorry, buddy," he declared. "You're in trouble now. I warned you."

Leash in hand, he dived forward onto his hands and knees. Pepe, startled, scrambled up into a sit.

Mark crept toward the front table legs. He threaded between them. He moved deliberately, for ominous effect.

"Doom. Doom. Doom. Doom," he taunted in a voice as deep in his chest as he could get it, alternating high and low notes, like drumbeats, to mark the progress of each knee.

When he was close enough Mark lifted his left hand and crooked his fingers into a claw. Pepe focused on it uneasily. Mark thought of how a cobra sways, which he'd seen recently on one of those nature channels. He imitated the inverted pendulum motion with his forearm. He watched Pepe's eyes track the slow arc of his palm and talons.

When Paige had come home for Christmas she'd produced, to Mark's delight, a surprise companion out of the pocket of her long woolen coat: a gopher snake. She'd bought it and smuggled it into her dorm room, she confided to Mark, to keep as a clandestine pet. Because pets were forbidden.

They found a deep cardboard box from the basement for Gofy, and got some dirt and sticks from the yard for it to hide under, and put it next to the register so the stick-side would be warm. The snake's presence in Paige's room remained secret from their mother too until it disappeared the day after New Year's. (Explanation of their urgent ransacking of the whole upstairs could not be avoided, especially when the search proved fruitless. Imagine their mother coming face-to-face with Gofy unwarned. Luckily it turned up at the bottom of a clothes hamper when Paige finally did her washing to return to school.)

Mark had helped her feed Gofy white mice.

Wincing, he'd drop them by their scaly pink tails into the box, and they'd scamper around – and then go into this same sort of trance at the instant they realized a lethal lifeform was coiled in front of them. Gracile forked tongue flicking, the reptile would range in on the rodent's body heat and scent; the mouse would freeze in its explorations, pink nose twitching, beady eyes bulging in instinctive dismay....

Like the snake, Mark struck.

Pepe yelped and spun up onto his hind legs, but Mark's hand came in at him too fast to dodge. Mark snared Pepe under the chin, just above the collar. The poodle's sheared throat in the fork of his grip, he clamped his fingertips into the curly fleece along the sides of Pepe's neck. He shoved the little dog into the corner, upright against the walls, and improved his chokehold.

"Hghaahgh!" Mark barked in triumph.

His upper teeth were exposed in a grimace. The feral gurgle was produced by the grate of his tongue and his uvula in the back of his throat and the thin surge of saliva between his parted molars. It came naturally. He felt like a panther that had pounced on its prey. He wanted Pepe to share the experience.

Pepe jittered in panic on his hind legs. Extended this way, they resembled the drumsticks and thighs that dangled from a chicken when his mother rinsed one under the tap. The viscid pink nib of Pepe's penis poked out of its stubby sheath, then retracted, but not completely. It was a horrible-looking thing. It made Mark angry at the dog, to be indulging such a disgusting fright reaction. Mark didn't want to be distracted. He didn't want to be reminded at this moment of his own penis... of sex, of erections, of vaginas, of how the scenes in movies and the concept of intercourse went together with the girls he knew, of wet dreams and experimental whacking off, of when he would start to grow hair down there like his Dad, like most of his schoolmates and teammates already had, of what his Dad and Karen – whose pleasing face and lush body disturbed Mark's imagination – were doing when he heard her gasps in the darkness from their bedroom....

Pepe couldn't have sex with that ugly thing, though. Or want to, or whatever. No impulse to "mount" bitches. He had no balls. Abuelita Jeanne had had them snipped off. She called it "fixed." Male dogs are a lot calmer that way, she explained. Which was why Pepe was such a sissy, Mark thought.

"Sissy!" he sneered. "You're a wimp-dog! You haven't got any balls! You think you can escape the lightning-quick claw of death? Of a superior being like me? Hah! Next time you better learn to listen when I tell you to do something. I'm your master!"

Pepe had stopped writhing. Head back, Mark's hand gripping his windpipe, Pepe goggled around his upwrenched snout. His jaws were ajar, the weirdly corrugated roof of his mouth, like a Klingon's forehead, visible behind his miniature fangs. They were pearly white above pink gums thanks to Abuelita Jeanne's veterinary care. Pepe's tongue licked out to moisten his lips as if in sudden and desperate thirst.

"Don't worry. I'm not gonna hurt you," Mark said. "I'm just teaching you a lesson. You gotta do what I say. Otherwise it means you'll be punished."

He began backing out from under the table. It was awkward, what with trying to maintain a grasp on Pepe's wattles. When the dog's underlying muscles contracted Mark ended up with flesh and fur bunched in his fist. He managed to hook his ring and little fingers under Pepe's collar too. He was plenty strong enough to keep the flyweight poodle up stilt-walking on his hind legs. There had to be just enough pressure so Pepe's back wouldn't buckle but not so little he'd give up and try to tuck inward around Mark's forearm. As soon as the unwilling dog staggered forward and planted his paws underneath his bodyweight, Mark used him as a crutch to reposition his off hand.

Pepe squalled shrilly. You'd think he were being tortured. Mark had a twinge of worry that his mother was going to hear the ruckus and come down to see what was going on. Pepe had started pawing frenetically at the air and at Mark's wrist, exposed below the cuff of his 49ers sweatshirt. Regular walks on pavement had blunted Pepe's tiny nails, but even flattened they hurt like hell when the ragged edges rasped skin.

"Hey! Ow! Stop it! Ouch! Stop it!" Mark demanded.

He gave Pepe a couple of brisk shakes, to parry and discourage him, the way you'd fling a spider or bee off the back of your hand the instant it stung. Except that Mark wasn't letting go. And it only caused Pepe to punch and scratch at Mark's welted wrist more frenetically.

"Damn! You little creep! You creep-o!"

He wrenched Pepe down onto his ribs on the tile floor. He was mindful not to apply such force that Pepe might crack his skull. Mark rocked his shoulder forward and leaned onto his arm to make sure Pepe stayed down. Air wheezed out of the poodle's chest.

"Remember how I had to drag you out from under the car when you hurt your leg?" Mark rebuked him. "Well, I've been trying to be nicer to you this time. Let you walk out like a man."

The phrase, the concept, had popped into his head, and he snickered at his cleverness. He wasn't really being nice, of course. Since Pepe was obviously a dog, not a man. Although Pepe wasn't supposedly all that clear on the distinction. Abuelita Jeanne herself liked to coax Pepe into doing a quick lurch across a rug on his hind legs in pursuit of a treat every now and then. Pepe would rear up, totter and twirl, proudly smirking, just as pleased with himself as was his owner.

"Mommy's little mannikin," Abuelita Jeanne would simper approvingly. "Such a good walker!" And she'd let him gobble down the proffered "doggy-candy. Mmm! Yummy-yummy!"

So how bad was it, Mark reasoned, that he'd tried to frog-march the disobedient Pepe out from under the table? Pepe was only mad because it wasn't his own idea. He always wanted everything to happen on his terms. And things in life don't go that way. Even at 13, maybe especially at 13, you can figure that one out. Pepe needed to learn about real life.

Pepe lay momentarily submissive. But rigid –

neck twisted to keep his head off the floor, one haunch cocked to protect against a blow to the genitals, one forepaw tensed and lifted toward Mark obsequiously. The corners of his mouth were pulled back to his cheeks. His lips were slightly parted and his row-teeth were clenched beneath. He breathed in soft, irregular snorts, a liquid film of snot bubbling in his flat pinkish nostrils. His eyes – well, only one was visible – were fixed on the middle distance, as if incoming danger could best be spied peripherally.

"Look at me!" Mark said.

He bent lower and rocked his head back and forth, trying to intrude on Pepe's line of sight, trying unsuccessfully to get Pepe's pupil to flick to his.

"What do you think?" That I'm gonna hit you? I'm not gonna hit you!"

Pepe winced at the stressed words. But he resolutely declined to meet Mark's gaze. From above Mark could see the translucence of Pepe's curved lens, like a glass marble; the iris and dilated pupil were flat disks under the aqueous bowl. That was pretty fascinating. The way the tuft of Pepe's eyebrow bulged you could tell his forehead was knitted in worry or something. Not enjoying himself.

Dogs have amazingly expressive faces, Mark had come to appreciate. It was easy to read their minds.

Pepe's exaggerated apprehension was really a disappointment, though. True, Mark had just now seized him and handled him a little roughly. But what did the dumb dog expect, when he wouldn't come when bidden, over and over? Mark had been as nice as could be to Pepe for the past two weeks. Never ever had he been mean to the dog. More than that, it was he who'd been the good Samaritan, it was he who'd leaped to Pepe's aid the minute he'd been injured and helped get him to the doctor to have his leg and paw fixed up so that they were as good as new. In thanks for which Pepe treated him as if were some kind of cruel monster.

Mark sighed. "Okay," he relented. "You can get up."

He eased back onto his heels and removed his hand. "See? I'm not such a terrible meanie. Allst I was doing was trying to get you to obey."

M ark whipped the spring-loaded clasp of the leash closer to his right knee and pinched it between his right thumb and forefinger, poised to snap it onto the ring on Pepe's collar as soon as the dog flounced up. Pepe's claws had made raw tracks along the inside of Mark's left wrist. A couple bore tiny beads of capillary blood.

Stupid poodle! Not that it wasn't understandable, even admirable, that Pepe had put up resistance. Feeble as it had been. Mark raised his wrist to his mouth and salved the scratches with his tongue.

Pepe, after a moment's hesitation, lowered his head to the floor. But his ham and his upper foreleg were still on guard, frozen in that truckling pose, as if to relax completely would only reignite Mark's momentarily suspended wrath. There was a certain calculation to the behavior too, Mark suspected. Pepe was now exploiting his victimhood. Pepe wanted Mark to feel guilty. He'd resumed the game of wills.

Mark brought the flat of his hand down sharply

on Pepe's ribs.

Pepe yawped, rebounded like a basketball when you compress it to restart a lost dribble. He shied into the corner again.

"If you act like somebody's gonna do somethin' to you, they will, you doo-doo," Mark explained. "Don't be such a little dick-head. Peepee Le Dickhead. Show some balls, even if you haven't got any."

Pepe stood with his rump jammed against the wall. The pompom on the tip of his tail was hoisted, his shoulders humped, his head forward. His chest heaved and his shanks trembled. He was glaring at Mark now.

Well, in fact, his expression wasn't all that easy to decipher, actually. Mark could impute anger, resentment, indignation. Or maybe resolve – the courage of a trapped rat. Had Pepe finally been pushed to the limit of canine tolerance?

On the other hand, maybe he was just confused. Sometimes you could tell that even Pepe's vaunted poodle brain was lost amid the ambiguities of interspecies communication.

As if "walkies" were a difficult concept.

Mark recalled having read a thing in the paper once about how to test your dog's intelligence. You throw a blanket over it and see how long it takes for the dog to scooch out from under.

More carefully than last time, Mark extricated himself from the overhang of the table. There was a tall antique cabinet against the near wall in whose glass-fronted top shelves his mother kept the good china and in whose bottom drawers were the silverware and table linens. He got out a green tablecloth, a cheap Guatemalan design with white lines and birds with dashed wings woven through it, and roughly fringed ends, and faint oil and wine and candlewax stains that no longer came out in the washing machine. His mother spread it every so often on the kitchen table at dinnertime. He unfolded it while he was standing, then balled it loosely and got down on his knees again and crawled to Pepe.

He wasn't going to be able to see the digital clock on the microwave oven from back under here. He needed Pepe out in the middle of the floor. He shoved the inside rear chair up against its neighbor by one of its scarred wooden legs, to create more clearance. Then he stretched a hem of the tablecloth between his fists and, before the poodle could react, caged him in with his elbows and looped the fabric over Pepe's arched back, slid it down the wall behind his rump and jerked it under his four paws.

Pepe tumbled, yipping as he was netted. Mark snatched together all the loose ends and bunched them tightly. Then he scrambled backwards out from under the table towing the twitching bundle.

"Okay, buddy," he said, "Abuelita Jeanne always says you're this great genius. Let's see."

Mark checked the squared-off green numbers glowing on the microwave panel – 5:52, the colon flashing every second – and relinquished the makeshift neck of the parcel.

Pepe immediately squirted out.

"Whoa!" Mark exclaimed. "Good job!"

Pepe streaked toward the kitchen door but abruptly skidded to a halt to give himself a thorough shaking in relief. The convulsion that rippled through his body from head to rump was so intense it set him tap-dancing, his little toenails scuffing the pavers to the metallic jingle of his collar-tags.

The hesitation allowed Mark to recover a hem of the tablecloth and, with a quick knee-walk and sacrificial headlong dive, parachute it over Pepe once again before he could escape.

Mark landed on his elbows – "ouch!" he objected. Using them as fulcrums, and lifting himself on his toes so he could wrench loose the part of the tablecloth trapped under his thighs and knees, he gathered the drape tight over the thrashing dog-lump. Meanwhile, he lowered his chin and upper chest to force Pepe flat.

When Pepe's legs finally yielded – Pepe yelped in complaint – Mark wormed forward and lay atop him for a few heartbeats until Pepe stopped squirming. Mark eased up. Pepe whimpered and lurched beneath him. Mark let gravity press his chest down hard once more. Finally Pepe quieted under the weight.

Prone, feeling the warmth and the laborious rise and fall of the little ribcage beneath his own, Mark experienced a flush of affection for Pepe. They were like two puppies snuggled together. Sometimes, truth be told, Mark's arm still flopped over drowsily on top of the familiar teddy bear that had sprawled beside his pillow between the wall and the headboard for as long as he could remember. Its fusty smell and worn plush matte of brown fur were a comfort in the night. Too bad Pepe had never wanted to be his sleeping companion. That could have been nice.

Mark pushed up gradually on his elbows. Cautiously he skated his knees forward on the runners of the fabric. Pepe didn't react. When Mark was crouched at arm's-length above the compliant shape he spoke to it softly.

"That was too easy," he explained. He waited to see if his voice would animate Pepe to renewed scuffling. There was no movement. "It wasn't a good test. Probably you *are* a really smart dog. But I didn't have this thing over you all the way, so we've gotta try one more time to really make it official. Okay? Sorry."

Mark rechecked the oven clock. 5:54. He considered the lie of the tablecloth. Its skirts were fairly evenly distributed around Pepe. He gave the swaddled body an open-handed whack and rocked backwards onto his toes – the starting signal. And incentive.

Pepe bleated, floundered up under the tenting, hesitated for a moment, apparently disoriented, then began to weave slowly across the tiles. The tablecloth tracked along with him, of course. It molded his head and withers and rump. You could tell when he lifted his nose and swiveled his neck beneath it in blind confusion. The sight was hilarious.

"Hey, you're a ghost! You're Casper the Friendly Ghost's friendly little dog-ghost companion," Mark teased.

He thought of the silhouette of the elephant swallowed by the python in The Little Prince, which used to be one of his favorite books. Pepe under the tablecloth would form the same hat-shape if you were looking at him from floor-level. From Mark's perspective, a three-quarters angle from above, Pepe was the crown of the fedora in 3-D!

Pepe collided headfirst with the projecting bottom ledge of the antique cabinet.

Mark laughed aloud.

Pepe leaned with his forehead bowed against the unseen obstacle, as if totally stymied, with no other direction in which to move except straight ahead, which was blocked. He was like one of those dumb losers at birthday parties when he was a kid, who used to get so frustrated and humiliated at pin-the-tail-on-the-donkey or smash-the-piñata that they'd simply give up and start blubbering under their blindfolds.

"What's the matter? You *are* stupid, aren't you?" Mark scoffed. "After all!"

He glanced at the clock. It read 5:55. But of course he didn't know how many seconds had elapsed. It could be less than a minute, or it could be more. He should've had a stop-watch, like the one his soccer coach wore on a black shoelace around his neck. Mark could run the forty in five-point-six seconds before his feet started growing; he was still the second-fastest guy on his team. Or third, anyway. By fall he was going to be down to near five-flat, he vowed. That wouldn't be bad for a fourteen-year-old. Someday he'd be able to beat Barry Sanders. Run a four-two or something. Unfortunately, he didn't know what a comparable canine intelligence score was supposed to be, though. Surely quicker than this.

He took a swipe at Pepe's haunch. The shrouded figure skidded sideways, slumping as its legs were batted out from under it.

"Better hurry up, buddy," Mark threatened. "Otherwise the invisible monster's gonna get you!"

The little lump under the tablecloth heaved up and resumed its blind travel, gimping along against the lip of the cupboard. Pepe was still holding his head low. The very contour of the shroud projected woe. Poor Pepe was feeling sorely put upon, Mark recognized. Hey, it occurred to him – that's where the

43

expression "hangdog" must come from.

Pepe had finally begun to rub the tablecloth off. The friction between his shoulder and the cabinet gradually peeled it away. Now he was just wearing a cowl – Pepe looked like some old peasant lady doddering along under a shawl. Or one of those medieval monks, stooped in prayer, his nose and whiskers just beginning to peek out from under the hood. Mark chuckled to himself at the comic resemblances.

Pepe tossed his head, and finally was able to see what was in front of him. He veered to avoid the forest of furniture legs he was about to blunder into.

But the invisible monster still had the advantage. Mark reached out his monster-claws and rained a quick drumbeat of open-palmed pitty-pats on Pepe's spine from above, to encourage him.

Pepe hunched his butt, shrugged his shoulders and scooted free of the tablecloth altogether.

Dutifully, because it was an aspect of the experiment, Mark consulted the microwave: 5:56. For whatever that was worth.

P epe celebrated his release with another fur-fluffing spasm. A halo of particles swirled up off him in the bluish backlight. Pepe was standing three-legged, Mark noticed, his tufted left front paw off the ground, bony elbow bent gingerly.

"Whoa, now what's the matter?" Mark frowned.

Pepe's expression had gone opaque again.

"Let's see," Mark murmured. He crouched forward and beckoned for Pepe's paw.

Pepe hobbled sideways in evasion.

Mark belly-flopped toward the little poodle – his foolproof maneuver – and snagged a front leg before Pepe could find traction to scuttle out of reach.

Pepe tried to tug loose. He squeaked in pain. Mark, down on his stomach, crawled back up onto his hands and knees – being very careful to keep his left forearm planted firmly on the tile, the fist that clamped Pepe's brittle shin immobile so as not to stress the tender limb any more than necessary.

Pepe jerked and whimpered in Mark's grasp nonetheless.

"Relax, relax," Mark soothed him. "I just want to see what's wrong." With his right hand he flexed the froufroued joint above Pepe's stubby toes gently, experimentally....

Pepe whined and began to tremble. He gazed up into Mark's face. He lowered his little rump as if about to sit. Suddenly Mark smelled it.

"Aw... ," Mark groaned, aghast.

He heard the soft sizzle. A pool appeared and spread on the tile, bleeding into and along the grout lines.

"Aw! Darn it all? *Darn* it all! Pee-pee? How could you *do* that? You idiot, ridiculous dog?"

Mark felt betrayed. "That's why I was trying to take you outside!" he complained. "Couldn't you *figure* that?"

Pepe looked up at Mark sadly. As if he'd been unable to contain himself any longer. As if he were ashamed and beseeching forgiveness. But Mark knew any remorse on Pepe's part was feigned. He'd pissed on purpose. Payback.

"Okay," Mark sighed. "Okay, then. You did it... you clean it up!"

Still vising the leg, Mark grabbed a fistful of lank curls between Pepe's shoulderblades with his other hand and flipped Pepe hard onto his side. Pepe shrieked. Angrily Mark scrubbed the little body back and forth across the puddle, using Pepe's mane like the mop it was pruned to resemble. One way that people housebreak puppies, Paige had told him, is by rubbing their faces in their own pee whenever they make a mistake. Another approach is to swat the puppy with a rolled-up newspaper. He knew Abuelita Jeanne would disapprove of either method.

Anyway, Pepe wasn't a puppy. And no question he was trained. That's why Mark had only muttered reproachfully and reeled off paper towels to turn yellow in the mess after Pepe's two previous "accidents" – both of which Mark was willing to accept some blame for. In those cases he'd neglected to take Pepe outside because his mother hadn't asked him to, explicitly. Later, after dinner, she'd questioned him about the suspicious wet patches that glistened next to the kitchen door. From Pepe's general demeanor – keeping himself scarce, wincing and flinching when spoken to – (plus a closeup sniff) they'd determined what the mysterious liquid was.

But this was different. This was rank defiance. This was what his mother called passive aggression.

"There. How do you like it?" Mark snarled as he swabbed the floor with the limp dog. "You like bein' a piss-rag? You like havin' your own smelly pee all sopped up in your precious poodle fur?"

Pepe looked stricken, but after that first yawp he'd gone silent. He didn't cry or snap or thrash.

"You stink! You're a stinker! Now you're *really* Pee-pee Le Pew. Pew-ee! You smell like *piss*, buddy! You smell like a *toilet*. Serves you right. Maybe you'll think twice before you try this trick again!"

Pepe offered no struggle. Like the big husky, Mark had apparently stunned Pepe into abject submission.

"Damn! You are *such* a *wimp!*" Mark said.

He flung his hands away to dramatize his disgust. And as his right arm flew up, he balled his fist.

For an instant he had an impulse to slice it down as hard as he could on the contemptible little animal. Just punch him flush on the snout. Or in the ribs or in the soft underbelly. Punish him for being so runtish. For acting so faggish. As if being a toy poodle were a matter of choice, and a despicable one at that. A failure of will.

But he didn't.

Pepe lay still, cringing in expectation of the blow. At which Mark clenched his knuckles and drew his arm back abruptly again, feigning the launch of a roundhouse just to see Pepe wince.

"I told you not to *do* that!" Mark lectured. "Don't act so *scared* all the time! It only makes people *want* to hurt you."

Pepe blinked fearfully in rhythm with Mark's phrases, like one of those electronic audio-level meters on a really good stereo system. Like his Dad and Karen had.

"Aaaagh...," Mark growled dismissively.

Pepe scrabbled at the air with the paw he'd been favoring, wheedling clemency.

Mark shook his head. "...You're a lost cause," he said. He opened his fist and showed Pepe his spread fingers. "Don't worry. I promised I wouldn't hit you."

He lowered the hand gently toward Pepe's withers. Naturally, Pepe quailed – rolled onto his spine and bicycled his legs defensively like a terrified mealy bug. Mark massaged the curly wool and the sharp sternal ridge between Pepe's forelegs.

"It's all right. It's all right," he purred. "You're a sissy and a loser. But I guess there's nothing we can do about it. Is there? Pepe's Pepe. A stupid little poodle who's lost his balls… and can't tell where to find 'em. Leave 'em alone and they'll come home. Yeah, right."

He kneaded the tense little animal's chest. "Too bad, buddy. I'll still love you, though. Allst I hope is you've learned your lesson."

O f course, there was still the problem of the dog-piss smeared on the floor. Pepe had not proved a sufficient mop. And now that he was all yucky he couldn't be allowed to just jump up and shake himself off.

Mark kept his hand firmly on Pepe while he considered. If he went for the roll of paper towels in the holder above the sink, Pepe would take the opportunity to dart for refuge under the table again. Carom around off the walls, cabinets, doors, floors, furniture… contaminating whatever he came into contact with.

The tablecloth was ruined: Mark couldn't just replace it in the drawer, already infused as it was with Pepe's cooties and dog-stink, to be spread out innocently some other evening under stuff that went into people's mouths. Bleaagh.

Mark hooked the fingers of his left hand under Pepe's collar at the throat. Leaning on Pepe's torso with his right, he kicked his leg out straight behind him and toed the crumpled tablecloth into reach.

Pepe's breath hissed out of him under the momentary pressure – he scratched reflexively at Mark's wrist as Mark removed it to gather the green fabric against his knee. Mark wadded it thick enough so that the pee wouldn't soak through to his hand, wiped the damp pavers around Pepe's near side, then hoisted Pepe abruptly by the collar and wiped the sworls of moisture that remained under Pepe's shuffling hind tippy-toes. Finally Mark rearranged the tablecloth with his fingertips – nose pigged in disgust – and jerked Pepe from side to side in unwilling half-pirouettes so he could dab gruffly at the poodle's soggy mane and flanks.

Pepe sparred, bobbed, weaved, suspended from the noose of his collar.

"I guess this is a hung-dog look," Mark suggested. "I mean 'hanged.'" There'd been a discussion of the proper past tense of the executionary verb – with lots of quips and protruding tongues and grisly stick-figure cartoons – in his English class only a few weeks earlier. "All you gotta do is hang in there for a second more, buddy."

He toweled Pepe against the grain and set him back down on all fours. Pepe hacked and gagged and immediately convulsed to rid himself of the horrid experience. He gave off the rancid odor of dank dog-fur. With an added uric taint. Mark was starting to regret having used Pepe for a blotter.

"You need a bath, is what you really need," Mark told him. He thought of hefting Pepe up into the stainless steel basin and holding him under the long spigot for a rinse at least. That would be a project. A disaster: piss-water splattering everywhere, especially on his own clothes.

Mark had an inspiration. He scurried to his feet and whisked Pepe up with him. Dangling the poodle at his hip by the collar-handle the way he'd carry a gym-bag – "this is the last time," Mark promised, "I'll make you be a hanged dog" – and kicking the tablecloth along ahead of him in flabby arcs like a deflated soccer ball, he crossed the kitchen toward the cubby they called the "laundry room." It was where they kept Pepe's food and water bowls too.

Mark opened the louvered accordion doors, reached inside and flipped up the lid of the toploading washer alongside the dryer.

"In you go," he said.

He swung Pepe up over the hole.

Pepe, not surprisingly, acted less than enthusiastic about the prospect of a descent into the dingy cavern of gray perforated metal beneath him. Then too, he was probably frightened by the jutting central stalagmite, the finned agitator that Mark was going to have to fold him around. In fact, as soon as he realized Mark's intent, Pepe went crazy. He flailed and gyrated, eyes pinballing. He tucked his tail – his slimy red inner dick-squib was protruding again – and, as Mark lowered him toward the opening, managed to vee his hind legs wide enough apart so that his pawpads lodged against the rim of the hole a good 90 degrees apart. That gave him a solid purchase. Legs rigid, hams quivering under strain, Pepe braced for all he was worth against insertion.

"You must have.. what do they call it? Acro.... Or, no. Claus... claustrophobia. *Claws*trophobia! With dogs is what it is, huh?"

Mark laughed in delight at his success in

plumbing memory. And at the breadth of his vocabulary. He'd learned lots of polysyllabic words from his Dad, including the word *polysyllabic.* His Dad was a sportswriter. Used to be with the Oakland *Tribune.* Now the Seattle *P-I.* He was unbeatable at Scrabble, his Dad. He'd written books, too. Most of all Mark laughed at his own clever pun. He wished somebody besides Pepe were there to hear it. Well, his Dad, of course. But the two words sounded the same, he reflected – a homonym – so you'd have to kind of spell out the claws variation if you were telling it to people.

Meanwhile, Pepe had gotten his forepaws jammed into the gap between the rim of the washer and the rubber gasket over the drum. No way was he going to allow himself to be crammed into this torture-chamber.

Mark tried to force Pepe's rump down through the hole. He grasped the base of Pepe's tail as a handle – Pepe let out a yawp as if scalded. Mark leaned on the heel of his fist. Pepe caterwauled and bucked with resurgent energy but didn't yield his leg-holds, even when Mark switched to prying and swatting them loose one after the other. Somehow Pepe always maintained a tripodal underpinning.

Mark relaxed slightly. "You're just making me mad," he said through gritted teeth. "I can get you into this thing, you know." His breath was starting to come faster from the exertion. "I just don't want to break something on you. But if that's what you're after. "

Pepe had not been lulled. Still, in a ruthless blitzkrieg Mark succeeded in capturing Pepe's hindquarters and crimping and folding the squealing little dog headfirst into the cavity. When he'd wrestled Pepe down between the agitator and the drum-wall, he released Pepe's tail and slammed the lid shut. Actually, he brought it down on his own left forearm before letting go of Pepe's collar. He snaked his arm free quickly and leaned on the lid to keep it tamped tight. He listened with satisfaction to the muffled whimpers and scrapings and thumps within.

"Told you," Mark gloated.

His mother made him do his own laundry, mostly. So Mark was familiar with the machine's operation. He twisted the chrome knob on the dial panel to the first position. "Normal load." He glanced at the temperature setting to make it sure it was on "cold." He pulled out on the knob.

Water hissed through the rubber hose attached to the brass faucet in the wall. It gurgled hollowly inside the tub where Pepe huddled.

The water would run for a few minutes, Mark knew, filling the tub before the agitator would begin to churn. That would obviously be dangerous for the dog. All he wanted to do was sluice Pepe down. Dilute the pee and rinse it away.

He was proud of this improvisation. Pepe was neatly contained, no splashing – and if Pepe found the mode frightening, all the better. Pepe had been one bad dog.

There was, true, the question of how Mark was going to dry Pepe off.

Stick him in the microwave. Yeah, and explode the little creep. Somebody had supposedly tried that once with a toy poodle. Producing just such a gruesome result. When he'd brought that story home from school, though, his Dad had dismissed it as an "urban legend." Still, it would be an interesting experiment.

Abuelita Jeanne and his mother would probably not be all that understanding, though, if Mark had to confess he'd made a youthful error in judgment and had had to scrape poor Pepe's remains out of the microwave.

He pictured himself with a rubber spatula, wiping bloody gobbets of gristle and fur into the paper garbage bag. Rooting around curiously in the steaming red goo for the two eyeballs.

Would he be sad? Well, of course he would. He felt a little ashamed, a bit shocked, actually, that the depraved fantasy had popped into his brain.

A more realistic option would be to give Pepe a tumble in the dryer. Put it on "permanent press" or "fluff" so it wouldn't get too hot inside. Might work, he thought – certainly Pepe would fit comfortably into the capacious bin. But twirling and bouncing a dog around in the humid, clangorous darkness of a clothes dryer would be truly cruel in itself, Mark had to acknowledge. Unless Pepe could run along on the bin's ribs as they rotated, like a hamster on an exercise wheel. Maybe that's how he could trim Pepe down and avoid the annoyance of the evening walks, Mark snickered to himself: Stick Pepe in the dryer every night for a half-hour's spin.

He was tempted in fact to try it. But he supposed there was too much risk that Pepe could be injured in there. Machinery was daunting – harsh and impersonal, not fully controllable. Maybe if Pepe really did have claustrophobia he'd be driven insane. Can dogs go insane? Mark wasn't sure. How would a poodle behave, he wondered, if it were insane? Dash around biting at its tail? Howl like a coyote? Foam at the mouth? That's what dogs supposedly do when they're rabid, which as he understood it was a form of insanity.

The grungy tablecloth lay at his feet. Couldn't dry Pepe with that, obviously. He recalled Abuelita Jeanne saying that the dog groomer used a blow-dryer, like his mother's in the upstairs bathroom. An ingenious solution!

Except he'd have to go get it. Trying to be surreptitious. Think up some innocent rationale if she saw him taking it downstairs. Find something to weight the washer lid while he scurried up and back. Anyway, the method would demand too much effort and patience – once he thought beyond the immediate pleasure of pointing a pistol-shaped gadget at Pepe and blasting him. Powpowpowpowpow. Not shots, but one continuous beam of hot air, like a laser, a ray-gun. Pepe would absolutely hate it, he was sure. Like the vacuum cleaner. At least if Mark doing it to him, not the groomer.

There was a big plastic bucket on top of the dryer full of rumpled stuff. Mark plucked at the topmost item, which he recognized as a sheet from his mother's bed, and released a bubble of maroon terrycloth from beneath. He wasn't sure if these things were clean or dirty. He bent to nose the sheet. He sniffed his mother's perfume. Good, dirty.

The enameled lid jumped under Mark's left hand as some part of Pepe's anatomy whanged tinnily against it. Maybe the rising water level was spooking him, Mark thought. He tugged the cuffs of his sweatshirt up over his elbows one after the other, cracked the lid cautiously and insinuated his right arm to block the gap while he fingered around for the poodle's furry body.

Goaded by the sliver of daylight, Pepe scuffled and heaved in the slippery, curved canyon between the conical agitator and the tub wall.

Mark caught a fistful of Pepe's frizzy nape and squeezed. He pressed down hard, immobilizing all but rump and tail. He flipped the hinged lid back, open all the way so he could slide Pepe clockwise around the tub. It was the only feasible direction, though awkward: Mark had to twist at the waist, his hip hard against the machine, and lift his elbow in a kind of backhand grip as he fought Pepe around the rear of the agitator to where the water burbled into the tub.

"Just pretend you're a car, going through a carwash," Mark counseled. He dragged Pepe under the tongue of cold water that cascaded from the upper right corner of the machine. "First your hood-ornament."

Pepe snorted and sputtered, although Mark gave only a cursory dousing to his curly topknot.

"You act like you're being drowned!" Mark chided. "And you hardly even got any into your little grille. Did you! 'Cause I was being very careful, so you wouldn't. See, your nose is your hood ornament. And your mouth is your grille, with your teeth. And your eyes are your windshield.... Use your wipers!"

Pepe blinked furiously, licked at his wet chops. He was desperate to shake himself. Mark plunged his left hand into the machine to keep Pepe's legs and squirrelly rump under control. He made sure the water soaked into the fleece covering the dog's shoulder and the pufflets on his flanks. "We have to do this part real good, though. This is your body, and those are your fenders. And finally your little butt-butt, which is your trunk compartment. And your tail... 's like, what. Your radio antenna, I guess. And Pepe's all done!"

Mark eased up and allowed Pepe to scootch himself along the narrow crevice out away from the horrible shower of icy water. Mark's own hands and wrists and forearms had gotten wet, along with the right cuff of his sweatshirt. He helped Pepe squirm back onto his feet again, to hunch shivering in the two or three inches of water that had risen around the base of the agitator. It would click into action at any moment now. Although there'd be a warning pause when the water shut off.

Mark punched the knob on the timer dial. The torrent abruptly ceased. He exchanged hands – grasping Pepe's collar with his left hand to free his right – and tugged the sheet out of the tangle in the laundry bucket.

Like a giant Kleenex in a dispenser, the sheet brought up with it from below the intertwined maroon bath towel, a balled pink sock, one of his mother's flowered flannel nightgowns, and a crinkled washcloth that had dried as stiffly as if it had been starched. They all snowed to the floor. The sock bounced into Pepe's water bowl. Instantly it began to darken and swell.

Mark shook the bunched sheet partially open. With the palm of his hand he splayed it out across the cramped space atop the two appliances, between the washer mouth and the plastic bucket. He snatched Pepe up off the bottom of the tub, let plaits of water drool off his rump for a couple of seconds, then threaded the sodden poodle up through the opening and plumped him onto the sheet. He bunched it around and over Pepe the way his mother crimped dough around the meat filling of a piroshki or a Chinese bao.

(His mother mostly cooked weird stuff. Mark and Paige had a standard joke about her menus: dinner that night, one would cheerfully inform the other, was going to be zucchini fritatta. Or eggplant casserole. Both of which she'd actually served them, to their utter disgust and undying sarcastic amusement. Their Dad's specialties, by contrast, were "five-alarm chile" and "Lieutenant j.g. Daddy's Ohio fried chicken with 27 secret herbs and spices.")

Pepe's fur was so wet it soaked through the thin sheeting immediately.

Mark lifted the poke he'd created to layer more plies under and around it. Brusquely he kneaded and patted the enclosed dog-lump, blotting his own forearms on the billows.

The squishy bottom of the bundle started to leave watery snail-trails on the white-enamel dryer top.

He hoisted the floundering poodle like a stork delivering a baby, and a few inches off the floor slacked his grip on the neck of the sack.

Pepe tumbled out.

Water slide! Wheee! Like at Raging Waters," Mark exclaimed as Pepe skidded across the slick pavers, on his side.

Pepe's frantic claws bit at a grout line. He hopped up three-legged and staggered a couple of steps, dazed by the kaleidoscope of experience.

"Wasn't that fun?" Mark leered.

With his coat plastered to his skinny body, Pepe

had lost half his mass. He looked like a rat, Mark thought. The diminution was astounding. Not to mention the complete subtraction of any vestige of poodle presence.

Mark had never seen Pepe wet before. His muzzle seemed more pointy, positively rodent-like, his chest frail and mousy, his legs twiggy, his tail stunted, as if bitten off or lost to a trap or disease. The straggly scraps of fur that clung to him here and there made him look like a mangy muskrat.

"Jeez," Mark commiserated, "you're really sorry-lookin' when you're wet! A sorry-lookin' specimen."

Pepe was seized by the inevitable spasm.

"No!" Mark objected, futilely.

He twisted, just as futilely, and by reflex lifted his right shoe and pressed his knees together to defend his fly.

The walls and the appliance fronts and his khaki pants were mottled by the shadow-pattern of the droplets Pepe had sprayed, as efficiently as a garden sprinkler.

"Darn you!" Mark wailed.

His mother would see. She'd suspect something funny had been going on. He didn't want to have to explain. He didn't think she'd like the idea of his having put Pepe in the washer. To put it mildly. And he knew Pepe would shake himself again.

Mark shoved the saturated sheet into the machine to rid himself of it and turned back to Pepe.

"Sit!" he snapped. He thrust out his right hand, palm flat and reversed, and gave it a peremptory upward jerk.

Paige had always fancied herself gifted at

communing with animals. When they'd first dogsat Pepe, she'd undertaken to teach him basic obedience. And she'd shown Mark what she said were the conventional hand signals. She'd seen them used by her best friend Naomi: palm up and lifted with "sit," palm to the ground and slowly lowered with "down," palm upraised and vertical, in the universal "halt" position, to reinforce "stay." Or sometimes they'd just level an index finger meaningfully.

Eventually, Paige said, Pepe would do what they wanted simply in response to the gesture. Naomi's collie-shepherd Sinclair had had to pass that test to graduate from obedience school, Paige noted. Unfortunately, she and Mark lost interest in repeating the gestures, and the boring commands, before Pepe displayed any willingness to recognize them.

Or at least to react appropriately. He'd take the bribe, all right. ("You give 'em a treat when you're first starting out," Paige lectured, "and you praise 'em like mad every time they get the trick right, and after a while they'll just do it for the praise, because dogs love praise. They're really into pleasing people.") But Pepe never got beyond the dog candy.

He'd eye the fist it was in avidly as Mark or Paige, or both, urged him to assume a posture. ("Only one person's supposed to be giving the command," Paige objected. Though when it was Mark's turn she had no hesitancy about butting in. "You aren't doing it right," she'd chide. "You're confusing him.") Finally, reluctantly, Pepe would sink back on his haunches for a nervous instant, or crouch, or roll over, or rear on his hind legs, or let out an irritable yap or two, or proffer a paw to shake ... all of them, in fact, if necessary, in random sequence until he hit on the position that triggered his trainers' Pavlovian instinct to reward him. If they refused to be gulled, he'd curl up dismissively on his pillow or stalk away to lap from his waterbowl. He was hopeless, Paige ultimately declared.

("Oh, Pepe's much too smart to do tricks like ordinary dogs," Abuelita Jeanne agreed when she returned. "He thinks he's a *mannikin!* That's why he'll walk like a little *mannikin!* For his *mommy*, though. Sometimes. Won't he, snookums?")

To Mark's astonishment, Pepe sat.

"Good... boy!" Mark acknowledged.

The compliment wasn't as heartfelt as the command. He was simply relieved at the unexpected reaction and preoccupied by the need to seize this fleeting window of opportunity to police up the incriminating evidence – the soiled tablecloth, his mother's nightgown, the petrified washrag, the sock steeping in the water-bowl....

He snatched and slam-dunked them in whirlwind series into the washer, bent for the maroon towel. He flapped it open as he straightened, caught two corners, switched them around so he could stretch it lengthwise like a bullfighter's cape before his knees, and pounced.

Pepe's reward—another lightning envelopment. Heck, he hadn't been all *that* obedient. At Mark's flurry he'd bolted up out of the sit....

"Ooh, you can never escape me!" Mark chortled in self-congratulation.

He was surprised himself at the unbroken string of easy captures. "You're totally at my mercy! I am inwincible!"

He'd heard his Dad use that pronunciation while mockingly flexing his biceps after opening jars for his mother here in the kitchen.

Mark pinioned Pepe against his thighs and subjected him to yet another quick-and-dirty rubdown. It was impossible to be very thorough, what with the wiggly little animal a constant threat to spurt free. Pepe felt almost boneless under the toweling, like a banana slug, except for the matchstick protuberances scissoring feebly....

Actually, a slug has eye-stalks, Mark remembered, only they're limber and retractable.

Perhaps it was because he'd entertained the idea of using the automatic clothes-dryer a few minutes ago, or maybe because he'd thought of his Dad in connection with the kitchen – his Dad rinsing lettuce leaves under the tap, then stepping outside with the colander and showily twirling it in big vertical loops, arm at full extension, to spin off the water and demonstrate the magic of centrifugal force. It was a trick Mark loved to emulate to his mother's disapproval and notwithstanding an occasional accident. Flying lettuce.

In any case, Mark impulsively bagged up Pepe in the towel, bobbed erect, secured his grip on the pouch with both hands, cocked it toward his left hip for momentum, then reversed the swing and heaved Pepe on up overhead in a giant counterclockwise circle.

"I'm givin' ya a spin-dry, buddy," Mark gasped in explanation, widening his stance..

He put Pepe through four measured revolutions. Uh-one, uh-two, uh-three, uh-four – the little dog's mass a palpable drag on Mark's shoulders and triceps at the nadir of the circuit, lightening as Pepe sheered to the acme, where he shucked gravity altogether.

That's how the astronauts train, Mark realized. He'd seen pictures of grinning men and women in jumpsuits paddling upside down or heels-over-head in thin air inside big cargo planes that were flying loop-de-loops. He might even want to be an astronaut himself someday, he thought. If he didn't play in the NFL. Or a professional soccer league. Or the NBA.

"Whooo!" he crooned in a high voice. "Whoooo! Pepe's an astronaut! Pepe's a dog-o-naut! Dogs in space!"

If he let go, of course, or if part of the towel slipped from his grasp, the hapless Pepe would sail across the kitchen: an acrobat, a dogobat – Pepe the Fearless Flying Poodle. No net, no trapeze. Wheee-ee-haw!

...Whomp!

He'd smack against the wall or a cabinet. Slowly trickle down, muzzle all bent like a fender, spitting his toy teeth through a rueful, sickly grin like Wile E. Coyote after Roadrunner has tricked him into yet another ridiculous try at leaping the canyon. Cartoon characters always recover immediately, though.

Pepe couldn't weigh more than ten pounds. So Mark would've had no difficulty keeping him awhirl almost indefinitely. But four orbits seemed like enough. He didn't want to make Pepe so sick he'd puke.

Mark relaxed, let the Ferris wheel pendulum to a halt. He dumped Pepe out on the floor.

Like a cat, Pepe tried to land on his paws. But his outstretched legs collapsed under him. Drunkenly he wobbled upright. He was favoring the left foreleg still. He reeled away from Mark, listing precariously. The gimpy forepaw failed, and he had to half-sit to recover. Pepe bounced up, rattled his head in annoyance as if he had a foxtail in his ear, set out once more indefatigably – but crabbing left, like a car with a tire out of balance, or a sailboat being set downwind. Pepe shuffled his paws in an awkward jitterbug to compensate, lost it again. He pitched sideways onto his rosetted rump. He lurched up, zigzagged another few steps....

Mark haw-hawed out loud. This was hilarious! Even more hilarious than watching Pepe chug along under the blanket! Pepe was dizzy! Hell of dizzy!

He hadn't consciously aimed at this outcome, but it was elementary, my dear Watson: Of course a dog would be woozy after you'd spun it around and around like that – just the way Mark used to make the world tilt and wheel by ratcheting himself about in tight circles when he was little. The disorientation was fun. Like the way it had happened just this evening, earlier, when the blood had rushed to his brain. But he'd never seen a dog acting dizzy before. It was fascinating.

"Pee-pee, you idiot dog. You're drunk!" Mark chuckled. "You're fallin' on your ear! You're drunk outta your gourd!"

Pepe seemed to be recovering, though – more rapidly than Mark would have preferred.

Pepe got his legs under him, swayed to a halt, and was immediately wracked by another of those tag-clinking, whole-body temblors. A cleansing instinct, Mark recognized. Boy, he thought – shrinking from the heavy mist Pepe was shedding – dogs sure do practice what the coaches and his Dad always preach when you've gotten the wind knocked out of you, or turned an ankle coming down with a rebound on somebody's shoe, or started to snivel because you've bloodied a knee: "Shake it off," they say.

An effective remedy, too, on the evidence of Pepe's spasm. It instantaneously restored some semblance of bouffant shape to Pepe's crest, corselet and pantaloons. Pepe bore a much closer resemblance to a poodle than to a rodent again, anyway.

And the ebbing tremors kicked him into flight. Butt-wiggle translated into beeline before Mark reacted. He was rapt in contemplation of how a dog-brain would process vertigo, how Pepe was interpreting the sudden weird kink in perception. Although apparently it had largely worn off.

Except for a hitch in his gait, Pepe darted capably enough toward the familiar recess deep behind the table from which he'd been so unceremoniously extracted.

"Sit!" Mark blurted. "Stay!"

Yeah, as if.

Pepe scuttled into hiding.

Yeah. As if.

Mark became aware of a sour, garlicky odor from the towel that trailed in his hand: stale flecks of dried-off human skin, hair, the cooking smells that permeated the house, potentiated by moisture from dog.

His mother was always chiding him for leaving towels in states like this to putrefy on the floor of his bedroom. Dark crescent stains mottled the hardwood in a couple of places as a result. He felt bad about how upset and angry she'd been when she'd found the documentation of his carelessness burned into the wood – just one more thing, she'd mourned, that would lower the sales value of the house. Which he'd truly be sorry about, she said, when it was his turn to go to college.

He'd get an athletic scholarship, he promised her sullenly – a "full ride," his Dad called it. But he really ought to try harder, Mark knew, to remember to discard used-up wet towels in the white wicker hamper in the bathroom, the way she wanted.

Trouble was, he had to tuck something around his waist for modesty's sake for the trip from shower to sequestration behind his bedroom door. Never mind how his Dad felt and acted on this issue – his bleary-eyed Dad with his hairytopped prong hanging out at countertop level, grinding coffee beans in the morning. Yuuch! Disgusting. And embarrassing! His Dad was always interviewing guys without any clothes on in the locker room, Mark knew. Too bad. No one was ever going to see *him* naked!

He swiveled toward the washer to flick the towel into it. He wanted to make Pepe dizzy one more time. Intensify the sensation. Watch him career around drunkenly – another human experience for Abuelita Jeanne's precious species-conflicted pet.

Mark knew what it felt like. The first time he'd been drunk was two New Year's Eves ago, when his mother and Dad had had a raucous party downstairs and Paige and Naomi had managed to filch a bottle of vodka from the kitchen to spike the cups of non-alcoholic fruit punch they kept fetching up to Paige's room.

Mark had spied what they were about. He'd even smelled cigarette smoke through the crack under Paige's door. Eventually they'd tired of his snooping and invited him into the room with them. It was smoggy despite the wide-open window. Music was thumping from Paige's boombox. Giggly and boisterous, the two girls enlisted the little brother in a sort of science project. The same motivation as his with Pepe.

The punch Mark let them ply him with went down easily – it was supersweet, like cherry Koolaid, with floating slivers of orange and lemon that got in the way and dammed up against your lips while you sipped, and a metallic off-taste that lingered on your tongue. That was because it was fermented potato-juice, Paige said, which was what the clear vodka was distilled from.

Nasty. But Mark was game. They offered him cigarettes, which he refused. Naomi had a joint. She'd scammed it from her older brother's stash. Mark took his turns sipping at the dwindling roach, its twisted tip damp with nasty girl-spit, and holding the harsh smoke in his chest until the cough reflex exploded it out of his nose and mouth. By the time they heard everybody downstairs starting to chant the seconds left to midnight, he and Paige and Naomi were cackling uncontrollably, pitching out of their chairs, weaving around bouncing against walls, doing pratfalls over the end of the bed. They stayed up till three moaning proudly between long silences about how incredibly wasted they were. And it was true. When Mark stared at the ceiling it slowly revolved. When he stood up to go back to his bedroom the floor undulated gently underfoot, as if the rug were floating on a current – a flying carpet. Like out of the *1,001 Nights*.

Paige and Naomi both threw up during the night. Or so they reported when they crept sunken-eyed out of her bedroom at noon. Mark had a cast-iron constitution, like his Dad. He'd admit only to being a little headachy and queasy.

He'd never seen his Dad drunk. Or his mother either, for that matter, although she acted kind of different at night after she'd poured herself a cocktail to sip while she cooked and quizzed him about his day or gossiped with her friend Sylvie on the phone – she became more coquettish and hyper. Usually she had a bottle of wine on the table with dinner. And she kept her tumbler filled with ice and Scotch while she watched television or read or murmured into the telephone some more.

He'd realized she was crying a couple of times during those conversations, overhearing her from up in his room as he worked math problems or tapped at his computer. He was vaguely distressed, curious to hear more of the exchange, except he wasn't. It was none of his business. He also kind of wanted to go down and comfort her, except he didn't know how to, and there was something about the idea of confronting such emotion in his mother that made him squirmy.

His Dad mostly drank beer out of the can or bottle. He'd have a cocktail too, though. A lot of times, before his Dad was no longer around, this kitchen would reverberate with the bitterness in their voices after dinner. His mother's and his Dad's. Yelling at each other behind the closed door, or just declaiming loudly, profanely.

Sometimes the conversation would rise in vituperous crescendo, to be punctuated by the sharp sound of something breaking, and the house would shake as the front door slammed, and Mark would scowl more intensely at the computer screen. Next morning there'd be shards of glass or pieces of a dinner plate in the garbage bag.

Mark didn't make much of a connection between their fights and their evening alcohol intake. And it wasn't as if they were always squabbling. Far from it. Lots of nights things were just peaceful and homey, or the four of them would play a game together, like Chinese checkers or Monopoly or hearts, or his Dad would snuggle up to his mother on the couch and the two of them would mug at the children self-consciously, like love-birds in some stupid romantic movie.

What would be neat, Mark thought, the ideal research methodology if he wanted to see Pepe drunk, would be to somehow get actual booze into him. But trying to pour it down his gullet out of a bottle would be another impossibly messy operation. And he was sure Pepe couldn't be enticed into voluntarily slurping it out of his bowl. Beer's too bitter, red wine tastes like cough medicine, white wine suggests piss with a little sugar in it, Scotch and bourbon sear your throat as if you'd swallowed smoke from a grassfire, even gin and vodka, which are conveniently camouflaged as water, have a faintly overripe pungency, like the inside of a garbage can. (Mark knew; he'd sampled them all – once with Paige when she was supposedly baby-sitting him and they tried a little bit from every single bottle in the liquor cabinet above the sink. A few gross combinations too. They'd found a pamphlet with stained, sticky pages full of recipes for things like "Side Car" and "Pink Lady" sandwiched between an empty pocket-flask with a red tartan case—it had been his Dad's in college—and a leaky pyramidal bottle of something yellow and viscous that tasted horrible. The sink came in handy that time. As did, he had to admit, the toilet.)

He might as well start the washer, he thought; it was already full of water and the dirty tablecloth, sheet and towel. Excetera.

He tipped the laundry basket over the opening and fed the rest of its contents into the tub. He distributed them more or less proportionally around the agitator so the machine wouldn't shimmy. He reached up and dug out a scoopful of fragrant detergent from the box on the shelf above the appliances. He sprinkled it over the clothes.

You're supposed to put the detergent in first, he always recalled too late. As usual, there was a dusting of spilled granules around the top of the machine, lost in the scoop-ride from box to bombs-away. He brushed them into the opening with the edge of his hand. He lowered the lid and plucked at the knob. The water started gurgling, and immediately shut itself off with a hollow clunk. After an instant the machine began its rhythmic sloshing.

He had it in mind to get one of the brown paper supermarket bags that his mother refolded flat and stacked under the sink after they'd been emptied. It would be a perfect vehicle to twirl Pepe in – the exact right size, and gratifyingly unpleasant for the dog when Mark muffled him up, once again, inside it.

Mark felt the way he imagined his mother did when she announced that he was grounded. Or his Dad when he used to order Mark to lie across his lap for three or four stinging open handed whaps on the underpantsed behind. Or his soccer coach when he made guys run lung-busting laps on the quarter-mile track when they'd been horsing around during practice. Kind of regretful at having been forced to administer punishment by the subject's ridiculous misbehavior, and yet not altogether displeased to have been given the opportunity to offer needed instruction, correction. Just retribution. Getting off – you know they were, even if they wouldn't admit it – on the power trip.

Power is... better than not having any.

Only trouble with a grocery bag, though, was that if Pepe was still damp, the bottom of the bag could quickly dissolve the way they do in your arms on the way into the house from the car if a milk carton has dribbled, or eggshells have cracked and oozed. He could visualize the fibers darkening, parting, a squawking Pepe tearing through – like a chick hatching.

Anyway, Mark was uneasy enough that his eye registered the pulsing colon on the microwave clock: it read 6:10 now. His mother would be coming down soon. And there still hadn't been a walk.

He went to the end of the table, squatted and retrieved the discarded leash. He stared at Pepe, who crouched shivering against the baseboard, eyes studiously averted.

"Hell-*o*-o!" Mark taunted. "I'm *ba*-ack."

Pepe winced slightly at Mark's horror-movie

inflections, but didn't turn his head.

"What, do you think I didn't see you come under here? You're Peepee the Ostrich-Dog, huh? As long as you don't look at me you're invisible!"

Pepe adjusted himself lower and flattened his jaw against the floor-pavers disconsolately, still refusing eye contact.

"Gosh, where's Pepe?" Mark inquired in a high, innocent tone. He swiveled his neck like a blind person, scanning the corners of the ceiling. "Oh where, oh where..." The tune proved irresistible. "...Can my little dog be? Oh where, oh where can he be? With his ears so long, and his tail so short...."

Pepe shut his eyelids, as if a nap were the best way to avoid this tedious human being's latest annoyance. His body was still trembling.

"C'mon, Peepee. All is forgiven. Everything's okay now. I've decided I won't get you shnockered again. Let's go for our walkies. Here, boy. C'mon, boy."

Mark pitched forward onto his hands and knees. He proffered the clasp of the leash.

"I know you've already done it, you bad, bad doggy. But prob'ly there's still some more in there. Right? And prob'ly you've gotta poop. So come on. Be a good boy now. We'll just take a short little walk. Huh? Here, Peepee."

The poodle's visible eye cracked open, and the eyeball twitched nervously, according Mark a wary peep from under his brow and lashes.

Mark crawled forward two shin-lengths, paused. "Don't tell me we're gonna have to go through this again," he said.

Pepe squirmed onto his side, exposing his belly. He parted his hind legs, the upper one tensed as if to absorb another blow.

"Darn it all!" Mark exclaimed in disgust. "Stop that! I'm not gonna do anything to you, you dumb little shit! And even if I were… that's just so damn… sickening! God! Show a little more fuckin'… something!"

He couldn't say "balls." Pepe no longer had any.

Pepe lifted his head slightly to assess the danger. As did Mark, invariably made uneasy when the eff-word emerged from his mouth.

The house was silent.

Pepe blinked at Mark, then lay his head back and probed the air twice with his forepaw in that pleading canine way.

"Up!" Mark clapped the palm of his left hand against the heel of his right. He was relieved to return to normal discourse. The leash occupied his thumb and index finger. "Get up! Peepee! Come! Come!"

Pepe flinched at each command, but he remained supine.

"Pepe! Come!"

Nothing.

"Okay, that's it," Mark declared. "You wanna play dead dog, I'll show y' a dead dog. I've had it with you! You are really gonna be sorry now!"

He scrambled forward and hovered menacingly over Pepe, whose only response had been to lift his defensive leg higher and saucer his eyes in fearful expectation. He still adamantly directed his gaze into space, though.

How many times had his Dad instructed Mark to always look people in the eye? Stand tall. Shake hands firmly. (His Dad had demonstrated: web of thumb slotted snugly into web of thumb, a steady squeeze for one or two pumps. Not like you're trying to show you can break the other person's knuckles –

although you can make him squawk in pain if you grab onto his fingers prematurely and work them back and forth. Not limp like a dishrag – which renders you vulnerable to the previous tactic, besides making you seem like a pussy. And not too clingy – like you're gay. Another way guys messed around with handshakes was by tickling the other guy's palm with the tips of their fingers when they withdrew, while making kissy-kissy sounds with their lips and wiggling their eyebrows. That was supposed to be how gay people gave each other the signal or something. Although his Dad and his mother and Paige were always telling Mark there was nothing wrong with being gay. O-o-kay.)

"Be a man," was what his Dad and his coaches urged. Even when you're getting chewed out – especially when you're getting chewed out. When you know you're in deep shit and something very disagreeable is about to come down on you, be brave. Don't bow your chin to your chest, don't slouch and toe-scuff the ground, don't mumble. Don't cry – once you're old enough to help it. Nod crisply, reply politely but curtly – his Dad recommended "yes, sir," or "no, ma'am" – all the while meeting the other person's eyes. Like an equal. Just because you're a kid doesn't mean adults shouldn't treat you with respect, his Dad said. But you've got to earn it. And if you've done something wrong and you know it's wrong, take your medicine.

"Don't do the crime if you can't do the time," was a neat little rhyming joke for it. His Dad had made that up.

But Pepe. His Dad had never met Pepe. He'd hate this little dog, Mark was sure. Just like Maurice... well, maybe not quite as bad as Maurice. Pepe wasn't as fat. And Pepe couldn't quite muster the same infuriating air of… what was it his Dad had called it? "Supercilious. Supercilious entitlement."

Although when it came to it, Mark doubted that Maurice would have put up with the crap Pepe was taking so docilely. Maurice had had that mean streak that underpins self-importance. Maybe runts are most likely to display it, Mark reflected, dog or human – compensation for their physical inadequacy.

It was always the short guys who played dirty, in Marks's experience, always some cocky, insult-spewing, sawed-off little jerk who'd kick you in the ankles going for the ball, try to rake your heel or your Achilles tendon with his cleats if you got by him, grab the tail of your jersey or the waistband of your shorts from behind, flail at you with his elbows and then flop, pretending it was you who'd tripped or fouled... and act all pissed off, like he wanted to fight you, when the game was over. Win or lose. True, that kind of trouble could also come occasionally from one of those muscle-bound Neanderthals a head taller, with a deep voice and five-o'clock shadow, and a face crimson with zits, whose hormones had kicked in preternaturally early. Especially if you'd outplayed him or scored a goal on him.

In either case, they'd usually back down if you didn't allow yourself to be intimidated. Glowered at 'em, stood in your tracks, went off on your own in righteous denunciation of the unwarranted challenge, the insult of it, which you refused to dignify by responding the way *they* wanted you to. "*I'm* not going to fight you!" Not to mention that you were scared shitless to. But fear, he'd found, translated easily into anger if you just let it. Your body fizzed with adrenaline identically. And anger made you crazy. Which was the best preemptive defense.

Mark imagined Maurice's snub muzzle viciously wrinkled, lips peeled back from the needle-sharp fangs, yapping and snapping, dog spittle flying... crazy with rage if Mark had tried to stuff *him* into a washing machine. Maurice would *never* have brooked such disrespect from an inferior. Which Mark figured was how Maurice would have regarded him. Maurice was a toy poodle: as Abuelita Jeanne once said admiringly, "They think they're God's chosen creatures."

Not that Mark, twice as big as he had been when he'd last seen Maurice alive, wouldn't be able to crush a dog that size now if he chose to. Stomp him flat. Swing him hard by a leg or his tail against a wall and batter his fucking brains out.

Which was what Pepe, the realist, understood. Mark had to give him that. Animals didn't necessarily behave like humans, like Americans. On the nature shows Mark had seen how all kinds of animals – walruses, monkeys, wolves, he could recall offhand – grovel before superiors of their own species. Any run-of-the-pack young male who dares or blunders into direct eye contact with an alpha is in for a savage attack. But as soon as he goes limp, rolls on his back, offers himself completely to the mercy of the stronger, he's spared. At least usually, supposedly. Whereas with people, surrender is deadly.

Weakness is deadly.

The world's scary, if you think too much about it. In the movies, on the TV news, you were always seeing weak, helpless people get hurt and killed, even if they had their hands up or were crying and begging for their lives. Like in *Schindler's List*, which they'd shown at his school.

A lion, though…. A lion, he'd read, will kill a rival lion's pups.

So that's just as mean.

The world's scary, if you think too much about it.

In Abuelita Jeanne's house, Pepe was the alpha male. But here it was Mark, which Pepe had damn well better have figured out finally. And seemed to have. Maybe, in fact, that demotion was why he was always acting so glum around here.

Except that Pepe still wasn't obeying him. Pepe was using surrender as resistance. Like that guy Gandhi, from India. And Martin Luther King, Jr. Passive resistance. Pepe kind of reminded Mark of the picture of Gandhi in his social science text: skinny, long nosed, banded here and there in puffy white, one of those Indian togas or whatever they call them. Obviously a complete weenie. No wonder he'd adopted a jellyfish strategy. Whereas Martin Luther King, Jr., looked like a linebacker. Probably if he hadn't been all religious he could have kicked some serious ass. Which white people and Mark was a member of the evil race, to his shame, not that he could do anything to change it – richly deserved.

Well, if Pepe wouldn't walk, Mark had conceived one more project for animal testing. He put down the leash, reached into his back pocket and fished out his pooper-scooper bag.

"Hey, Mark," Paige used to propose when he was bothering her. "Why don't you go play with a plastic bag?"

"Yuck-yuck," he'd reply sardonically.

He uncrumpled the transparent wad and smoothed it flat against the pavers. Pepe twisted his head up off the floor and glanced around nervously at the source of the softly ominous sound.

Sure enough, Mark confirmed, there it was, as his mother and Dad had stressed so often when he was little, stamped in green ink in tiny letters below the supermarket's logo: "WARNING: DANGER OF SUFFOCATION – KEEP THIS BAG AWAY FROM BABIES AND SMALL CHILDREN."

Nothing about dogs.

Mark and Paige had always scoffed at the silly concern of adults: As if the most obvious thing for a kid to do was go, "Ooh, here's a plastic bag! I think I'll stick my head in it!"

If they were dumb enough to do that, they were too dumb to live, he and Paige agreed. "That's how you improve the species. It's called 'survival of the fittest,'" she told him, chuckling. "That's how evolution works."

Mark had always been curious about how suffocation would work. How long would it take before you'd pass out? He and Paige had had timed contests at holding their breath. Both of them could go for more than a minute and a half. They used to play a game when they were in the back seat of the car approaching a tunnel; they'd crank up the windows as fast as they could and, at the instant of entry, suck in a huge gulp of air, clamp their teeth, compress their lips, sit back and try to last to the other side.

Nothing to it for the first thirty seconds or so, of course. But then the internal pressure would start to build. You began to dribble the air out of your lungs in careful rations, exhalation a substitute for inhalation. Saliva ponded behind your molars. Squeezing it over your tongue and swallowing it became another sublimation for breathing. Muscles all over your body began to tingle impatiently, especially around your ribcage and constricted stomach. Hungry for its air-meal, your gut responded with a twinge of nausea. You could feel your heart dully pulsing behind your windpipe. In the unbreathing stillness you could almost hear the cartilage creaking as you began to wiggle your ears, tighten and relax your temples, in the last desperate exertion of will.

Ahead, irising wider between your parents' shoulders through the windshield, was the semicircle of blue sky and gray asphalt and sun-glinting cars on the open freeway – the end of the bore. You were almost there. You couldn't let your sister beat you. You rocked back and forth in your seatbelt, forcing your shoulders into the upholstery to distract yourself – nostrils flared, eyes bugged, cheeks and forehead raddled... dramatizing to yourself and to your supposed audience your agony and your incredible self-mastery....

And then suddenly you were in the daylight! In joyful, stentorian chorus, you'd both heave in the delicious oxygen – reborn. The car might still be filled with the sickly tunnel-taint of exhaust that had inspired this exercise. Carbon monoxide, his Dad said. But each triumphant gasp slaked your insides like cool water in a paper cup at halftime when you straggle off the field all furry-mouthed with thirst, sweat-soaked and sun-fried, tail dragging

Or maybe you couldn't manage to make it all the way through the tunnel. Then you'd bow your head and revive yourself as silently as possible, checking out of the corner of your eye to make sure your rival too had been defeated before confessing your own failure. Which Mark always did in any case, because disappointment, he'd found, was harder to bottle up than satisfaction. And though he considered himself fairly tough, his resolve had never been strong enough to push him anywhere close to unconsciousness. Probably you couldn't even get there by determination alone.

Mark was a knee-jerk empiricist. Thinking about holding his breath had caused him to do it.

Pepe lay on his side quivering, waiting out the sudden, curiously prolonged and obviously sinister inactivity of the biped looming over him. But, in fact, Mark was absorbed in his own sensation. And as soon as actual discomfort set in to refine his memory of it – like when you're little, scribbling a few crude lines into each outlined shape in a coloring book with your crayons to evoke the finished picture – he loudly snorkeled air.

That spooked Pepe, who bounded upright.

Mark belled the plastic bag and slipped it over Pepe's head.

T he advantage of the clear plastic was that you could observe the dog's reaction.

Pepe tried to sluff out of the sheath, but Mark held the hem of the bag tight against the matted wool on Pepe's neck while backing him into the corner. He scooted up closer, fencing Pepe with his arms, until he had the dog snugly corralled in the vee between his thighs.

Pepe struggled, then calmed temporarily. There was air trapped in the bag to start with, of course. So Pepe had no inkling yet of what was happening to him. Except that his head was disagreeably enclosed, haloed by a clammy membrane as if he'd walked into a spiderweb.

And the bag wasn't opaque – he wasn't enveloped in darkness with peril woo-wooing all around him outside, unseen, as he'd been when Mark had thrown the tablecloth over him. As he would've been if Mark had followed through on the idea of popping him into a brown paper grocery sack.

Which would've been a different experiment. Just a boring continuation of the previous one, though, since paper breathes.

He watched Pepe looking out through the clear film. Pepe's nose was thrust forward into one corner of the bag so that the end seam ran on a diagonal across his muzzle. The opposite corner jutted like the peak of a jaunty ski-cap above Pepe's right ear, the one with the straggling ribbon ends. Mark rearranged his grip on the bag and on Pepe, managed to spread his fingers and wrap them, first one hand and then the other, around Pepe's mane on either side so that the plastic bag was snubbed securely under his chokehold. His thumbs overlapped on the underside of Pepe's jaw, at the windpipe, just above the collar. But Mark didn't exert pressure there. Or at least no more than necessary to keep the slick plastic from crinkling loose, out from under his encircling hands, when Pepe started to wriggle. He didn't want to throttle Pepe – allst he wanted was to observe the natural course of oxygen deprivation.

Pepe's big round black poodle-eyes weren't avoiding Mark's any longer. Pepe gazed plaintively into Mark's face from behind his translucent hood – like a bubble-boy or something. A winsome bubble-dog. A hospital patient in an oxygen mask – a veterinary hospital. Only this was a *reverse* oxygen mask. Pepe was trying to puzzle out what his tormentor might have in store for him, though he still blinked and bowed his head deferentially as if to avoid provoking it. Pepe seemed to recognize the situation as demeaning. But not yet dangerous. Pepe's distress so far came from being restrained, not from being smothered.

Paige and Naomi used to have arguments about whether dogs thought like people. Actually, *they* didn't argue – Naomi was just as dubious as Paige about the contention of Sinclair's trainer that dog psychology is completely different.

Naomi had a couple of books on canine behavior, though, that said the same thing. According to these theorists, beyond recognizing that a dog is hungry or in pain or territorial or afraid or confused – acting out of the most elemental of drives – humans are simply wrong if they impute complex emotions and motives like love (as opposed to loyalty) or spite or revenge to their pets.

If you leave a dog at home and it tears up the couch and the drapes and your slippers, for example, it isn't doing those things to get back at you for abandoning it – it's because the dog was cooped up and bored. If a dog defends you against an assailant, it's simply honoring the pack bond. Dogs chew and dig and fight by instinct, not calculus. Obedience is just another survival skill.

In fact, to the extent that dogs relate to people (watching 'em on the street or in a park left Mark with no doubt about which of the two species truly fascinates 'em) it's as honorary dogs, not the other way around. Contrary to what Abuelita Jeanne believed, then, Pepe didn't think he was a very small human; he thought Abuelita Jeanne and Paige and Mark and everybody else were very large canines. Some sort of weird, hairless, odd-smelling, hind-leg-walking, totally quirky breed, it's true, but masterful.

His Dad agreed with the books. Even Maurice couldn't help it that he'd been bred to certain unfortunate traits and spoiled by his owner, his Dad allowed. There was a word for it, his Dad said. If you thought Maurice was "arrogant," "disdainful," "manipulative" – adjectives that really only describe human behavioral constructs....

Except Mark couldn't think of the word right off.

And basically he was in Page and Naomi's camp. No doubt Pepe's thought processes were a lot more limited than a person's, but it seemed pretty clear to Mark that Pepe could reason to his own interests and consciously tailor actions to ends.

Anthro...!

Anthro...po....

...Pomorphizing!

Almost as long as *antidisestablishmentarianism*, his favorite word. Which his Dad had taught him to define as well as spell: "Being against being *against* being *for* having a state religion. "

Or whatever. Crazy!

Yeah, anthropomorphizing. He'd remembered it. And there was another one, too. The... fallacy... something. The... *really pathetic* fallacy!

That was it. That was the way his Dad had

explained it. Because he said people had the concept completely backwards. The fallacy lay in not recognizing that inanimate objects actually *do* have it in for people. Coffee or Coke or ice cream will invariably jump out of the container to spill down your shirt-front in a car, his Dad pointed out. Clothes dryers eat socks. Nails bend just to psych you out. Hammers aim at thumbs. Clothes hangers multiply like rabbits in closets but scuttle off into hiding when you need one. Excetera.

Once in Seattle his Dad had actually pulled over to the curb and gotten out and hurled his half-eaten hamburger as hard as he could against a telephone pole after catsup had dribbled from the wrapper onto his lap.

"*Bad* burger!" he'd shouted angrily. "Take *that*, you *son of a bitch*!"

He'd frowned at the stain on his khaki pants, dabbed at it disconsolately with a napkin and then slid back in behind the wheel, explaining lightly, "You can't just let 'em get away with stuff like that."

Karen hadn't looked too happy. In fact, she'd told his Dad it was a pretty pathetic example to set.

So whereas all kinds of things would be racing through Mark's brain if he were in Pepe's place – how did I get into this predicament and what are my alternatives for getting out and what'll be the consequences on what time-scale if I don't and how serious are my adversary's intentions and why's he doing it to me and how can I use whatever I can infer about his character and motives to convince him to stop it or to save myself...? And, boy, the minute this is over I'll make sure he never tries it again by biting the shit out of him! Or cozying up to him as nicey-nicey as I can be!

Maybe it was true that all Pepe was aware of was immediate experience. Food equals pleasure. A smushed paw equals pain. Praise – a tone of voice, a facial expression – equals pleasure. Rebuke – ditto, ditto – equals displeasure. Nuzzle the button that pays off, avoid the one that keys a shock. Even mini-brained mice learn that. But maybe Pepe really couldn't discriminate context at all. He just knew what he liked. And what he didn't like. Demand a walk when he's not in the mood, unh-unh. Throw a blanket on him, unh-unh. Stick him in a washing machine, unh-unh. Try to asphyxiate him in a plastic bag, unh-unh.

Mark thought of the joke about a goldfish, swimming back and forth in a bowl all day thinking: "Oh, wow, a pretty castle! Oh, wow, a pretty castle! Oh, wow, a pretty castle! Oh, wow, a pretty castle...!"

Pepe, meanwhile, had begun to sense the atmospheric change inside the bag. The air would be warm and humid, Mark imagined, thicker with the vapor exuded from his lungs but thinner in nutritional content. Even though Pepe was still under the illusion that he was breathing, his cells knew they weren't getting the oxygen dose they expected. And that triggered a renewed rebellion.

But Mark had Pepe under perfect control. He pliered his thighs tighter around Pepe's heaving flanks and levered more of his upper-body weight onto Pepe's shoulders.

Pepe's eyes under the plastic seemed to protrude and to glisten more brightly with desperation.

"It's okay, Peepee," Mark lied. Although it wasn't altogether a lie – he had no intention of going so far as to kill the obnoxious little loser.

Pepe tossed his head and bucked. He worked his right foreleg free and raked Mark's trousered thigh, clabbering to scratch out of the bag. Mark parried with his forearms, which were protected, fortunately, because his cuffs had slid down to his wrists as he'd crawled under the table. One of Pepe's claws snagged on the damp sweatshirt fabric. That helped Mark pin the skinny limb under his left elbow, against his leg. Pepe jerked and let out a shriek. Mark leaned harder on him to cram his hindquarters even more firmly into the narrow prison between his knees. Pepe's spine was bent awkwardly under the pressure, against or at least to the limit of its natural curvature. Struggle was difficult if not painful.

"Take it easy," Mark cooed. "Easy. Easy. Just a minute more, buddy. You're gonna survive."

Pepe quieted, as if considering his options, or gathering his strength. Or maybe because he was burning up the oxygen available to him faster by struggling. He was breathing harder now. More deeply, anyway. The plastic bag had begun to expand and contract. At first it was barely noticeable, but within a few seconds the transparent membrane was pumping in and out, molding itself to Pepe's snout like shrink-wrap and then ballooning away, droplets of watery dog-snot clinging to the inside surface where it had indented itself briefly against Pepe's nostrils.

Mark was engrossed. Delighted. He thought of one of those bladders on respirators you see inflating and deflating in movies about hospital emergency rooms. (Or the TV shows with the doctors and nurses running around crazily doing stuff to people who're being wheeled in on stretchers, which Mark had caught a few times in the summer; most weeknights during the school year he'd fallen asleep by the time they came on.) Once again his experimental results were really gratifying. This was a dramatic illustration of what happens as all the air slowly gets used up in a nonporous container.

If he'd had a huge glass jar, say, to put Pepe in, the way he and Paige had kept grasshoppers and praying mantises they'd captured in the yard or the park – only without the torn up blades of grass and twigs and the holes they'd always stabbed into the lid with an ice-pick so the insect could breathe – well, the effect wouldn't have been anything like as visual. As instructive. As plain entertaining.

Would Pepe, bewildered, just have laid down and died? Or no, lain down, Mark corrected his interior monologue. English class: lie, lay, lain. Lay, laid, laid, is when something's in your hand. Or would Pepe have tried as hard as he could to climb out of the jar, like the bugs? Circling the base more and more frantically, jumping up and falling back – unfortunately lacking suckers or sticky stuff on the bottoms of his feet to walk himself up the sides, not that it would have done him any more good than it did the grasshoppers and mantises, what with the lid – until the lack of oxygen drained his strength and he collapsed on his back, tongue lolling, little puff-balled legs twitching limply in the vacuum, his eyes turning into Xs....

Probably the fact that Mark was keeping him squunched down, though, that Mark's hands were around his throat clinching the offending plastic shroud over his face, connected cause to effect for Pepe. And the effect was now unmistakably life-threatening.

Mark felt the little dog's body, wedged between his thighs, humped under his crotch, suddenly ripple and surge with panicky urgency.

But that only made Mark more determined to maintain final mastery. He felt his own heart thumping in his chest. He felt the heat of the blood suffusing his cheeks and forehead. He felt it thickening his penis. He felt the swirling adrenaline fizzing into his brain – almost like being drunk.

This wasn't a reaction to exertion, though. Not from grappling with Pepe. It was (he would later conclude, worrying over the sensations) what happens to you when you mess with pure evil. The evil, the weakness, you have inside you. Which feels like strength, in a way, because it's a test of your willingness to transgress what's forbidden.

Cruelty. Cruelty to an animal. Feels good. Because it feels so bad. Probably like one of those hard drugs they warn you about, crack, speed, heroin. The pleasure they give you is partly a function of the awfulness you sense is waiting for you – that you now have coming to you – after the pleasure's over....

He had the power to kill Pepe if he wanted to. Make this inferior creature cease to be.

Not that he would. If it weren't that he could.

Everything he'd done to Pepe, he realized, was only because he could. And because Pepe had brought it on himself. The little dipshit. The disobedient little sissy-dog. The stupid ingrate piss-poodle.

But Mark wouldn't. Wouldn't kill Pepe. Imagine, if nothing else, the trouble it would bring down.... Trying to secrete the little carcass. Throw off suspicion, disassociate himself somehow, improbably, from the mysterious disappearance....

But how close was he capable of actually coming?

Mark gritted his molars and clung to Pepe and the plastic. All he wanted was to see Pepe black out. Then he'd relent. Immediately revive him....

Pepe flexed his neck, the only thing he could move. He wrung his head about in anguish. The soft bubble within which he was suffocating flapped and pulsed with his thrashings. Pepe's jaws began to clamshell wider, the pink tongue flicked between his teeth and lips and then its heel curled back in his throat. Pepe started crying.

The continuous ululation – hardly muffled at all beneath the wrapping of extruded polyvinyl film — was higher and more plaintive and more tremulous even than when his paw had been slammed in the car-door. He sounded almost like a human baby. A human baby shrilling in a way that could only mean that somebody was doing something totally sick and horrible to it.

But Mark was not really hurting Pepe. He *wasn't!* Not physically. Except for the leg a little, maybe. Which Pepe could avoid by not wriggling. But Mark was making absolutely sure he wasn't strangling Pepe. Or stressing his spinal cord too much or whatever. Mark was gauging his subject's condition with the microscopic care and dispassion of the scientist.

Pepe's darting eyes were blinded by terror. If you could call it that. But probably it was more just intense discomfort and raw survival instinct. The way a fly flails to pull loose when it's tangled in a spiderweb, Mark thought. Flies obviously can't have learned about the deadly threat of spiders. They just know they aren't supposed to be caught. But Mark, luckily for Pepe, was no spider. Solicitude was part of the package – compassion stronger than dispassion. That, (he would also decide later) was why smothering Pepe was actually giving him an erection.

He was shaky, breathless, dizzy with nerves. Ashamed to his marrow. Of himself, of what he was experiencing. Not all that different from the way he felt when he lay on his bed squinting dry-mouthed at the pictures in the *Playboys* or *Penthouses* he sometimes turned up when he searched his Dad's bedroom. Scared. Brave: you have to be brave in a weird way to do what feels completely wrong, whether or not you know why. Proud, sort of, of the bravery; ashamed of the wrong.

Curious. Mostly curious. About what exactly there was to be scared about and how he was going to deal with it. His penis was engorged and straining to stick up more from auto-excitement at the revelations of his own unimagined potential for depravity – sneaking into his Dad's room, rifling through the closets and drawers, stealing the magazine, hiding behind closed doors (which might be banged open at any minute to reveal him in his humiliation) to pull down his pants and rub himself while trying to imagine the enormity of actually touching a girl's nipples, of sticking his dick inside her – than from the mere lust inspired by a few two-dimensional revelations of the female anatomy.

Or the meaningless power to make something weaker than you are suffer.

Mark had a conscience, all right. And suddenly he felt he was on the verge of damaging it irreparably. Like the drug in the syringe, the virus on the dirty needle. This experiment....

Okay, couldn't go on any further.

He let go of Pepe's neck.

He relaxed his thigh muscles.

Pepe erupted from between Mark's legs and, shaking his head violently, fled to the opposite rear corner of the alcove. But the plastic shroud clung. Pepe ricocheted off the table leg, bowed his head, reached up with his paw and peeled the bag down over his eyes and muzzle with a quick, deft swipe.

Mark slumped, watching Pepe around his shoulder. He smiled at the little poodle wanly.

"I told you," he murmured. "I wouldn't do anything really bad to you. Didn't I tell you?"

That gesture with the paw, he thought: It was so poignant, for some reason. Like a little human. So... cute!

His mother's voice, eerily close and totally unexpected, almost gave him a heart attack. He rocked back onto his heels – caught red-handed, at least in his weltering guilt.

Which he reflexively straightened to distance himself from. Cracking his crown hard on the low roof of the tabletop.

"Ow-*ow*!" he wailed, recoiling forward onto his hands and knees again.

The table legs clattered, knocked out of alignment with the walls. One of the chairs had been toppled backwards and rested on its top-rail against the windowsill.

Pepe, jaded or exhausted, matter-of-factly got up and edged toward the stove.

"What in the *world*?" his mother exclaimed from the doorway. "What are you doing under there?"

Mark grabbed his head. The second time! How stupid of a klutz, he whined inwardly, did that make him?

"You scared me!" Mark accused her. "I didn't hear you coming. You ought to warn people before you barge in a place!"

He noticed the empty plastic bag slowly deflating where Pepe had shucked it. He reached over, snatched it off the floor and hurriedly crammed it into his front-pocket.

"Excu-u-se *me* ," his mother drawled. "For walking into my own kitchen. To make *your* dinner. Next time you want me to knock?"

"Yes, please," Mark mumbled. Mollifying her by rounding out her ridicule with his own polite self-mockery. He was waiting for his heart to slow down.

He watched her disembodied calves scissor toward the refrigerator while the door thwop-thwopped behind her. The hem of a wine-colored skirt with some kind of tiny pattern flicked just below the dark horizontal top-frame of his view. She had on the ugly two-tone gray running shoes she wore commuting to work and sometimes actually ran in with her friend Sylvie. Sylvie had a

trace of a French accent still, which beguiled
Mark, especially because she liked to make him
blush by telling his mother in his presence how
incredibly handsome he was. Almost as if she were
flirting with him. ("You're her type," his mother
commented dryly once. Curious to learn something
about himself and what girls might find attractive
in him, Mark eagerly asked her what type he was.
"Male," his mother replied.)

Even though Sylvie was old like his mother she
wore fashionable lycra tights with her navel
showing and jog-bras you knew had nothing
beneath and perky headbands and expensive
shoes and actually looked sort of sexy in that
dried-up middle-aged way – as well as giving off
a disquieting, highly perfumed musk — when the
two of them stood in the kitchen drinking juice,
cooling down from their exercise.

His mother, on the other hand, was just plain
embarrassing. Coming in after one of their circuits
– "gotta stay svelte, now that I'm back on the
market," she'd panted bitterly at Mark one time,
recognizing his disapproval – her face and chest
and upper arms would be all blotchy red, her hair
straggly, her nipples disgustingly visible under her
sweat-stained tanktop and ordinary bra, the teensy
webs of broken blood vessels on her upper
thighs — as if somebody had been doodling on
her unsunned skin there with fine-nibbed blue and
red pens – revealed by her skimpy gym-shorts,
which were just an old pair of Paige's she'd
probably salvaged from the Goodwill basket. And
already the shoes, a cheap brand neither Mark nor
Paige would have gone around in without bags
over their heads, looked used and about two years

out of style.

"So you dived under the table because I startled you?" his mother proposed.

There was a sucking sound that indicated she'd pulled open the freezer door. You could hear she was amused. Prompting him less out of interest in the true explanation for his 13-year-old behavior – she could probably imagine almost any trivial rationale or none at all—than out of curiosity piqued by the particularly implausible implication.

"No," Mark grunted. He was crawling in reverse, head carefully bowed, veering backwards through the gap between the leaning chair and the front table-legs.

Behind Mark's butt, Pepe's tags tinkled and his claws tippy-tapped on the pavers, like a flourish on a toy snare-drum. Mark could picture the restorative shake and shimmy.

"Why was Peppy making that terrible racket?" his mother demanded, more pointedly. "It sounded like he was hurt."

"You could hear?"

"Of course I could hear."

"I was grabbing him," Mark explained. He righted the chair, lifted the table from underneath and squared it in the alcove. "I was holding him down, which got him upset. As usual, if you do *anything* to him. But he was so bad? He made me really mad. I guess," he admitted, "after he made me have to catch him I was a little rough with him. But he was just refusing to come with me. He knew he was being disobedient too. And then he did a pee, right in the middle of the floor."

"He did!"

Mark's mother, he saw when he turned and cranked himself up onto his feet – having made very certain he was well out from the overhang – had a blue plastic ice-tray in one hand and the other on her hip. She was frowning down at Pepe with her head cocked in that classic parental pose of dismay and disappointment.

"Yeah," he nodded eagerly like a prosecutor, encouraged by the jury's apparent sympathy. The colors in the kitchen suddenly faded. He thrust his hand out toward the table to steady himself but the brain-bubble immediately popped. "I cleaned it up," he added.

"I should hope so."

"That's why the washing machine's going."

"I *told* you he had to be taken out right away!"

"I know, Mother! I was trying! Remember, I called to you? I had to chase him all over the kitchen! Believe me. He wouldn't come to me. He *never* does. He was being a *very*... *bad*... little *animal*!"

The subject sat shivering slightly, halfway between the table and the stove in front of the Dutch door that opened to the backyard. At the word "bad," or perhaps the insult "animal" – Mark spat both words with a scowl beamed directly at Pepe – the little poodle rose and slunk around behind Mark's mother's ankles.

"Is Pepe limping again?"

"Gee," Mark replied evasively, "you think so?" Pepe did seem still to be favoring the leg, Mark had to agree ruefully.

"Maybe that's why he was being reluctant. Why's he all wet?"

"He's not really wet," Mark corrected her. "Just... damp."

"And that's because...?"

"Well.... I rinsed him off. I *tried* to get him

completely dry. I used a dirty towel. Don't worry, I put it in the washer too."

"What'd he need rinsing for?"

"I.... Okay. See, I rubbed him in it. His pee. So he'd learn."

"Oh, no, Mark. No. That's not right."

"I know." Mark hung his head and winced apologetically.

"Is that why he's limping?"

"Unh-unh," Mark insisted.

"You *know* you have to be careful about his leg. No wonder he was crying! If nothing else, you injured his pride! I don't even think that works. But the main thing is, it's not your place to punish Peppy. Mark? No, no, no. Mother has entrusted him to us. "

"Yeah, I know. But he just squatted right down in front of me."

"I don't care. Discipline is not a part of your job description. She'd be really upset if she heard you'd done something like that to him."

"I know," Mark nodded.

"He's a grownup dog. If he makes a mistake it's because he isn't being let out in time. It's our fault, not his."

Mark bowed his head. He winced dubiously. "Yeah. I guess. I know. I was sorry after I did it."

His mother set the ice-tray on the counter and hunkered alongside Pepe. She ruffled his topknot. She scrubbed his back, appraising him. Pepe lifted his head to her and pulled the corners of his lips back into what looked like a smile of pleasure.

"Are you all right, Mister Peppy?" she inquired. "*M'sieu* Pépé? *Le Moko*? *Du Casbah d'Algiers*? Such a *très grand nom*, for such a *p'tit* little *chien*. *Quel p'tit* li'l *mec que tu es*. And you're very proud of that fancy moniker, aren't you, *mon vieux*? That silly *nom* your silly Mommy gave you."

She scratched Pepe behind his ears.

"It's hard for you being around this house though, isn't it? Nobody spoils you here the way your own Mommy does. You don't get all that attention you've grown so accustomed to."

Mark thought of objecting. He'd just given Pepe plenty of attention. But his mother was right... it was not the kind Pepe was used to. Or the kind Mark would want to describe in detail.

"And then when you have an accident, some mean kid goes and shoves your nose in it."

"Not his nose," Mark countered, wounded by his mother's characterization. True as it was. "Just his... like, side fur."

"Well, it's still mean. A very undignified thing to have done to you. Isn't it, Peppy? As if you didn't know any better. You do know better, don't you?"

"But the thing was, I was already trying to take him outside," Mark defended himself.

"You just couldn't hold it any more, could you, fella? We let you go too long."

"I swear, Mother. He wouldn't come out from under the table and when I finally dragged him out he just deliberately piddled there."

"Well, you probably *were* being too rough with him. Probably you frightened him. In any case, I don't want to ever hear that you did that to him again. Right? Are we clear on that? No punishments. Anymore."

"Yes, Mother," Mark agreed.

"We've only got two more days left anyway. And then Abuelita Jeanne'll be here to take him home. We ought to be able to cope for that much longer, shouldn't we? All get along with one another?"

She worked her fingers in the thick thatch below Pepe's collar and down between his forelegs. "Even if you *are* sort of a pill, sometimes. Eh, little guy? What might be called a difficult dog? You *are* a difficult dog from time to time, aren't you, *M'sieu Pépé*? I guess we can't blame you too much, though. It's very stressful having to adapt to new circumstances."

Pepe shuffled in ecstasy as she tickled his chest. Abuelita Jeanne said he loved having French spoken to him. If there was anything wrong with any of his four legs it wasn't apparent now, Mark noted with gratitude. Pepe curled himself against his mother's calf to curry prolongation of the caresses.

"So you still," she said, "haven't taken him for his walkies, I gather."

"No, Mother," Mark acknowledged.

"Come on, Mark. It's been an hour now since I asked you."

"Not an hour."

"Okay. Forty-five minutes?" She gave Pepe a final stroke down his spine and stood. She spun to open the door of the upper cabinet where the glasses were kept. She took down a stubby one.

Mark bent and picked up the leash. "I'm gonna do it right now," he said. "I had to clean up after him and everything. I *started* the *wash!*"

"Gee. I guess you deserve the Congressional medal." She reached for the bottle of Scotch on the liquor shelf. "Just don't be gone too long. Dinner's gonna be ready fairly quickly tonight. I'm going out afterwards. I have a date. For a movie."

"Huh. What're you gonna see?"

"Some foreign thing. I can't even remember the name. You wouldn't be interested. You probably haven't heard of it. I'll be back early."

"Who're you going with?"

"Somebody you haven't heard of either. A new person. You'll meet him, when he comes to pick me up. That's why I wanted you to get Pepe's walk over with earlier, though. Look, it's not even light anymore."

"Yes it is," Mark argued, glancing out the window. The corner redwood tree and the brushy hillside rising behind the grape-stake fence were still visible in the post-sunset gloom. "What are you gonna make?"

"Babooty."

"That has curry in it, right?"

"Mm-hm. A little." She unscrewed the cap on the Scotch bottle. "Apples. Raisins. Ground beef. You know. And we have bananas. Over some rice?"

"I hate curry," Mark objected.

"No you don't," his mother assured him. "You'll love it."

Needless to say – what with there now being a witness for whom to cast doubt on Mark's version – Pepe sat as docile as a lamb when Mark genuflected to snap on the leash. And after a brief hesitation at the threshold for a precautionary sniff, Pepe resolutely plunged into the great world as if walkies were a treat he'd been impatient for all day.

Mark took him around the side of the house and out the front gate his Dad had built. It opened onto the paving square he remembered his mother and Dad pouring and troweling all one Saturday afternoon. When it was smooth everybody had gathered to press a palm into the gray goo, and his mother had scratched their four names and the date alongside.

"The Ahlquists."

Yeah, right. Mark was always bemused at the tiny cinquefoil print that was his hand then, next to cute little Paige's.

Pepe was walking fine now. There was only a very occasional skipped beat. Mark basically felt drained; he allowed Pepe to set his own pace. Which meant they lingered at virtually every distinct tuft of groundcover along the way.

Pepe would bury his nose in the stalks or leaves, like the magnetized tip of a compass needle locked on the pole, and inscribe quivering arcs around it, rump out, while painstakingly deconstructing the history of its canine visitations. Finally he'd decide on an appropriate position from which, gazing around superiorly, to overlay his own conclusive chapter. Then he'd trot off to snuffle at the next shrublet or tree-trunk or telephone pole.

(Although he was equally keen on decoding the aromatic texts imprinted on upright objects, Pepe couldn't really edit them – he'd just have to leave a kind of afterword on the surface alongside – since he wasn't into hiking his hind leg. Naomi said that big male dogs practically topple over sideways trying to pee on things as high up as they can, so that any dog who follows will be impressed by what a fearsome giant roams the territory. Mark wondered if that was why Pepe didn't even try. No way he could ever fake being anything but the lowly loser on the canine food-chain he was.)

The streetlamp at the corner opposite the park guttered alight just as they reached the grassy slope that led down to the swings and teetertotters. Mark's nerves always tingled warily near the park after nightfall. It had a curfew from sundown to sunrise. Not that Mark and Paige considered it applicable to them, as immediate neighbors. Paige and a bunch of kids from her school used to smoke grass and drink beer and giggle furtively there in the pitch-blackness sometimes on Saturday nights. Mark would play Indian scout and circle them silently in the wooded fringes. It was best to have a gang of people with you, though, to be safe. You also had to be ready to run if a cop-car showed up. Or a real gang, from the flats, roistering black guys or Chicanos with their caps backwards and baggy pants. An elderly man and his wife had been mugged not far from where Mark was standing now. That was a long time ago, though, and later at night. They'd been walking a cocker spaniel. So you could imagine how much protection Pepe would give him.

Mark tugged at Pepe's leash and, for variety, headed him across to the other sidewalk for the return trip.

Mark was feeling more morose with every step. When they were halfway home, Pepe found a spot of lawn that emitted whatever vibes set off sympathetic resonance in the canine bowel. He humped his back, tucked his rump, stiffened his tail and began a kind of nervous, circular duck walk around the target area. He gazed upward the way Mark had noticed some men do at stadium urinals, as if to divert attention away from the business at hand.

Pepe's expression was oddly sheepish too, Mark thought. When their eyes met Pepe glanced quickly away. He seemed to be imploring Mark by example to accord him visual privacy. You wondered if dogs – well, toy poodles, obviously – weren't as embarrassed as people to be observed at this basest of activities.

Everybody in Mark's family except his Dad would go ballistic if somebody blundered into the bathroom while they were on the toilet. The bathtub was different—he'd seen his mother in it a lot when he was little; could recall her pink-nippled breasts and brown wedge of pubic hair under the water, same as the Pets and Playmates when it comes to that.

His mother, the family album showed, was kind of a fox when she was young. Paige looked almost exactly like her at the same age. The last time he'd seen Paige naked was when her chest was still flat like a boy's, although she had a sleek dimple where a boy would have had a weenie. They all religiously threw the lock now. Except, of course, for his ridiculous Dad, who said the body and its functions were perfectly natural and you might as well get used to it. Excessive modesty is silly, a kind of vanity, he declared Once he even recited this long Latin gobbledygook which meant, he said, that everyone is born out of the place between where a woman shits and where she pees. Karen let out a squawk and said that was disgusting. And an inappropriate thing to say in front of a kid. Mark found the concept gross too, if graphically memorable. He couldn't help picturing it, trying to orient the parts alluded to, though he didn't really want to. His Dad added that he wasn't advocating being an exhibitionist, because that's just the other side of the same coin. Mark intended to take Latin in high school.)

Before Pepe uncrouched he'd extruded three gelatinous turds. Glistening in the dim light from the streetlamp filtered through the tops of the planter-strip trees, they appeared almost identical in color and consistency to the lumpy canned food that had gone in at the other end. Mark automatically patted his pants to locate the pocket he'd wadded the plastic bag into. Meanwhile, he was automatically surveying the scene of the crime. The sidewalks were empty in all directions. The curtains were drawn on the windows glowing from the house behind the lawn. Normally under those circumstances he'd have just left Pepe's poop where it was. It would dissolve with time. It was organic. He couldn't figure out why some people got so uptight about a little dogshit on their precious grass. But his mother's standing instructions were to clean up after Pepe. And Mark was feeling he'd cut too many moral corners already today.

Anyway there was something satisfying, righteous, about gloving up the loose stools (Paige had taught him that strange term, which had of course immediately provoked a round of gleeful punning: "excuse me, lady, you're sitting on my stool," "is that your stool on my stool?") heightened by the fact that nobody was around to see. Only Mark knew he was performing this good deed. Which made it all the more virtuous. Just as only Mark knew the bad deeds that were burdening his conscience. Which made them all the more torturous. Pepe would never be a stool pigeon.

The joke gave him no joy. To tell the truth, it wasn't even clear that Pepe, bopping along at the end of his leash – displaying no particular hesitancy about being in Mark's company – was anything but indifferent to the tribulations of the recent past now that they were past.

"Oh, wow, a fascinating stink! Oh, wow, a fascinating stink!"

Did he even have a memory? Certainly he had associations. This sycamore—equals squirrel, because he surprised one at its base once. That driveway—equals cat. Mark—equals pain. Or the distinct possibility of it. Something like that. Didn't matter whether Mark was actually responsible or not. Pepe didn't trust him; never had, never would. So what else was new?

Well, now Mark had the altogether unsettling understanding that he couldn't trust himself.

Pepe's shit was too soft to come up in intact blobs. Mark tried to minimize the residue and wipe it off the blunt blades of mown grass with the clean polyvinyl around the edges of the mass he was consolidating in his fist. The job was messy. When he decided he'd done the best he could – "good enough for government work," his Dad always said, enigmatically – Mark slid the loop of the leash over his left wrist to free his hand to remove the bag from his right. Pepe, toilet needs relieved, was ready to forge on; he flopped at the end of the leash like a hooked fish.

Mark gave it a sharp, annoyed yank to reel Pepe closer and create slack. Then he skinned the cuff of the plastic gantlet quickly down over his forearm and right wrist. But just as he was about to whip the bag completely inside out, contents securely pouched, Pepe tautened the leash again. The unexpected jerk caused the nails of Mark's index and middle fingers to brush one of the smears of dog-caca.

"Augh!" Mark reacted in revulsion, "Yuchh!"

He contorted his face into the Mask of Tragedy. He sneered at the contaminated fingernails. A few tiny flecks of brown jelly were indeed visible.

"Awww, Pepe?" Mark shuddered. He whinnied involuntarily. Hastily he shifted the horrible packet back to his right hand and snapped his left wrist up and down as if trying to detach the fouled fingers.

"God damn it! You *creep! Damn* you! See what you made me do?"

Mark had flung the handle of the leash off his wrist with the first downstroke. Pepe took the opportunity to scurry off to the bush whose siren scent had been beckoning. Mark hunkered and scraped his sullied fingernails on the grass, over and over, each time in a new clump, working them down into the moist dirt too, then wafting them under his nose, until no trace of the fecal stench adhered. He couldn't wait to get home to soap and hot water.

The flush of anger at Pepe had dissipated, though. Mark no longer had the heart for it. He'd used up all his energy. In fact, he had to concede, he deserved this. You could look on it as justice. Getting caca-ed by Pepe was appropriate. Doing the dirty work of cleaning up after a dumb little dog was the station he'd earned in life. His best hope, his penance. Although never having had religious training he could only intuit the concept. What goes around comes around. Shit for shit.

He let Pepe walk the rest of the way home

independently, trailing the leash. Mark bore the bag of dog feces in his hand humbly all the way to their own garbage can.

Although Pepe seemed satisfied, Mark gave him a small additional portion after the first bowlful of dinner had gone down. Pepe retired himself to the living room and the pillow by the sofa while Mark and his mother ate in the kitchen nook.

"You're very subdued tonight," she said after a while.

"I guess," he replied.

"I'm sorry if you don't really like the dinner. I hardly put any curry powder in it."

"No, it's okay," he said.

"I always thought you liked babooty. It's one of Paige's favorites."

"No it's not."

"I always thought it was."

"Whatever. It tastes fine."

"Are you feeling under the weather? Did you have a hard workout today at practice?"

"Unh-unh." He shrugged and shook his head.

She looked at him in silence for a minute and then smiled and arched an eyebrow. "Okay."

He ate another couple of forkfuls of the hot, sweet mixture of meat and onions and fruit, and the rice. He drank from his milk-glass.

"We're gonna miss Pepe after he's gone, aren't we?" his mother mused.

Mark raised his eyes. "I guess," he said.

"It's nice having another presence around the house. With Paige away and all. The place seems kind of empty. Doesn't it to you?"

Mark wasn't sure how to answer. He had the suspicion she was working toward another one of those depressing conversations about moving to some smaller place. Trying to enlist his alliance.

"Maybe we should get a dog of our own eventually," she proposed. "Have you ever thought of that? How does that idea strike you?"

"Huh!" he allowed.

"I'm not sure right now's the time. Things are too unsettled. We'll have Paige back with us for the summer, wherever we are. But then it'll just be you and me again, eh, kid?"

"I guess," he nodded.

"Would you like to have a dog?"

"I don't know. Not a poodle," he added. "Not a *toy* poodle anyway."

"No, no," she agreed.

"It would have to be big."

"Why big?"

"Just would."

"Big dogs are harder to take care of."

"You think so?"

"Well, they eat more. They take up more space. I don't know. I had in mind something along the lines of... say a beagle. They're a nice size. Aren't they? Or maybe just a mixed breed. A regular old mongrel. Some poor orphan dog we could get from the pound, who really needs a home, and a family. Hybrid vigor. With a nice disposition. They say mixed breeds have more even temperaments."

Mark thought for a moment. He'd never missed pets. The notion of having his own animal companion, in abstract, was appealing. Intimations of body warmth, thick redolent fur, romps, dependence, affection....

...But then the guilt. A low-level dread.

"No," he declared, "it would have to be more like a German shepherd. Or a husky. A malamute. Something like that. A dog that's really tough. And big. And mean. Like a wolf."

A TV image played in his mind: a pair of pale eyes staring coldly into his. A muzzle corrugated with feral menace. A snarl of warning from between two sets of fangs as slim as daggers....

"Good heavens," his mother exclaimed. She laughed dubiously. "I think a dog like that would scare me."

"Uh-huh," Mark nodded. "Me too."

Hoops

I just can't control him anymore. He's too big for me."

Weinert's diaphragm has tightened. He edges onto the squeaky metal draftsman's stool in front of his blackened computer screen and sets his half-empty beercan on the filing cabinet.

"He literally threw me down. Wrestled me to the floor. 'I can beat you up any time I feel like it,' he said. I told him I was calling the police. He laughed at me. Walked out."

"Where?" Weinert frowns. A new worry. Nighttime. Unnamed perils abroad. He pictures the nasty scene: their flushed faces, shrill invective, the scuffle. Caroline suddenly sprawled on her ample butt on the red-and-blue Persian rug. Nick, gangly, fists clenched, stalking out the carved front door. Vicious slam. Her Eskimo prints on the whitewashed walls suddenly rattled out of plumb.

"How should I know? Frankly, at that point I didn't really give much of a damn. For all I cared he was running away. Good riddance, too."

"So what'd you do? 'D you actually call the cops?" He doubts it, hopes not.

"No," Caroline admits. "No. But it was more than an idle threat. I warned him. Next time he lays a hand on me.... I won't put up with that!"

"Jesus, of course not!" Weinert exclaims.

"He probably just went down into the park. Till he cooled off. He's up in his room now."

Weinert exhales. "I don't like 'em going in that park after dark."

"Christ, Richard! Neither do I. You know that! Normally. But, hey, listen. If he'd gotten you in a headlock.... Then wrestled you to the ground."

"Right," Weinert scoffs. "I mean," he sighs, overcoming a flicker of amusement at the plight she's pictured, "I know. I don't blame you."

He wonders how many martinis she's soaked up so far this evening. He shifts the receiver to his left ear and humps low over his elbow, cradling the weight of his head and heart.

"The point is," she says, "I can't fight him. He's just gotten too strong."

"Yeah. You shouldn't have to fight him anyway."

"He thinks he doesn't have to obey me anymore. He said: 'Don't touch me, don't tell me what to do!' He figures that now because he's taller than me he's a law unto himself. Than I."

"Mm-hm." Their seventeen years of marriage have quickened her grammatical reflexes. Weinert swallows the correction he probably would have thought better of voicing anyway. "Well, he's testing."

"Great. Penetrating insight, Richard. Thanks. Let him test on somebody else for a while. I've had it. I'm not gonna be his punching bag."

"Good God no."

"It's time for you to take him."

"Well...."

"Or if you don't want to deal with it....maybe the answer's a foster home."

"Caroline..."

"No, I'm serious. This kid's in desperate need of somebody who'll put the fear of God in him! He's a bad citizen. Right now anyway. He's got to be reined in. And I can't do it."

"Okay, okay, listen. You know I'm perfectly willing to have him come back here."

"Not that you're the one, either. You're way too easy on him. You let all those kids ride roughshod. That's what makes it so tough on me. I try to lay down the law, establish some discipline, and they object: 'Aw, gee, that's not the way it is at *Daddy's* house.'" Her voice has become a nasal, munchkin singsong. "'*Daddy* never makes us do that!' So I always come across as the bad guy."

"Listen," Weinert objects. "What they're telling you isn't true. They're just trying to get out of whatever it is. It's a scam. Divide and conquer tactics. In fact, I always back you up. You know that. And I've got the same rules as you do around here. Same chores, basically – our approaches to discipline are practically identical. It's just," he adds, "that I happen to be a nicer person."

"You probably are," she murmurs.

"Hey, I'm only kidding." He regrets his lapse in judgment.

"No, I have no doubt you are. I'm a bad mother and a harridan. Right? I drink too much and I fly off the handle... I'm mean-spirited... my instincts are always to say no when they ask me for something. Right? Isn't that your version?"

"No, no."

"Well, it's all true. Every bit of it. You've had me pegged from the start."

"Oh come on. "

"And you know what I say to you, Richard?" Her voice is husky. "I say fuck it. I'm tired of being a mother. I wasn't cut out for this kind of stress. You take 'em."

"Little late to be figuring that out, isn't it?"

She has begun to cry. "They'll be better off without me."

"Hey. Stop it, Caroline," Weinert says. "You've had a bad night. What Nick did was inexcusable. No wonder you're upset."

"D-damn right I'm upset!"

"Believe me, I know how frustrating it can be."

"Frustrating isn't the word! Impossible! I do my best... and what do I get? Thrown down! My own son. Grabs me around the neck. "

"Did he hurt you? Jeez, I should've asked. I got the impression. "

"Yeah, just my pride. Next time, though, he'd better watch it. I'll kick him in the balls!"

"Go for it," Weinert agrees. "He's asking for it."

"No, no," she whimpers. "I can't. can't compete, can't cope on that level. That's ridiculous! That's not the way, Richard. That's not a fight I can win. He's right. Damn all!"

"Mm." Weinert can almost hear her teeth grind.

"Oh, I wish I could. Still beat the stuffings out of the little… prick!"

"You always were a retaliator," he sympathizes.

"Aagh, I'm just blowing off steam. But it's what he needs. A man, somebody to make him toe the line. Ever since Curt left. "

"Hey," Weinert bristles. "It's not as if he hasn't got a real father! I'm not exactly absent from his life! I mean, he just moved up there two weeks ago. And before that, with me, he seemed fine."

"What I'm saying."

"Reasonably fine. Sure, he has his moments. It's a stage."

"Well, it's one he's gonna have to work his way through without my participation, thank you. I'm not gonna stand around and take any more of this baloney. I'm shipping 'im back down to you. You try whipping 'em into shape. Both of 'em!"

"Where was Tonio? He a witness to all this melodrama?"

"He'd gone up to bed, thankfully. Not that he isn't a handful in his own right. And with Nick's example."

"You think they all aren't? Dani and I had our usual shouting match over dinner tonight."

"What about?"

"Who can remember? It all blurs into one long mishmosh. Generalized howl of teenage dissatisfaction. The 'wonder years!'" He snorts, reaches for his beer and sips a mouthful.

"Tell me about it. No, don't bother. They're yours, and welcome to 'em. You raise 'em. All three. They can benefit from your lackadaisical outlook. They may turn out to be real messes, but so what? At least I won't have to bear the bruises."

"Look...."

"I know. You're really a terrific father, Richard."

"Caroline... "

"No, believe me, I mean that."

"Mm-hm."

"And I'm a walking disaster. Obviously. None of 'em wants to be around me. Nobody wants to be around me! Not you, not Curt. The kids'll be better off. They'll grow up just fine."

"You finished?"

"Yes, I certainly am. It's been nice knowing you, Richard."

"Now wait a minute. "

"What have I got to live for? My life is total shitshow. Everybody'd be better off without me."

"Oh boy."

"I mean, think about it. I've got nothing, absolutely nothing, to look forward to. I'm in a job I hate – going nowhere, no future. There's no man in my life. Not even the remotest prospect of one. I'm a two-time loser at marriage. I can't stop eating – I'm getting fatter by the day. My kids hate me. One of my ex-husbands won't even talk to me, he apparently finds me so frightening and loathsome. The other one can barely bring himself to patronize me."

"How am I patronizing?"

"Listen to yourself!"

"I have been. I think I've been very sympathetic and supportive, actually."

"Anyway, how do you know which one is you I'm talking about?"

"Well. I certainly don't find you loathsome."

"I guess that's something."

"Grotesque and repugnant a bit, maybe. No, no, no, no!"

She's silent.

"I'm sorry. Bite my tongue. I'm just trying to cozen you into a better humor."

"Cozzen?" she mutters.

"However you pronounce it. What's the word? Cajole. Noodge. Stupid, of course. I admit that. My usual ham-handed, inappropriate approach."

"To say the fucking least."

"I'm sorry. I'm a lousy suicide hotline, Caroline. Granted. The thing is... I mean, you know yourself you're just talking... shit. If you'll pardon the expression. Not that what you're saying isn't real. Authentic concerns, in your life. I accept that. But at the moment you're seeing everything through dung-colored glasses. It's not all that bad. Is it?

Truly?"

She doesn't reply.

"Well it isn't. You know it isn't. You've got all kinds of stuff to live for. Of course you're down in the dumps tonight. Anybody would be."

"You'd've killed him!"

"Damn right I would've! And as far as how I really regard you.... I mean what do I have to say? You're a wonderful person! Would I have married you otherwise? You're smart, witty. beautiful. Interesting. "

She snuffles, quietly attentive.

"I respect you," he goes on. "I like you."

It's all true, but he's suffused by Machiavellian satisfaction nonetheless. He's even about to venture "I love you," but decides against it. The implications are too furry without a bunch of mood-puncturing qualifiers. On a roll now, he's proud of his tact itself. "You're a great mother, too," he declares. "Despite what you say. It's the kid who's the shit."

"Well. It's just that he's got so much anger in him!"

"I know. He's not a shit. He's going through a bunch of stuff. It's a tough time."

"He needs counseling."

Weinert shrugs. "Don't we all? Anyway, we've already tried that."

"Yeah. Maybe with somebody else, though. He wouldn't talk to Chloe when he went by himself. He said he didn't like her."

"He's not gonna like anybody. It won't be any different. Teenagers are notoriously resistant. If it's not his own idea, his own impulse – and it never will be. "

Caroline sighs. "So. What do you suggest?"

"About what?"

"About *what!* About *tonight,* Richard! Jesus Christ! Are you all there? About the future of this family!"

"Mm." He takes a breath. Her phrase has made him wince.

"Well. For starters, I guess, I'll come up and get 'em. Huh? That's what you want?"

"Or I could bring 'em down. So you wouldn't have all the burden of driving. Seems only fair, since I'm the one who's kicking 'em out."

"Well.... It's up to you."

"It is late."

"It is," he concurs.

"I guess we shouldn't disturb Tonio. It's not as if he did anything."

"Sounds reasonable."

"Oh, Richard," she moans. "I don't know, anymore! I just feel like I'm losing it!"

"Hey, babe," he says. "Can I make a suggestion?" He glances at his wristwatch. "Nick's safely ensconced by now, right? Up in his lair?"

"Mm."

"So you're not likely to have any more interactions with him. Not tonight. He didn't say anything to you when he came back?"

"Nope."

"No apology."

"No nuthin."

"Boy, he is being a shitface. Okay. Here's the thing. You go to bed, get some sleep, you'll feel better in the morning. Then we can discuss it further. We'll figure out the appropriate punishment and the logistics of whatever we want to do next, when we're all brighter and fresher. Less wound up. Meanwhile. "

"You're just trying to brush me off."

"No I'm not. I'm just trying to maintain perspective on what's best for all involved. Not fly off half-cocked."

"I should have been in bed half an hour ago!" she moans. "I have to go to work in the morning!"

Weinert sighs. "Which is why. "

"I can't keep on this way! I just can't!"

"Caroline," he grimaces. "You're utterly stressed out. For good reason. And we'll deal with it, I promise you. Only not now. Now is the time for you to go to bed. Got that? This is my first, my key recommendation to you. Go. To. Bed."

"Okay," she murmurs. "I hear you. Once again I will accede to your vast wisdom."

"For which I thank you."

"Don't mention it. The upshot being, of course, that in fact nothing is going to happen. As usual. Until the next time. And then once again nothing is going to happen."

"There won't be a next time," he declares. "There doesn't have to be."

"Yes there will be. Sure there will. Unless he starts to feel some real consequences."

"Don't worry! He's going to! I'm gonna have a serious talk with him."

"Yeah. Great," she intones.

"Tomorrow. In the afternoon. I'll go up there before you get home."

"Good. Fine."

"Then we'll take it from there."

"Sounds very promising."

"I'm glad to hear that."

"Good night, Richard. Thanks for listening."

"Hey, it's my problem too."

"It certainly is. 'Bye."

Nick shambles down the long grassy slope from the gate, untied shoelaces on his scuffed hightops flopping, sockless, his shoulders narrowed inside a baggy red-white-and-blue "Australia" tee-shirt that Weinert brought him from a press junket a year or so ago. Nick's slack posture is the subject of frequent parental remonstrances. He's got on a pair of wide-legged purple soccer shorts that emphasize his coltish pipestems, all knee-knobs and ropy muscle. Strands of dark hair have begun to fringe his lower shins.

"Hi, Nick," Weinert greets him.

Nick scrunches up one side of his face in a lopsided squint and grunts back "Hi." Somehow he manages to convey reluctance, petulance, suspicion and cautious pleasure. Not an inconsiderable feat, Weinert reflects, working only with a slouch and a monosyllable.

The park is sparsely peopled, as usual on a weekday afternoon. A couple of 30ish mothers in jeans and a dazzlingly blonde, achingly nubile teenager – probably, Weinert has concluded after thorough study from behind his dark glasses, a Nordic *au pair* – are tending toddlers around the swings. There's also a carousel, a teeter-totter, a sandbox and a steep, curving concrete slide tucked up against the wooded eastern hillside. Cupped in the middle of the bowl is a flat meadow for blanket-spreading and Frisbee-tossing. It's bounded by a path leading to a narrow, echoing tunnel that crosses under the elevated street to the westerly tennis courts and a tiered municipal rose garden. Beyond the path is an asphalt court with two hoops on metal poles.

Caroline recently bought a rambling brown-shingle cottage shaded by redwoods at the northern edge of the park. She moved after splitting with Curt and selling the big four-story Mediterranean she and Weinert had owned before their divorce. Weinert drives up here often to juggle a soccer ball, heave a football or play twenty-one with whichever of the kids are staying with her. Their rendition of shared custody – part of a scrupulous settlement they drafted without lawyers or overt rancor – features random permutations in living arrangements keyed to work and school schedules and the shifting dynamics of sibling rivalry. ("California!" his lawyer brother in Chicago scoffs at their aberrant post-matrimonial accord.) Weinert's own tiny two-bedroom cottage is only a zip-code digit away, in the flats. It's a less prestigious neighborhood, but then Caroline had an extra $50,000 in equity to work with thanks to the remodeling job Curt had paid for on their old house before abruptly exiting the scene.

"How you doin'?" Weinert smiles.

Nick shrugs.

Weinert assesses him quizzically. He does appear to have elongated another couple of inches in the past week. You notice it more in time-lapse, Weinert thinks. Nick's at that ugly stage when his feet and florid nose have bloomed out of scale with the rest of his child's skinny body. The down on his upper lip is beginning to take on a tint. He has a pimple with a whitehead above one eyebrow. He hasn't yet learned to pop them.

"Shoot some hoops?" Weinert says.

It's a phrase he wouldn't normally utter – there's a plaintive, "wannabe" quality in the word *hoops* from his own Midwestern and generational perspective. But it's Nick's parlance.

Weinert has brought along his new indoor/outdoor basketball with the NBA logo stamped in silver on the pebbled surface. He flips it to Nick, who dribbles it deftly between his legs. The ball bounces off the grass with a hollow, mushy ring.

"Sure," Nick shrugs. Indifference is the soul of his new persona.

They stroll together toward the court, past the homeless man sprawled under a pyracanthus bush next to his neatly packed and tarpaulined Safeway cart. Why, Weinert wonders, do these derelicts decompose into formless mounds when they sleep? You have to look very carefully to discern feet and a human anatomy among the grubby rags. This particular wraith has lurked in the park's margins for months.

"I hear you and your mother had some problems last night," Weinert says over his shoulder as he takes off his sunglasses and stashes them with his wristwatch and keys on a bench by the tunnel entrance.

"She had a problem," Nick scowls. He rims his first layup. "I sure didn't."

Weinert bristles at the swagger implicit in his response. "Well, you do now, pal, I can assure you."

"She's nothing!" Nick sneers. "She's weak."

"Whoa, buddy...," Weinert cautions.

"Anyway, she always has problems."

Nick has abruptly shifted from surly to plaintive. "She's

constantly getting on my case. The least little thing! I don't know what's wrong with her!"

"Nothing's wrong with her. She's just looking out for you. For your welfare," Weinert replies. "Sometimes that means saying 'no.' Or telling you what to do, when you don't want to. It's not an easy job, being a parent."

Weinert is discomfited by the cliches he's just heard himself mouth. He wonders if Nick's equally conscious of the triteness of the sermon. Its truth notwithstanding.

"Here, lemme have that thing," he demands, "if you're not gonna use it." Weinert beckons for the ball.

Nick has gone inert. He stares disconsolately at the white key-line painted in the asphalt. Without looking up he drop-kicks the ball to Weinert.

"Hey!" Weinert scolds. "Don't do that with my good ball!"

He dribbles once with his left hand, steps right, hops and banks in a fifteen-footer.

Nick rouses himself to gather the fall-through and scurries away, head down, spine humped, elbows cocked, rat-tatting the ball in and out between his pumping knees as if threading a swarm of invisible defenders. Weinert is impressed at this mysteriously acquired dribbling skill. On the other hand, he's annoyed at the breach of courtesy.

"You're supposed to give that back," he grumbles.

Nick accords him no discernible attention. At the top of the key he whirls and flings up an offline set-shot that whangs hard against the metal backboard.

Weinert has automatically trotted into position to snag the rebound, and he flips the ball in off the crescent backboard with left-handed English.

"You oughtta come in a little closer," he advises Nick. "That's outside your range."

"No way," Nick insists. "Watch this."

Nick darts around Weinert and snatches the ball before Weinert can shield it. He flees to the top of the key and fires another lunging, stiff-armed push-shot that rattles the rim.

Weinert seizes the rebound and prepares to throw a hip if Nick tries to steal it again.

"Brick," he taunts. "You oughtta listen to me. You don't have enough arm-strength yet. That's a waste. Work on something in more around here, till you get so you can make it every time, or almost."

Weinert eases to his left this time, about ten feet from the basket, and drills another sharp bank-shot in demonstration. He gestures for the ball with an outstretched palm. Again Nick ignores him.

"Hey, I made that!" Weinert objects as Nick zigzags to the opposite wing.

Nick's reply is a jumper that's a fair imitation of Weinert's except he doesn't use the backboard. It swishes.

"Attaway. Nice," Weinert acknowledges. The ball drops through the net strings and bounces to him. He considers keeping it as his belated due, but returns it to Nick with a stinging, textbook pass—thumbs upside down after the snap of the wrists—as a reinforcing lesson in proper court etiquette.

Nick immediately dribbles toward him, veers, feints – an act of contrition and provocation. Weinert grins a warning and lifts his right hand. Nick nestles against him rump-first, quixotically applying all the leverage of his 98 pounds. Weinert jostles back, arms upstretched now, a hulking colossus on guard and standing firm at a bemused

185.

Suddenly Nick ducks out from under him, pivots and tries to sneak off an abbreviated hookshot. Without leaving the ground Weinert swats it away.

"Face!" he roisters. "In yo' face, boy! Better not be bringin' that cheap shit into yo' daddy!"

"You sound stupid," Nick snarls as he scampers to retrieve the ball from the grass at courtside. "You realize that? How stupid you sound? Why do you talk that way?"

Weinert, stung, doesn't have a ready answer. Somehow he feels he has the right to indulge the idiom in private mockery after a lifetime rubbing sweaty shoulders with black guys on public basketball courts. Nevertheless, he recognizes the justice in the criticism. His drawl grates in his own ear. As it is, Nick hears the authentic version of the patois every day at his school— Malcolm X, no less.

"Well, excuuuuuse me," Weinert sulks. "Certainly wouldn't want to offend anyone's tender sociological sensibilities. Here, gimme that. I'm tired of you hogging it. When a guy makes the shot, let him have the ball back. Otherwise people're gonna get pissed at you."

Nick's heavy eyebrows lour, but he does as instructed. When his face grows into his nose he's going to be a strikingly handsome young man, Caroline says. Like Dani's, they're his ex-wife's full-fleshed looks, though, not the thin-lipped, aquiline Weinert legacy. Only Tonio's snapshots resemble those of his father at the same age.

Weinert fields Nick's overhand toss, wheels and loops a high archer from behind the plane of the backboard. The ball clanks off the front of the rim. He ambles after it, dribbles to the half-court line, circles a stride or two closer and launches a bomb that uses his body and legs as well as his arms to achieve trajectory. The ball plummets through the net.

"Three," Weinert crows.

Nick dutifully feeds him this time. Weinert works his way right, from beyond the key, following an imaginary college three-point line, about 20 feet out from the basket. He's in a rhythm, and he sinks four in a row.

"What d'ya think?" he grins at Nick. "Think any of your other friends' fathers could hit like that?"

"Nope," Nick acknowledges.

"And they're probably ten years younger," Weinert says.

"Uh-huh," Nick agrees.

More than he'd care to analyze, Weinert's basketball prowess is a source of self-esteem. He suspects from a faint glint under the masking grimace that Nick is proud, respectful and at this stage envious of him for it too.

The game was Weinert's salvation after the split. Stunned by Caroline's renunciation, alone for the first time in years in a series of vacationing neighbors' houses, he'd hunch dutifully over his portable typewriter till lunch, down a sandwich, scribble notes through a couple of distracted telephone interviews, then hustle off to the catharsis he'd been anticipating since "Morning Edition" had awakened him in the strange, empty bed. Consoled, at least, by his aching muscles, fresh bruises and memories of one or another double-pump reverse layup or hurtling 15-foot jumper off a pick.

He lived for almost two years in basketball shoes and a warmup suit. Often – on weekends especially – he'd take Nick, Dani and Tonio with him to amuse themselves on the sidelines. They'd bat tennis balls against a wall, carve teetery skateboard figure-eights, exchange precocious banter with the guys sprawled along the chain-link fence waiting to run again. Caroline would have freaked at his notion of day-care. The air was full of casual profanity and the pungence of smoldering marijuana. Weinert even accepted a comradely sip from a joint himself now and then.

The kids soon knew the court regulars by their first names. That, in fact, was the zenith of intimacy among the lab assistants, security guards, writers, waiters, associate professors, laborers, computer programmers, students, subcontractors between jobs and felons between sentences who congregated each afternoon at about three under the square backboards atop a university parking garage.

They were a motley of races, heights and ages. Weinert, at six-foot-two (he'd have been listed as six-four on an NBA roster) and forty-plus, was among the tallest and already one of the oldest. Their only commonalities were gender and an unflagging fascination with the physics involved in propelling a ball whose diameter is nine-and-a-half-inches through a ten-foot high hoop whose diameter is eighteen inches. That plus more than a little skill at the complex exercise. Not to mention the license to keep odd daytime hours. But where else in American society, Weinert rationalized, could his children have observed such matter-of-fact communion among white, black, brown and yellow men? Even discounting for the contrapuntal howls of outrage and the occasional fistfight.

Over the years he has continued to visit the court

three or four times a week. It's only a couple of blocks away from this park. Dani, now a voluptuous 17, still shows up with him every so often to dandle a tennis racket and bask semi-obliviously in her new regard. Tonio, wearing his trademark Chicago Bulls cap, likes to cheer Weinert on – "Whoo, Daddy! Way to bust!" – when he isn't shying foul-shots at the far basket or perfecting the noisy skateboard hops known as "ollies." As for Nick, he's finally attained the minimal size that permits him to take part in the games sometimes.

"Five, four, three...!" Weinert suddenly starts counting, adding imaginary pressure to his next shot in the sequence. He's deep in the corner. "...Two, one... braaaagh!"

The ball whisks through the net just as he simulates the game-ending horn blast.

"Un-conscious," he winks at Nick. It was much more likely he'd miss, of course, which was part of his generous calculation. But, as often happens when he hasn't played for a while, Weinert is starting out incongruously hot.

He breaks into a jog, heading toward center-court. "Five, four...," he renews the chant.

Nick accommodates the pretense, rifles the ball. It's slightly underthrown, though, and Weinert has to brake and fling his right hand back, against his momentum, to snare the pass. "Four!" he repeats – the clock is, after all, in his own head. "Three, two...."

Falling sideways, he casts the ball high. He doesn't put as much rotation on the shot as he'd like, though. He stumbles, regains his balance as the ball curves, descends....

Stops.

Weinert and Nick both grunt in dismay. The freeze-frame, the sensation of a slip in time's sprocket, is jarring.

The ball, instead of ricocheting as their eyes, brains and muscles were tuned to expect, has wedged itself fast between the backboard and rim.

"Uh-oh," Nick chuckles. He gawks overhead and then turns to grin accusatorily at Weinert.

Weinert mugs chagrin.

Nick crouches, leaps and swings. "How close?" he asks. He does it again. "I'm almost touching the net, huh?"

"Yeah. Couple inches. That's all you need," Weinert assures him. "Here, watch it."

He waves Nick aside, trots in toward the basket, hops and bats at the ball to dislodge it.

He disturbs only air.

And himself. Annoyed, he springs once more.

Again he fails to graze the ball. He's puzzled. He takes two steps backward, draws a breath and lunges, flinging himself off the surface as hard as he can, straining for maximum extension. This is a situation that occurs routinely on basketball courts, and not within memory has he had the least trouble batting the ball loose. But he fails a third time even as he hears cartilage grate and feels a twinge under his shoulder-blade.

"Oh, my God," he lows. He stares at Nick, who's watching him intently. "I can't get it."

"Sure you can," Nick says.

"No. I can't."

"I've seen you."

"Of course you have," he snaps. "But I can't now. That's how much I've lost on my jump. My God, can you believe it?"

"You used to be able to dunk," Nick objects.

"Well, yeah. In college," Weinert agrees. "More or less."

Actually, he was never able to slam the ball through. Despite his long fingers, he had trouble palming it. But technically he was capable of dunking the ball. And he recalls not more than a year or so ago, it seems, hurling himself at the rim in disgust and dangling there with both hands for several minutes until the frustration after a lost game ebbed.

"Jesus," he winces. "The shits, huh?"

"Naah. Go on," Nick insists. "You can get that."

"Nope. Not if I have to try this hard. Never gonna do it. I've lost it, buddy. Gotta face it. That's what age does for you. I'm an old guy now."

Weinert is aware of the effort he's exerting to remain calm. He has a vision of himself at an accident scene, cooing flat descriptions of their injuries to the pinned victims so they won't panic. He believes in candor. Most of the dire power of the vile and fearsome, he has always believed, derives from the mystery in which they're cloaked by reticence. It's his rationale for iconoclastic wisecracking, for padding out of the bathroom naked, for swearing uninhibitedly before his children. But he can sense his own pallor. He's shaky.

He wheels, limps away.

Suddenly he goes lightheaded with rage.

"Fuck!" he retches voicelessly. "Fucking... *shit!*"

At least he's under enough control to keep it more or less private. No point rubbing Nick's nose in it. Demean himself further by impotent railing. This is life, after all. Mortality. Nothing you can do about it.

Still, he's wracked by another spasm of anger so intense he could easily relieve it in tears. A physical capability he's taken for granted – part of his identity as an athlete ("Hey, man, you can really sky!") – has abruptly been subtracted.

Veterans nearing the end of a career are said to have lost a step. That's a rhetorical measurement. Weinert has lost three inches off his jump – the aging process quantified with linear precision. And although it must have happened gradually, a concomitant to the sciatic throb he's long since learned to sleep with and the nagging bursitis in hips and groins he finally decided to palliate by staying off the court entirely for the past three weeks... not until this moment had it registered.

He shudders, rolls his head, hammers his fist against his thigh and lips the same useless, unimaginative curse. Useless. Then he turns back to Nick. "White man's disease," he groans. "Finally got me."

Nick looks dubious, as if this were some willful ploy by his father to shirk the responsibility attendant on noble stature.

"Which means," Weinert sighs, "you better start climbing, pal."

Nick frees the ball without difficulty. All Weinert's kids glory in shinnying. It's a family joke that they have monkey in them.

Weinert proposed it when Dani was about ten and had just descended from the crossbar of a football field goalpost, where she'd watched one of Nick's soccer games. She cheerfully agreed, proffering her chubby arms and bending her neck to display whorls of fine white nap.

"I'm the hairiest person in my school," she boasted. Then she sank into a crouch, jutted her lower jaw and started hooting like the chimpanzee they'd recently seen at the zoo. (It's a startling imitation she still performs now and then when she's feeling zany or craves attention.)

Once aloft, Nick stays a while. He braces himself spraddle-legged against the horizontal support struts so he can lean out over the backboard from behind and intercept Weinert's shots. Nick then jams them through the hoop from above.

"Okay, enough," Weinert says finally. He's having a hard time appreciating the pleasure Nick's getting out of this silly exercise. But Nick, in his airy perch, looks mischievously happy for the first time this afternoon.

"Come on, get down from there," Weinert commands after a couple more obliging lobs. "This is boring."

"Two more," Nick pleads. "Three more."

"One more," Weinert relents. He loops the ball up, Nick grabs it and stuffs it through the basket.

"Feed," Nick demands.

"Nope, that's it," Weinert declares. "C'mon down."

Nick remains poised with hands apart.

"What kind of fun are you getting out of this?" Weinert scoffs.

Nick says nothing, just waits for the toss.

"I'm not going to throw it to you," Weinert assures him.

"Come on," Nick wheedles. "One more. That's all."

"Listen, buddy," Weinert says. "You're in no position to keep on push-pushing. You're in very bad odor as it is. Which, in fact, is what I came up here to talk to you about. Now do what I say. Get down from there. I already gave you an extra shot anyway."

"One last one," Nick insists.

"No! This is ridiculous!" Weinert exclaims.

Nick smirks at him defiantly, hands still beckoning.

"I don't suppose you realize how vulnerable you are," Weinert says. "Do you? Out there on a limb – kind of treed? And you're messing with someone down below you who has a deadly missile in his hand?"

He strolls closer, ostentatiously juggling the ball from palm to palm. "Not a whole lot of protection up there, I wouldn't say."

"Deadly missile," Nick snickers. "Boy, I'm quaking in fear. Go ahead. Let's see if you can hit me."

He clutches the backboard and peers down at Weinert, who's prowling underneath him with the ball now cocked threateningly.

Weinert circles the post. Nick scrambles to change footholds so he can face the danger.

"Careful," Weinert breathes. As soon as Nick looks to have a good grip, though, Weinert slings the ball at him. He aims low to graze a foot or knee, at most. And he doesn't put too much velocity on the peg.

Nick cringes aside but gropes with one arm in a tentative, defiant attempt to snatch the ball. It caroms off the bottom edge of the backboard.

"Ha! Missed!" Nick taunts.

"That was just a warning shot," Weinert smiles.

"You're re a sitting duck, you know." He brandishes the ball. "You really want to challenge me?"

"You're soup," Nick gibes.

"Soup, huh?"

"Yeah. You couldn't hit me even if I didn't try to get outta the way." He nestles against the backboard for balance and lifts his hands. "Go ahead, I dare you."

"Dare me! What, are you banking on the fact that I wouldn't wanna see my son's brains splattered all over the cement? Some dumb calculus like that?"

"Yeah. Watch it or I'll get blood all over your nice new Nikes." Nick picks up the thread eagerly. "Make 'em all yucky."

"Not very much in the way of brains to worry about, though," Weinert muses. "And blood... comes off easy. I know from experience. You used to have *four* brothers! You aware of that?"

"Ha!"

"Fritz, Earl and Nebuchadnezzar," Weinert says. He pauses for a beat to delight in the names that have popped to tongue.

"Yeah, right," Nick snickers. "You're hilarious."

"Nebbie was the oldest. Fritz and Earl were twins. All born before Dani, actually. When they were growing up, though, they started not obeying me. Like you. Started thinking they could get away with whatever they wanted. Always raising the ante. Talking back. Fighting with each other – vicious stuff, the way you do with Tonio, sometimes. Then the last straw. The unpardonable sin. They laid a hand on their mother. Any of this sound familiar?"

Nick's face has clouded.

"So that was it. I had to kill 'em."

"Mm-hm."

"Funny thing is, now I find you in exactly the same situation," Weinert says. "And totally at my mercy. Only too stupid to realize it. So what should I do?"

"How should I know?"

"Just knock you right out of there? You seriously think I can't?"

Nick glowers at him.

"Come on. Give it a bit of thought. What d'you deserve?"

"Whatever," Nick mutters. "Kill me too, I guess."

"Mm. Maybe," Weinert agrees. "You're in luck, though. I'm gonna give you a break. The only thing you gotta do is get down nice and snappy. Okay? That's all I'm asking."

Nick studies him glumly for a moment, then crouches and duckwalks out along the struts, straddles the pole and slithers to the ground.

"Great," Weinert says. "Now. The next item on our agenda is a game of twenty-one. We're gonna find out just how bad this old, crippled guy can still whomp your teenybopper ass. This is the real stuff, buddy – the primal struggle! It's your turn to slay the father – figuratively, of course. Only you ain't got it in you yet, I don't believe."

At Weinert's instruction, Nick starts off. He refuses the warmups Weinert suggests, and promptly airballs his first shot from the line. He loiters dispiritedly in the key as Weinert retreats to deep Three-Point-Land and misses in turn. Weinert isn't particularly keen to break a sweat. He makes no effort to hector Nick, or to scuttle for rebounds. Still, it takes Nick three attempts before he finally sinks a clumsy, driving layup that

Weinert simply backs away from.

"The matador defense," Weinert quips. He bows and sweeps his arms as if waving a bull past with a cape. *"Olé!"*

Nick isn't amused. He misses the follow-up foul-shot. Weinert collects the rebound and saunters to the right perimeter, maintaining his self-imposed distance handicap. As luck would have it, though, the shot drops.

"Ah. Radar still functioning," Weinert observes.

He steps to the line and sinks all three of his freethrows. "Two. Four – for the first one – five, six," he counts up his score. "To two."

He takes the ball out at the half-court line, dribbles two paces in and shoots. Although he's at the limit of his range, he's reasonably consistent from here, dead-center atop the key. It's a swish. "Eight," Weinert says. He toes the stripe and strokes the free-throws. "Eleven."

Nick returns the ball and Weinert once again initiates play from half-court. "You're gonna have to come out here and start guarding me," he warns. "Otherwise you don't stand a prayer."

Nick shuffles toward him, then stops. "Naah, go ahead," he says. "I'll let you have it from there. Your luck isn't going to hold up forever."

"Bad decision," Weinert grins. "Luck has nothing to do with it." He hops and fires. The ball swirls around the inside of the rim three or four full cycles before suddenly skidding out.

"See? What'd I tell you? Choke!" Nick whoops.

"Hey, that was a fluke," Weinert objects. "That was in all the way! I got robbed."

"Yeah, yeah," Nick chortles. "Soup."

"What soup?" Weinert snorts. "I finally get a bad

roll after sixteen in a row or so? And you have the gall to call me soup? You, who's... what, oh-for-about-a-hundred-and-eight?"

"I made one," Nick protests.

"Yeah. An uncontested bunny," Weinert says. "Let's see how you do if I get serious."

Abruptly he darts at Nick, who's drilling the ball off the pavement with stately nonchalance.

Nick's eyes bug. He hunches protectively and recoils, spinning away from Weinert's charge with a quick through-the-legs dribble. He has sound instincts and a facility – even a flair – that's remarkable. Weinert himself, for all the lonely hours spent pounding up and down gym floors in his youth, never managed to develop anything more than workmanlike ball-handling skills. His own between-the-legs and behind-the-back maneuvers are pretty much confined to slo-mo, time-killing drills on the sidelines.

But Weinert does have fast hands. And long arms. He bellies up to Nick from the rear, taps his rump, feints right, anticipates the reactive dribble and lunges left. His snaking fingertips tick the ball away. He clambers after it, blithely elbowing Nick off-stride to make the recovery.

"Foul!" Nick squawks. "Hey, that's a foul!"

"No way," Weinert grins. "Incidental contact. The pick was clean."

"Bullshit," Nick says. "Incidental contact is in football."

"Aw, come on," Weinert says. "Okay. What the hell. Call it a foul. Here." He underhands the ball to Nick. "Go ahead. Take it out."

"Fuck it. You can have it," Nick shrugs. He bats the ball back as if minimizing touch to avoid a gob of spit.

"Hey, watch your language. I'm respecting your call!" Weinert insists. "Maybe I did foul you. Go on, take it." He bounce-passes the ball to Nick with crisp, no-nonsense backspin.

Nick scuffs reluctantly toward the sideline. He turns and dribbles inbounds. He's wary now, crouched forward, head bent, eyeing Weinert's feet from under his brow.

"Keep your head up," Weinert counsels. "Don't look at the ball. If you're gonna be a guard, you've gotta see what's going all around you so you can be aware of the cuts."

Nick gives no indication he's registered the advice. He continues his measured, hunchbacked circuit of the periphery. Weinert sidles along with him, a soft eight or ten feet off, casually maintaining the cutoff angle to the basket.

"What's this, the stall?" Weinert teases. "The four-corners offense? You trying to lull me to sleep?"

Nick doesn't respond. He just keeps dribbling in metronomic largo.

"Twenty-four second clock's up. Forty-five second clock's up," Weinert declares. "Turnover in any league. Bzzzz. My ball."

"I don't see any clocks," Nick says.

"C'mon. Get on with it," Weinert urges. "You sure do have a peculiar idea of fun."

"This is fun," Nick says. "Dribbling's fun."

"So's shooting."

"I like to dribble."

"Okay," Weinert sighs. "Guess I'm gonna have to come out there and steal it from you again."

"Only way you're going to get it from me," Nick counters, "is if you foul. Like last time."

"That was a ticky-tacky call. You were just making excuses because I picked you clean," Weinert says, closing the gap.

Nick retreats. Then suddenly he bursts into high gear and flees toward the baseline. Weinert has to run to stay abreast. Nick spins and slices for the basket. Weinert does a cocky counterspin. Only the moment he plants his left leg to shift direction, he feels a searing pain in his hip. The leg almost collapses under him.

Nick scoots open and banks in a five-footer.

Weinert gimps around for a moment, testing the pelvic ball-and-socket system—which seems to be intact. The tweak of pain ebbs to a dull ache he can't localize. This unsettling phenomenon is part of a new syndrome. His doctor ordered X-rays a while back but said they showed nothing except a few undefined "pre-arthritic" changes in the lumbar vertebrae.

"Someday, maybe," the doctor added with a chuckle, "we'll have to give you a couple of Teflon hip joints." Then he lit up a Marlboro Light and wrote Weinert a prescription for a serious anti-inflammatory.

Nick must have heard Weinert grunt and realized he'd pulled up. He shows no particular concern or sympathy, though. He's seen enough of his wincing father walking off sprained ankles after coming down on somebody else's foot, or heading for his car and the emergency room with a split lip or a double-dislocated finger wrapped in a bloody tee-shirt. He ambles expressionlessly to the line.

"Good bring," Weinert compliments him. He takes station gingerly for the free-throw.

Nick doesn't acknowledge. He gives the ball a couple of preparatory bounces, scowls at the basket, flexes his knees and shoots. It goes in.

"So what's that?" Weinert says. "Five."

Nick nods. He repeats the motions and cans his second.

"Six," Weinert counts for him. "See? Now you're finding the range." He returns the ball to Nick with an insouciant no-look flick.

Nick keeps a poker face. He aims and thrusts the ball at the basket. It strikes the flat metal bracket where the hoop joins the backboard.

"Fuck!" Nick howls.

"Hey, man!" Weinert chides as he gathers in the rebound. He glances toward the far swings and slides. The few kids and supervising adults in the park seem oblivious. The knockout blonde has long since wheeled her charges away into the tunnel in a double stroller – Weinert saw her go while Nick was cavorting atop the backboard.

"Keep it down if you're gonna overreact like that," he says. "That's ridiculous. And save the fucks for when you really need 'em."

"Jesus Christ. I can't make shit," Nick whines. He slumps at the line in despair.

Nick's profanity is both unseemly for his age and disproportionate, Weinert thinks. But he's long since surrendered to the weight of hypocrisy.

"What're you expecting, perfection?" Weinert soothes him. "You just hit two out of three. Sixty-six percent. Not great, but...."

"Doesn't matter. I suck at foul-shots," Nick

declares.

"So work on 'em," Weinert sighs. "That's what this game's about."

"I don't care about working on 'em," Nick says. "Who gives a shit, anyway? I hate basketball."

"Ah," Weinert says. "Aren't we in a beautiful mood today?"

"It's the mood I'm always in."

"That so? Why do you think that is?"

"How should I know?"

"Who else'd be in a better position to know?"

"It's Mommy," Nick says. "I hate living at her house."

"Hm! As I recall it was you who said you thought it was time you should come back up here."

"Yeah. Well, I forgot what a bitch she is."

"Hey, man...," Weinert rumbles. He draws a breath, lets it out. "So. Why's she a bitch?"

"How'm I supposed to know!" Nick retorts.

"Listen. You know what I'm saying. In what way is she being a bitch to you?"

"Every way."

Weinert sighs again. The conversation, as usual with his children, is degenerating into the absurd.

"Name one," he says.

"Mn-mn," Nick shrugs. "She's just a fucking bitch all the time! All she does.... "

"Whoa!" Weinert interrupts. "That's enough. I don't want to hear you say that word again. Either one. Your mother's not. What you've been calling her. She's just a caring parent. Who's looking out for your welfare. We both are. Now, what were you gonna say?"

"Nothing," Nick mutters.

"Yes you were. Go ahead."

"I 'n' know."

"Sure you do. I want to hear it. Tell me what's bothering you."

Nick doesn't speak. He rounds his shoulders and gnaws his lower lip, working to pinch off the tears that have suddenly begun to shimmer in his eyes. One drips from his thick underlashes and splats on the patched asphalt.

"Hey, Nick...!" Weinert murmurs solicitously. He starts forward. His right arm curls....

Nick reacts to Weinert's telegraphed intention by dodging angrily away.

Weinert is startled. Not that this is the first time his embraces have been spurned by children in a pet. Nick lurks warily, hugging himself, eyebrows beetled fiercely, pursed lips twitching.

Weinert squints at him, conscious of the interval. Of not breaching it with quick movements—as if he were trying to hand-feed a spooky squirrel or deer. He inhales a cleansing breath. That's a term, he realizes, he learned in the Lamaze classes they took when Nick was a tiny homunculus thrashing in Caroline's belly.

"What's going on?" he asks quietly.

"Nothing!" Nick hisses. He scrubs brusquely at his eyes and nose with the back of his hand. He's managed to sublimate the weepy impulse.

"If you won't tell me, how'm I supposed to deal with it?"

"Why should you deal with it?" Nick growls. "It's none of your business."

"Actually, it is," Weinert says. "I'm your father. You and Mommy are part of my life. Even if we're not together anymore. I love you."

Nick hangs his head.

"I want you to be happy," Weinert adds. "I want everyone in my family to be happy."

"Tell Mommy to quit bugging me then," Nick mumbles.

"Bugging you about what?"

"About everything."

Weinert sighs. "Look, this is getting circuitous," he says. "Tell me. What exactly started the trouble between you two last night?"

"Mn-mn," Nick shrugs.

"Strain your memory."

"Just... her usual bullshit! I got tired of it, that's all! I'm not gonna keep listening to her crap. She's driving me crazy!"

"What, with 'clean up your room?' 'Put the dishes in the dishwasher?' Stuff like that? The normal chores and responsibilities you have as a member of a household?"

Nick grunts equivocally. "I'm tired of talking about it," he says.

"Gee, isn't that too bad?" Weinert bristles. "Because it's gonna get talked about. Especially since your response was absolutely unacceptable. Whatever it was she told you to do, you can't simply act out your displeasure by attacking her physically. Beating her up. I mean, that's just beyond the pale."

"All I did...," Nick whines.

"Was step over the boundary. Even if you didn't hurt her – lucky for you. But it's never gonna happen again. You got that clear?"

Nick scowls at his frayed shoelaces.

"You hear me? I'm telling you right now. No more rough stuff with your mother. No matter how pissed off you get, that's not an option. Got it?"

"Then she better stop buggin' the shit out of me,"

143

Nick mutters.

"No, she'd better not!" Weinert erupts. "You'd better get it into your thick skull that you've gotta obey your parents! We're not making unreasonable requests. We're not depriving you of anything. Making you do slave labor. Violating the child labor laws. I mean, the few measly chores we assign you? You've got it so cushy...! That's the trouble, I guess. You don't realize how fortunate you are. What an easy life you lead. If anything, we've been too permissive."

Nick flares the downturned corners of his mouth and exhales loudly through his nostrils, deflating his sunken chest even further.

"Ah yes, I know," Weinert leers, "this is all very boring to you, isn't it? Well, I'm teddibly sorry about that, Your Royal Pain-in-the-Assness. But until I see some evidence from your behavior that what I'm telling you has finally begun to sink in, you're gonna keep hearing the same litany over and over."

Nick glowers in silence.

"And there'll be no privileges. That goes without saying. You're grounded until further notice."

Weinert studies Nick for a reaction. Nick's transgression obviously requires punishment, which is supposed to provoke remorse, penitence. Those would satisfy Weinert's retributive impulses at least. Unfortunately, he can't engineer what he'd really like: some miraculous dawning in the kid of good-natured rationality.

Nick casts him a baleful glance. "What's that mean?" he challenges.

"You know as well as I do. No going to friends' houses, no having anybody over, no movies or whatever... until we're satisfied you're doing what we ask of you. With reasonable good will. Till you've demonstrated to us that you're a civilized member of society again. TV's off limits too."

"She's already got it locked up."

"Good for her."

Nick expels a bitter chuckle.

"Obviously, since you're at Mommy's house," Weinert adds, "she's gonna have to be the one that decides when you've earned a reprieve."

Nick shrugs.

"I'll be keeping an eye on you too, though. You're in fairly deep shit for the moment, my man. But all you have to do to get yourself out of it is start shaping up. So. There. Any lingering questions?"

Nick snorts derisively.

"I beg your pardon," Weinert frowns. "I didn't quite catch that reply."

"Nn."

"Nn?"

"No."

"No, what?"

"Questions!"

"Ah. Wonderful," Weinert nods. "Golly, I'm so glad we had this little meeting of the minds. So we could air out any misunderstandings before they festered. Wouldn't you concur?"

Nick doesn't respond to Weinert's chipper sarcasm.

"And while we're at it, let's extend the ban on violence to your brother," Weinert adds. "I know he's annoying sometimes, but that doesn't give you license to whack him."

"I'm just making sure he knows who's boss," Nick snarls.

"You're not his boss!"

"Yes I am."

"Oh no you're not, bud! He's an autonomous human being. You may be bigger and stronger, but you're not his boss. And you're just being a bully when you try to impose your will on him by force."

"I gotta teach him who's in charge," Nick maintains. "I only mess him up when he deserves it."

"Listen, Nick. Nick. I don't like to hear you talking this way. It disturbs me. There's no justification for beating up on Tonio. You're not in charge of him. Sure, brothers fight sometimes. A lot! I did with my younger brother. You and Dani fight. I expect that. It's natural. But it's a question of degree. All I'm saying is, don't be a bully. A little scuffling around is one thing, but when you're whamming him, constantly making him cry."

"He starts crying the minute I touch him! It's all a fake! He's just trying to get Mommy and you to take his side."

"Well... yeah, I suspect that's true to some extent."

"All I have to do is walk up to him...." Nick pokes an index finger illustratively.

"Okay, okay," Weinert says. "I know, it's hard. Tonio can be a real pain. But it's not all him. I see you starting plenty. The point is... the point is, let's have a truce for a while. We need to stop infringing on each other's personal space. All of us."

"Can I go now?"

Weinert peers at him, grimaces and shakes his head. "Have you been listening to anything I'm saying?"

"Mmm-hmm," Nick grants without inflection.

"What? What was the last thing?"

He shrugs. "Truce."

"Truce," Weinert echoes. "What about it?"

"Nn-nn. Like not interfering."

Weinert flaps his fingers, beckoning for amplification.

"'Infringing on anybody else's personal space,'" Nick parrots.

"Ah. Wow. Fantastic. Meaning...?" Weinert demands.

Nick bows his head with a disgusted wince. "You don't think I know?"

"Okay," Weinert relents. "Let's see how well you put it into action then. That's the real test. Right?"

"I got homework," Nick sighs.

"I know. Fine. I guess we're done," Weinert nods. "Unless you'd like to finish up our game."

"You're gonna win anyway."

"Maybe. Who knows? I'm not that far ahead though, really, am I?"

Nick shrugs.

"What was it? I don't remember. Eleven-eight or something?"

"Six," Nick says.

"You sure? I thought you had more. I mean, even that's not so bad. But we could start over, since. "

"Doesn't matter," Nick declares. "You'll win."

"Why do you say that?"

"'Cuz it's true."

"Well, whatever," Weinert concedes. "If you don't have confidence. Though I still *oughtta* win most of the time, don't you think?"

Nick shrugs. "I guess."

"So. Anyway. You want to go get started on your homework now. That it? Sounds like a good plan."

"I don't care. We could play it out, I guess. If you want."

"Up to you."

Nick shakes his head. He hasn't moved.

"You're going to win one of these days," Weinert assures him.

"Maybe," Nick agrees.

"Could be this game even. All it's gotta do is start falling for you."

"Mm-hm," Nick says. "Okay. Go ahead."

"Nah, you go ahead," Weinert counters. He bounce-passes the ball to Nick. "We'll keep the score the same, but it's your out."

"Why's that?" Nick asks.

"Because," Weinert explains, "when I stupidly tried to come put my arm around you, it was a traveling violation."

Nick immediately drives on Weinert again, a mistake. Not even an extra desperate stride enables him to corkscrew out from under Weinert's splay-fingered paw, poised this time for the swat.

"Sorry," Weinert says, "but I can't give you that any more."

Nick chases down the ball.

"Actually, you just walked, too," Weinert observes. "You know that, don't you? Probably wouldn't get called in the NBA, I'll admit. Maybe not even in college or high school anymore."

"What'd I do?" Nick inquires innocently.

"You traveled. After you picked up the ball you went boom, boom...," Weinert stamps his soles in exaggerated demonstration, "before you took off. You're only allowed one step."

"I get one-and-a-half, you told me."

"Yeah. But what you took was two-and-a-half. See? Boomp, pick up dribble, boomp... *boomp!* And then up. Instead of...."

Nick interrupts the lesson with a shot. He's about fifteen feet away, squared to the basket from the right. Weinert completes the soliloquy while eyeing the ball's flight: "But I see people on TV getting away with it – there you go! – all the time nowadays. So maybe I'm old-fashioned. Maybe they've loosened up on the rules. Good one."

"Eight," Nick murmurs. Deadpan, of course. A shy smile is as close as Weinert has ever seen Nick come to exultance. When he kicks a goal in soccer—which he does infrequently, though he's a skillful midfielder—he simply turns and trots away, head down, looking almost embarrassed.

Weinert himself has always believed that the most effective way to celebrate one's own prowess is to act as if it were taken for granted, not as if some bizarre fluke, some divine intervention had just occurred. Nor, being white, is he much given to gloating jigs or boastful finger-waggling. So maybe that attitude osmosed to Nick. (Tonio, on the other hand – whose friends at school seem almost all to be black—has picked up a disquieting tendency to bluster. Weinert is much more attuned to Nick's diffidence.)

Nick makes his first freethrow. The second ricochets from rim to backboard. The ball arches back over the lane.

"Shit," Nick exclaims. But he darts reflexively for the rebound.

Weinert lunges in front of him and brushes him

aside with a haunch. He plucks the ball from the air.

It's a glancing collision, but it does bring Weinert down with his full weight over his left heel. Once again he's jolted by an intense pain, as if his femur has just skewered his pelvis.

"Aanh, aanh!" he gasps. He reels, hopping for balance on his right leg. Again the pain diffuses almost instantaneously.

"Ah, Jesus!" he winces, kneading the meat of his rump, trying to get at the bone-ache that's tantalizingly there and yet, as soon as he thumbs it, not there.

"What's the matter?" Nick inquires.

"Aah, my fuckin' hip," Weinert says. "I don't know what the fuck it is! Pardon my language. God damn it! Fucking old age is what it is! I might as well hang it up. Here."

He rids himself of the ball and hobbles for the backboard pole. He dives to clutch it with both hands and leans there flexing his left knee, rotating the hip.

Nick dribbles idly for a moment, then begins to shoot. Every time the ball strikes the backboard overhead, the clammy galvanized pole vibrates annoyingly under Weinert's palms. He has to stay wary, too – muscles of his nape tensed – to duck when the ball drops through the net. The faded red-white-and-blue mesh has been ripped and stretched by lead-footed would-be dunkers.

Nick's thoughtless indifference suddenly angers Weinert. Although, he rationalizes, Nick is just observing masculine convention – pretending not to see his pain, according him the privacy to come to terms with it. That's certainly behavior he's learned at the court: a guy goes down, you check to see how bad it is, commiserate briefly, then wander off to noodle with growing impatience till he asks for a hand up or drags himself over to the sideline so somebody else can come into the game to take his place.

"You gonna be okay?" Nick finally wonders.

"Oh, yeah! Just great. Crackerjack!" Weinert replies.

"Probably we should quit, huh?"

"Hell no! Just gimme a second. ... Ah, screw it. C'mon. That's okay. I'm good as I'll ever be, I guess. Let's go. Go on. Your ball."

He pushes off from the pole and advances slowly toward Nick, twisting his hips to determine how much torque he can tolerate. In fact, the ache proves difficult to evoke. He realizes how odd his gait looks and finishes off with a hula shimmy.

"Still got my beautiful moves, though," he simpers at Nick, "eh, honey?"

"Don't do that!" Nick shudders.

Weinert cocks an eyebrow. "What's the matter, darling? You got some kind of problem with... effeminacy?"

"Don't be stupid!" Nick says, rolling his eyes.

"I'm just wondering why what I did makes you so uncomfortable," Weinert persists. "Maybe...." His teasing voice drips with syrupy concern. "...We should explore that."

"C'mon, Daddy," Nick says. He shudders. "You sound like Mommy." He proffers the ball. "Anyway, you had it."

"Aah, I walked," Weinert demurs. "You take it. It's eleven. what, nine?"

"Mm."

"Catchin' up," Weinert observes.

Nick dribbles back and forth until he's sure

Weinert's ready, then tries a set shot from deep. The ball slants hard off the board, missing the basket entirely. Nick races after the rebound – Weinert only limps a couple of token steps in pursuit – and repeats the shot from the opposite quadrant.

"God damn!" Nick mourns.

"At least this time you got rim," Weinert notes.

Again the ball has kicked out long over his head. Nick jogs to retrieve it. He's beginning to pant from the effort of milling those outsize feet from one side of the court to the other. He slumps to catch his breath.

"I'll give you another piece of coaching advice," Weinert says. "This is when you ought to be bringing it, instead of shooting from outside. Drive on me, so you're taking advantage of my bad leg. Figure I've lost mobility. You've gotta exploit an opponent's weakness."

Nick squints at him, considering. Then he fires from where he stands. Weinert can see that the shot is off-line in time to shuffle into position for the carom.

"God damn!" Nick keens. "Jesus Christ!" He bobs his head, bolos his fists, stamps his foot and spins in paroxysmic frustration. "What's goin' *on?* I can't hit *shit!*"

Molars clenched, Weinert dribbles to midcourt and continues down the left sideline. When Nick finally rouses himself to wander nearer, Weinert shoots. The ball rims out. Nick grabs it, stalks to the spot where he missed his last shot and launches another. The ball brushes the net – but below, not through, the hoop.

"*Mother... fuck!*" Nick shrieks.

Weinert slogs grimly after the ball as it bounces off the court and comes to rest in a bed of ivy beside the bench where he stowed his watch, keys and sunglasses. Except for a grey-haired woman in an oversized sweatshirt trudging up the far slope behind a frisking Irish setter, and the dormant ragpile under the shopping cart in the bushes, he and Nick have the park to themselves now. Thank goodness. Weinert stoops to check his watch. Caroline ought to be home from work soon if she isn't already. He strolls back toward the basket.

"Look," he admonishes Nick. "I'm getting fed up with your foul-mouthed tantrums. Either cool it or give it up and go do your homework. I'm not gonna stick around listening to you bellyache that way after every shot. It's ridiculous!"

"I never shoot this bad!" Nick whines. "I can't figure it out!"

"You're too far away," Weinert says.

"That's my range!" Nick insists. "I can always make 'em from there usually!"

"Usually always, eh? Well, then, you're just in a slump. Everybody gets into a slump now and then. Even the stars. And you know what they say? How to break it?"

Nick shakes his head.

"How do you think?"

Nick shrugs. "'Shoot your way out,'" he grudgingly parrots the cliché.

"Absolutely," Weinert nods. "Only way to get out of a slump is to shoot your way out."

"That's what I'm *doing!*" Nick wails. "And it's not *working!*"

"So keep at it. That's the whole point. A shooter has no conscience. Even if you weren't being incredibly impatient... even if it takes you fifteen, twenty... who knows how many shots? Miss, miss,

miss, miss, miss, miss. You just have to keep at it. Till they start dropping for you again. Shoot your way out. That's what it means!"

The homily fails to wipe the pout off Nick's face.

"So what's it gonna be?" Weinert demands. "Should we wrap it up? Or you think we can finish this game without you going bonkers every time you don't make one from now on? Choice is yours."

"Sure. Maybe. I guess," Nick mutters. "I 'n' know."

"I'm warning you," Weinert stresses. "One more outburst."

"Okay, okay."

Weinert's mouth tildes into the tight-lipped, not altogether assuaged smile these interchanges with his children so often inspire.

"So guard me," he sighs. "I'm gonna make fast work of this."

W einert steps across the out-of-bounds line, dribbles the ball twice, whirls and flicks off a high-arching, fall-away eighteen-footer. It rattles through.

"Thirteen," he announces. He marches to the foul-line and rips the free-throws fwip-fwip-fwip. Nothing but net. "Sixteen-nine," he scores. "Come out and get me."

Nick does bring the ball to the top of the key before relinquishing it. And he waits there as Weinert backpedals behind the midcourt stripe, then dribbles inbounds to renew play.

Weinert advances directly on Nick. Nick hunches,

knuckly hands on bony knees. Weinert can sympathize with his halfhearted readiness. It works two ways: It's a signal of disdain, but it's simultaneously self-protection against humiliation. If you're not really playing hard, losing's no comment on your ability. Weinert knows his kids – losing to anyone at anything is torment. It challenges their megalomaniac delusions. Still, he's never believed in throwing games to coddle them. Not that he goes all out.

But he does intend to force Nick to play defense. He lowers his shoulders and begins to crab right to shield the ball behind his interposed body. Nick hunkers deeper too as Weinert closes. He spreads his arms and cautiously fingers the small of Weinert's back. He gives ground. Weinert works to his right, dribbling the ball at arm's length from his inside hip. He carries his left elbow akimbo to fend off the harrying whisks of Nick's free hand.

Suddenly he spins toward Nick, changing to a left-handed dribble with a behind-the-back bounce. At this tempo it is part of his repertoire. He repeats the maneuver twice more, tacking right, then left again. Nick responds sluggishly the third time. That gives Weinert the opening he'd need against a taller opponent. He breaks into a lope, parallels the paint and shucks up a stiff-wristed running hook from about eight feet out. It banks off the board into the basket.

"Lefty," Weinert points out with a self-satisfied waggle of eyebrows.

Nick turns away to capture the ball.

"No way you could block that," Weinert consoles him. "Too much height advantage. See? I could do that all day on you... from the right, for sure. But that wouldn't be much of a contest, would it?"

Nick shrugs and smirks at him patronizingly. It's a dead-eyed, mocking expression that startles Weinert. He doesn't quite understand what it signifies in this context. Nick has taken to making the face a lot these days, though. Weinert finds it infuriating.

"Ball, please," he growls. "I've got eighteen."

He adjusts himself quickly at the line: feet apart, toes nuzzling the paint stripe, weight evenly distributed. He cups the ball in his left hand, waist-high, and fans the fingertips of his right hand atop it, locating the seams. He locks his eyes on the narrow orange oval of the elevated rim in front of him, sinks on bent knees, as if readying a tennis serve... and brings the ball up smoothly through his cone of vision until it rests just above his brow, a peripheral brown moon poised at apogee from the mother-hoop. Then he snaps his wrist. The ball twirls off the pads of his fingers and threads the goal without a sound except the rustle of nylon cords.

"Nineteen," he informs Nick, who clubs the ball back to him with a perfunctory rap of his ankle. Weinert starts to carp, then decides against it. The impact was too blunt to be considered a kick. He bounces the ball twice and repeats the free-throw sequence.

Brain, eyes and muscles are still in synchrony. "Twenty," he notes. He looks at Nick and throws in a little good-natured personal ante: "Moment of truth."

"You'll miss," Nick mutters. "You're goin' back."

"Unh-unh. Sorry. This is game."

When he plays Tonio, the hex is delivered with characteristic brio: squinty telepathic glares, elaborate gestures – wiggly fingers emanating off-putting vibes or throttling the windpipe – and a chant on the order of "oo-ee, Daddy, oo-ee, gonna brick, gonna brick, choke, choke, choke!"

Nick, naturally, relies on understatement – a contemptuous assurance Weinert will fail.

Justified, as it happens. For all Weinert's confidence, his visceral knowledge of the exact chain of motions and forces to be exerted, his clear mental image of the ballistic path he will impart... rehearsed in five straight flawless shots... some short-circuit in the neural firing pattern this time causes the heel of his thumb to cling to the ball's grain a couple of nanoseconds too long. The yaw is apparent instantly.

He refuses Nick the satisfaction of hearing him curse. The familiar fricative takes shape between his incisors and lip, but he bites it back – tranformed into a toothy grimace as he watches the ball clank off the side of the rim.

"What'd I tell you?" Nick jeers.

"Yup," Weinert acknowledges. "My bad. I blew it. First time that's ever happened. Won't happen again, though."

"Sure won't," Nick taunts, hugging the rebound. "That's the last chance you're gonna get."

"Think so? Think you're gonna make a comeback on me?"

"Twelve-nine" is all Nick says. That's the revised score – Weinert's penalty for missing the potentially winning freethrow.

Nick skips away from the basket, tattoos the ball between his legs, about-faces and puts up one of his herky-jerky set shots. "Count it," he declares.

But bravado isn't the absent ingredient. The ball spirals around the rim... and skids out.

"Yaagh!" Nick bawls. He dances into the air in a gawky pirouette of dashed expectation and thwarted body English.

"Don't say it," Weinert cautions.

Nick doesn't. He expels his frustration in a guttural rumble instead. He bows his head abjectly.

"Congratulations," Weinert encourages him. "Anyway that was a good shot. Should've gone. You're just havin' a bad run. It's like there's a lid on it for you."

Nick is not to be so easily mollified. He still droops, chin on chest, arms dangling.

Weinert withdraws to the wing. No point prolonging Nick's misery, he's decided. He wheels, aims for the backboard and sinks the gimme. It's a signature bank shot he'll probably be able to can when he's eighty-five and so frozen up with arthritis they'll have to trundle him out to the spot on an appliance dolly.

The first two free-throws fall for him too, now that there's no real stake. But he pulls the string on the third. Nick listlessly clears the rebound and emphasizes his frame of mind by shying a nineteen-foot hook shot at the basket. From twenty feet deep.

"What's that?" Weinert sneers.

"That's nothing," Nick replies.

"That's right. A total waste," Weinert agrees. "Disgusting. That's just giving up. Is that what you're doing?"

Nick shrugs. "I 'n' know. Sure. Why the fuck not? I'm playin' like a piece of crap, aren't I?"

"Fine," Weinert says. He pivots and flips the ball in off the backboard, a dink-shot his father always called a "bunny" – an anachronistic term nobody seems to recognize these days when Weinert lets it slip.

"Eighteen," he declares. "I'll end it the right way now anyway."

He stalks toward the line.

"How much?" Nick mutters.

"What?"

"How much? You wanna bet?"

"What – that I make 'em? The foul-shots?"

"Mm-hm. Bet you fifty dollars you'll miss one."

"Right. Fifty dollars."

"Okay," Nick concedes. "Five dollars."

"You don't have five dollars," Weinert scoffs.

"I do so."

"Where'd you get it?"

"Mommy. I moved some wood for her on Saturday."

"Wow, amazing. Miracles never cease. And you want to bet it?"

"Mm-hm."

"That's a real wise use of your hard-earned money."

"Nothing else to do with it. Not if I'm grounded. Anyway," he declares archly, "I'm gonna have ten dollars in about two minutes."

"You're gonna be flat broke in about two minutes. If I take your bet, which I'm not, 'cause I don't believe in that kind of stuff."

Especially, Weinert might add, since a couple of years ago, on a slow Saturday, when he broke his own rule. Hazarded five bucks on a game of one-on-one HORSE with another court regular – a guy his own age and of similar ability, a meat inspector for the city. Ended up dropping thirty.

Stung by the first loss, E to S, Weinert agreed to

two follow-up double-or-nothing matches, with the same results. His Achilles heel turned out to be a back-to-the bucket trick shot from the foul line. Maybe the outlay was worth it after all, despite the galling frivolity. An object reminder of his own fatuity.

"Tell you what," Weinert decides. "Just this one time I think I will bet you. So you can learn how stupid it is. Five bucks, huh? And all I've gotta do is make these three foul-shots."

"Mm-hm," Nick nods.

Weinert shakes his head sadly. "Feel sorry for you, buddy. Ever heard the expression 'taking candy from a baby?'"

Weinert rarely misses from inside the circle during the flurry of a game, when it's essential to pull the trigger the second you grab the pass or slide free off the pick. The complex vector analysis and simultaneous gyroscopic integrations his brain can routinely order, often from only a sort of aural sense of where he is in relationship to the bucket, never cease to astonish him in retrospect. Over the years Weinert has experimented with various methods to achieve that same autonomic mind-body unity when the shot is deliberate. That's why free-throws are so troublesome – they're static and lull you into thinking.

Back in the days when he was still spending a couple of nights a week shivering in a sleeveless yellow mesh jersey with shiny blue plastic iron-on numbers (14), getting hacked and mauled as a center-forward on a rec-league B team (under six-feet-four), Weinert tried to improve his free-throw percentage by shooting them as jumpers. That only seemed to make him more erratic. So he started not looking at the hoop until the instant he was ready to release the ball. Worked sometimes, didn't others.

Pickup players never get to shoot when fouled, but they need a reliable free-throw too. The line's usually where those who will make up the teams are winnowed at the outset from those who're going to sit and watch. So Weinert has continued all his life to hone this skill. And to tinker with it. His technique as it has evolved is once again methodical. Maybe 80-, 85-percent effective. Probably higher this afternoon. All it takes is one brick, though. Like the one he put up in the clutch before. This time he'll shoot faster, he decides. Get more fluidity from more spontaneity....

See? Thinking again, he realizes. Already mulling departures from the routine he's found most successful.

He bounces the ball once, twice. Spins it in his palms. Scrutinizes the rim, visualizes the swish. Crouches, still visualizing. brings the ball up. Flicks.

Swish.

"One," he declares.

Nick taps the ball back impassively. Weinert suddenly wonders what Nick's actually hoping for. The obvious answer is a miss, of course: Win the wager, humble his father, gloat, feel superior....

Or maybe just feel equal. Prove Weinert's fallible too – the hulking authority-figure as prone to miscue as the weedy kid.

Not that that's much of an issue with the authority-figure. All this macho, in-your-face verbal swagger's just the stylistic hallmark of the game. Caroline would be quick to point out the puerile insecurity that underlies this *de rigueur gasconade*. Every athlete knows he's going to fail. Those who do it least are those who're best at suppressing the certainty in any given situation.

Like being a husband, it occurs to Weinert. Or a parent.

"So which," he grins at Nick, "is gonna make you feel better, you really think? If I mess up and show you I've got feet of clay, so you end up with your ten bucks? Or if I make 'em, the way I'm gonna, and show you I'm still Power-Pop? Deadeye Dad. Mister Basketball USA, Senior Division. Leave you poorer but with your Pride in Poppa intact."

Nick snorts. "Yeah, right."

"Just wondering."

"Which one you think?" Nick mutters.

"Mm-hm," Weinert nods. "I can imagine."

He bounces the ball and squares to the hoop. "But you know what, Nick?" he says. "Either way the bet's off. I've changed my mind."

"Why?"

"Just have," Weinert says.

"You're scared."

"Nah. I just don't like putting money on it. Gambling's a real waste, as far as I'm concerned. I don't want to be giving you the wrong message. There's enough excitement in just competing, one on one, or against yourself – that's where the real thrill of victory and the agony of defeat is. You got a problem if you've gotta artificially spice it up."

Nick shrugs. "You wouldn't 've paid me anyway. I already figured that."

"Sure I would've. If I said I would."

"Whatever."

"No, I *would've!*" Weinert insists. "Not that

I'd've had to, of course. I'm gonna *win* this bet. Only it's... what d'you call it? A gentleman's bet. Right? No money. Just every ounce of self-respect you and I have got. That's what's riding on it. Right? My very manhood. "

He dribbles the ball.

"...Depends on.... "

He springs off his toes and only then, ball cocked overhead, does he switch his gaze from Nick to the target.

"...Whether I bury this or not. Whoops! Guess what. Bingo! I'm still a man."

Nick slouches at the edge of the key with his right wrist snagged loosely behind his back in his left hand. Chest caved, face blank, he watches the ball fall through the net and bounce in front of him. He doesn't stir.

"Hey. You gonna get that for me?" Weinert inquires as the ball trickles away toward the ivy bed.

Nick stares off as if entranced by a big black-and-white dog snuffling for picnic leavings in the sand under the playground slides. He shakes his head.

"Ah. What? Copping a bit of an attitude, are we? Do I detect the scent of poor sportsmanship?"

"You got legs," Nick replies.

"Mm. So I do," Weinert acknowledges. "Thanks a lot for reminding me."

He sighs and goes to fetch the ball. He understands. This is customary: the hex. Nick is trying to interrupt his rhythm, scramble his psychic attunement.

The light is getting thicker. The sky over the eastern ridge is a limpid indigo, but a bank of evening fog has risen off the bay, above the treetops to the west. Time to let Nick get back home, Weinert thinks. Tonio'll be up in his loft, rap music thudding through the walls. Caroline at the kitchen table reading her day's mail, nursing her first martini. Maybe even pouring the refill already. Quarter-inch of French vermouth carefully dripped from the bottlecap, followed by a generous slug of discount gin over the freshened ice-cubes. The image is vivid. Mixing the cocktails was among their most pleasurable moments together – the evening ritual before the squabbling got underway. Still a ritual now that they're apart. He's beginning to anticipate the martini he'll sip while he figures out what to cook for himself and Dani tonight. Spaghetti?

"Okay, whatever happens, this is it, game's over," Weinert declares as he returns to the line. "If I miss, you're the winner by default. Hurrah for you. If I make... well, you'll just have to live with the fact that you're pond scum. Eh?"

Nick doesn't meet Weinert's eye. He curls his mouth in that exaggerated, derisive smirk.

"I'll even make it harder on myself," Weinert offers, out of a sudden access of generosity and puckish spite. "Backboard."

He bends over the line, takes his preparatory dribble, looks up at the basket and immediately lets fly. He has to hit a spot on the board neither too high above nor too low against the flat bracket by which the rim is bolted to the metal crescent. And he has to strike dead-center so that the carom will pierce the hoop, not glance off it. The shot is tricky from straight on.

His aim is up to it.

"Ha-hah!" Weinert chortles. "Twenty-one! There you go – game! Sorry about that, bud. Guess we've found out who's the man and who's the pond scum. Who's the despicable slime mold."

"Eat shit," Nick grunts.

"Ah, c'mon, Nick," Weinert immediately soft-pedals. "I'm only teasing."

"Suck my dick."

"What?"

Nick glowers at the ball. Abruptly he lashes his foot at it – boots it high and far out over the grass. "Hey!" Weinert bellows. "God damn it! What the fuck...? What'd you just say to me?"

Nick turns his back and stalks away.

"Hey, I'm talking to you, man!" Weinert barks.

"Fuck you," Nick mutters.

Weinert lunges after him. "Whoa. Hold it! You wait a minute, buddy."

Nick doesn't stop. Weinert double-times, catches up and grabs Nick by the shoulder from behind. Nick ducks, twists free.

"I told you to wait up!" Weinert roars. "You *listen* to me when I'm talking to you."

"Yeah, yeah," Nick sneers.

Weinert darts for him again and tries to halt him by the arm. Nick windmills out of his grasp and starts to run. Weinert snatches at Nick's tee-shirt and snags a finger in the collar along with a fistful of sleeve. He jerks Nick to a flailing halt.

"Let go of me!" Nick snarls. His face is crimson, puckered with fury. The collar-band of the kinked tee-shirt bells around his scrawny neck as he bucks. Weinert gives ground, like a wrangler playing a lassoed bronc, so the straining fabric won't rip.

"I said I want to talk to you."

"Get your fuckin' hands off me!" Nick bawls. Tears brim from his lashes. "Fuckin' asshole!"

"Shut up, Nick."

Weinert is making an effort, staying calm. Reasonable. "You're only diggin' yourself deeper. "

Clutching the bunched shirt with his left hand, dancing in tandem, Weinert is at least subliminally wary. But Nick has never tried to hit him before.

There's not much he can do to fend off the punch anyway. It has snap and all Nick's sinewy bodyweight behind it. It lands at the base of Weinert's left pec – resounds, amplified, through the hollows of his lungs. He feels the pain simultaneously in tender muscle and brittle bone.

No apparent calculation is involved. Reflex knits Weinert's fist and launches the instantaneous counterpunch. His knuckles clack off the ridge above Nick's left eye. Nick sprawls to the ground.

It's the first time since he was younger than Nick that Weinert has swung at anyone. He's aghast — as if his arm were Dr. Strangelove's, governed by some synaptic pathway and malign agenda all its own.

Nick lies at his feet, arms and legs splayed. His cheeks are flushed, nostrils a brilliant sniveling scarlet, brow aflame. It's only that big ripe pimple, though, Weinert recognizes.

No, Nick shows no marks. Not yet, anyway. No pallid incipient bruise, no nascent technicolor shiner. Too soon. But really, Weinert's sure, the punch couldn't have done all that much damage – he was on his back foot when he threw it. And Nick was recoiling. Which is mostly why he fell. Hey, rule it a slip, not a knockdown.

He'd obviously compensated for Nick's evasive dip, though. And desperately upflung hand. No question, he was aiming to connect. His blood thrums in his temples. He's appalled.

"I'm sorry," he blurts. "That wasn't right. I shouldn't have punched you."

Nick struggles up on an elbow. His eyes are filmed by tears. The pupils don't seem to be dilated, though. Nah, nah. No way, Weinert tells himself, he could've caused a concussion.

Nevertheless, the punch was for real. A flashing, compact overhand right. Bam on the money, even though the target was bobbing....

Ah God, Weinert moans inwardly. Shameful. Inexcusable. Striking his kid with a closed fist. The very definition of child abuse.

"I shouldn't have done that," he apologizes again. He shakes his head in anguish. "I didn't mean to. I'm sorry. I'm sorry. Although if you swing at me. "

He's been swung on maybe three times in his life. The last occasion not much more than a year ago, actually. It's fresh in his memory. He was playing at an unfamiliar neighborhood court, three on three, a smooth-faced, intense young black guy with dreadlocks guarding him. All over him – constantly pushing, shouldering, hand-checking. Every time Weinert broke free inside, the guy simply tackled him. Disgusted, Weinert finally took the ball back about 30 feet, until the guy relaxed, then launched a rainbow that wrung whoops of incredulity from the spectators on the courtside bleachers when it fell. Weinert sauntered toward the guy to set a screen for the inbounds play and was greeted by a punch in the face.

Fortunately he reacted to the in-rocketing fist in time to flinch aside. It grazed his cheekbone – he found a tiny welt when he showered that evening. Fingered it with reminiscent pride for a day or two. To have annoyed the guy that much! Flamboyantly burned by some old white dude. Who then nimbly slipped the sucker punch too.

But old white dude didn't swing back. You kidding?

Trumpeting his outraged dignity, Weinert stalked to the bleachers and resolutely sat.

"Fuck that!" he declaimed to the assemblage. "I'm out. That's bullshit, man! I'm forty-five years old, and I'm supposed to fight some twenty-year-old kid 'cause I make a bucket on him? That's fucked, man! Somebody take my place."

The guy just glowered. And Weinert in fact did eventually allow himself to be coaxed back out on the court to finish the game.

"C'mon, baby, be cool," the other players admonished his antagonist. Who slacked off enough to yield Weinert the winning tip-in.

"I thought that's what you were comin' to do to me," the guy mumbled afterwards – the implausible explanation for his preemptive strike.

Doubly crazy. Because Weinert has *never* struck. Certainly not first. Not even second.

"I'd've put that motherfucker *down*," a burly, bearded black spectator who looked to be about his own age observed jovially to Weinert after the game. But Weinert didn't regret his principled retreat. He'd fractured a metacarpal once punching a wall after a bad loss. He knew exactly how little satisfaction he'd have felt nursing another throbbing, knuckle-sprung hand – not to mention a flattened nose, split lip or frozen jaw – expended in defense of some chimeric honor. Even if he decked the son-of-a-bitch, he knew, he'd only feel sullied. Invincibly immature.

And that's the point. No matter how grave the provocation, Weinert has always found reason to hold back. He's always avoided mixing it up, always refused to retaliate.

Though he's never fled. Never cringed. He takes major comfort in that. Nick and Tonio have heard the story of how, well after midnight one New Year's Eve when he was 18, Weinert and two friends returned the shouts of a passing carload of guys from another high school after a dance at a downtown hotel. The car veered to a halt on the deserted street and the three occupants lurched out belligerently. Weinert's companions immediately bolted. Weinert was startled by his abject abandonment, scared but unwilling to sacrifice self-respect. Hands in pockets, he sauntered on. The three toughs roistered up behind him.

"What'd you say, pussy?" one demanded.

Suddenly he felt a muffled thump against the nape of his neck. He was wearing a cotton teeshirt, a blue Oxford-cloth shirt, a rep tie, a V-neck wool sweater, a sportcoat, a plaid wool scarf and a thick tweed overcoat with the collar turned up. The rabbit-punch barely registered through all that padding. But the concept – assault from behind – infuriated him. He wheeled.

"Did you just hit me, God damn it?" he roared. "What the hell's your problem?"

The louts eyed him uncertainly.

"All we said," Weinert squawked righteously, "was 'Happy New Year!' You got ear trouble? Anyway, I'm not gonna fight you! I don't have any reason to fight you! Three," he snorted, "on one."

He turned his back and resumed his deliberate

stroll. He spotted his fair-weather pals two blocks ahead, crouched behind a parked car, timorously watching. His would-be assailants drifted away.

One twilit evening at the U.S. Naval Station, Subic Bay, afoot and bound for the officer's club in his tropical whites, Lieutenant (junior grade) Weinert rounded a warehouse near his destroyer's berth and was met by an approaching enlisted man. The seaman was unknown to him – presumably headed back to the carrier in whose wake they'd been riding plane-guard for the past two weeks. As their paths converged, Weinert noticed that the guy's jumper was soiled and his hat mashed askew over booze-bleared eyes. They drew abreast and the seaman cocked his arm. Weinert's right hand dutifully twitched toward the bill of his cover to return the salute – a laughable irony. Because this salute whistled in at his teeth.

Weinert jerked aside. His cap flew off but that was the only damage he suffered. Without a word, the sailor took to his heels. Weinert snatched up his cap and – anger supplanting astonishment – sprinted after him.

For about six strides. Until he imagined what would happen if he caught up. Reflected on the unpleasant scenario that would follow – the futile, sordid *lèse majesté* of a fistfight between an officer and a drunken enlisted man.

Anyway the guy was so bombed he didn't even keep running. Weinert trailed along at a curious distance. Was the poor weaving sap *compos mentis* enough to appreciate the shit he'd just wallowed into? Striking an officer! Attempting to, anyway, thanks only to Weinert's lightning reflexes. Either way a court-martial offense.

He must be working off some smoldering generic grudge inspired by some particular officer, Weinert mused. And God knows, there were assholes aplenty sporting bars on their collars. Especially on carriers. He'd almost talked himself into forgiving and forgetting – after all, the crux of the incident was that the guy hadn't managed to lay a glove on him. But then he emerged from behind a shed and found his quarry had mysteriously vanished. Weinert scouted the side alleys with mounting bile and urgency, dashed up the gangplank to the carrier's quarterdeck, festooned with brass and fancywork, to ask the Marine guards if anyone had just come aboard.

"No, sir," he was told.

He wondered if the jarheads were lying to him, noncoms protecting one of their own against the enemy. His attitude had undergone a one-hundred and eighty-degree turn. Mercy's one thing, fumbling the initiative's another. Once the guy had gotten away with it – and safe from actual confrontation – Weinert seethed with vengeful fantasies of the punchout *perdu*.

Safe. From real physical jeopardy. That's what bothers him now.

Nick lolls on the grass. His facial muscles have gone slack. He's opaque again, interior inaccessible. "It's okay," he says. "Don't worry about it."

Nick doesn't seem to be in pain. He hasn't lifted a hand to caress the spot where Weinert socked him. His lashes are still gummy but he's not crying. He's absolutely composed, matter-of-fact. Almost amiable.

"I didn't hurt you," Weinert inquires.

"Mn-mn." Nick shakes his head and wrinkles his nose dismissively. "You can't hurt me."

"Ah, Nick." Remorse enables Weinert to swallow back the urge to argue the contrary. "I certainly don't mean to hurt you. I don't *want* to hurt you. I never want that."

"You didn't," Nick repeats. "It's okay."

"No it's not – not okay, punching you," Weinert insists. "That's wrong. And I apologize."

"It's nothing, really. Forget it."

"I'll tell you something, though," Weinert says, cupping his sore pectoral. "You sure as hell hurt *me*." Nick regards him in sharpened focus.

"Naah."

"What do you mean, 'naah?' I'm the one who's feelin' it."

"I didn't hit you that hard."

"You did so! Right under the muscle, you got me. One of those sharp, pointy little knucklebones of yours. Diggin' in. Right here in the side of the boob."

Weinert massages the spongy tissue – muscle and fat, the only place on his body besides his abdomen that's begun to accumulate an extra layer. "Vulnerable spot. Even on a man. And the rib. Ouch. You pack more of a wallop than you realize. Little creep."

Nick is getting good at masking his reactions. But Weinert's tone and flinty half-grin are reflected by a tic.

"Which is one reason you'd better never try it again," Weinert adds soberly. "You take a poke at me and I can guarantee you I'll defend myself exactly the same way. You're just gettin' too big and too dangerous. Next time I might do you some real harm, too. Not that I'd like to, or want to, or mean to, but it's just an automatic reaction. So take warning. I may not believe in hitting you. "

"Yeah," Nick grunts. "Right."

"I've never hit you! Have I? Punched you?" Weinert objects. "Until now?"

Nick smiles sardonically.

"Hey. I've given you spankings. I've slapped your cheek a few times. You're right. I *have* lashed out and whapped you kids. but only when you've really driven me to it. Some people would say that's bad. I'm not saying it's ideal. It's human." He gestures with his palm. "But I've never touched you with anything other than an open hand. Have I?"

Nick shrugs.

"Well I haven't, and you know it. And I've never done anything more than make you guys' booty-butts or your cheeks sting for a minute or two. Right?"

"When Mommy used to spank us it really hurt," Nick reminisces. "She always used that wooden hairbrush. Till we hid it."

"You hid it from her?"

"Yeah, Dani and me."

Weinert is amused at this revelation of sly enterprise. "Where?"

Nick narrows his eyes shrewdly. "Somewhere."

"Never mind," Weinert says. "Her method's too cold and calculated for me. I only believe in bare hands. And the violence of the moment."

"Like when you threw the mashed potatoes at Dani."

"Mm."

"I hated it the way she got all freaked out."

"Well. The way she was behaving I thought she deserved it," Weinert explains.

He has to modulate his grin. There's something exhilarating in the memory of these sudden, messy

173

outbursts, indulgences in pure id his loved ones have learned to respond to with equal vigor.

"And she threw hers back at me. So it was fair. "

"And her plate. And her milk."

"Yep."

"She went totally crazy. The way she was acting all hysterical?"

"She was pretty upset. But we screamed at each other for a while and then it was all over and we cleaned it up. We'd gotten everything out of our systems. That's the good part about when you just let go of your emotions, your anger."

"No. It's stupid! She didn't just get over it, like you say. Remember how freaked she was? What you did to her was really, incredibly," Nick sneers, "stupid!"

"Yes. It probably was," Weinert allows. "Obviously was. I do lots of stupid stuff."

"That time you pegged me with that little car? I've still got a thing here I can feel from that." Nick runs a finger along the helix of his ear.

"Yeah." Weinert winces. He nods. "I know, I know, that was a bad one too. That was a mistake. I thought it was just soft rubber. I wouldn't have thrown it otherwise. That was definitely something I'm sorry for. And you can still feel it?"

"Sometimes," Nick nods.

"I had a teacher in high school who had a keycase, one of those little leather things where the keys fold up inside 'em?" Weinert approximates the size and shape with pincered thumb and index finger. "And if somebody was talking in class, whispering behind his back – he'd be at the blackboard writing the lesson or something – and this teacher'd just quietly listen, and he'd kind of triangulate, and he'd narrow it down, and he'd figure out exactly where it was coming from, and meanwhile he'd just sort of casually stick his hand into the pocket of his cassock – which is this black robe they wear. "

"You had priests for your teachers?"

"I've told you that! You know that. I went to where?"

"How should I know? I forget. Saint Something."

"Mm-hm. Saint Xavier High School. Saint X. In Cincinnati, Ohio. Actually, most of our teachers were what's called scholastics. That's people who're still in training to become priests. Jesuit priests. But so anyway... all of a sudden this particular teacher, who was named Mister Bell. "

"Mister? How come not 'Father?'"

"Because he wasn't a priest yet. I just told you. I think it was Bell. Doesn't matter. Anyway, the point of this story... if there weren't so many interruptions... is that suddenly he'd whirl around and he'd just wing that keycase at the guy who'd been talking! Fwip! Tk!"

Weinert pops his tongue and pummels his left shoulder with the heel of his hand to illustrate the ricochet.

"And he'd always be right on target. And it'd be the right guy. We always wondered how he knew."

"How *did* he know?"

"I told you. He'd triangulate. We thought he was psychic or something, but all it was, was... he told us later... was that he'd just figure who sat where, and how far back the noise was coming from, and who was the most likely person in that part of the room, and which row, and which desk, to be the one providing the commentary. He was

175

uncanny, too. Not only at picking out the right guy, but he was a deadly shot. He'd get you on the arm, or the ear, and I'll tell you. When that thing even just nicked you, it hurt like hell. Sometimes he'd just spin around and whip off the piece of chalk he was writing with. Fwick! Tk! 'Ai-ee!'"

Weinert accompanies his sound effects with more wrist-snapping mime and a gawp of astonishment.

"How many times 'd he get *you*?"

"Actually, I'm not sure if he ever did. Although I certainly accounted for my share of talking in class."

"Boy, if anybody ever did something like that to me I'd kick their ass!"

"Mm-hm. A teacher."

Nick scowls. His voice has quickened with angry fervor. "I don't care who it is! If somebody threw a bunch of hard keys at me. Or a piece of chalk."

"Yeah, well, I hope you wouldn't."

"That could put your *eye* out or something! That's the stupidest thing I ever heard of! That guy must have been a total *asshole*!"

Nick's invocation of the motherly bromide— like "don't run with scissors"—strikes Weinert as droll. Especially juxtaposed against his truculent illusions. This from a kid who's supine after a solo jab. But he's annoyed at the moral Nick has drawn.

"We *liked* him," Weinert counters. "We thought he was cool."

Nick shakes his head. "Sounds like a real dickhead to me."

"He was a perfectly good guy!" Weinert exclaims. Nick's descriptive further offends him. "Wouldn't you respect somebody who had that... I guess you could call it a talent? And who wasn't always all uptight and prune-faced and bureaucratic about discipline? I mean, that was the main thing. We were kind of scared of him, sure. But personally I'd a lot rather get hit with a piece of chalk than get sent to jug."

"Jug?"

"Detention. After school. It's what we called it. Or get a bunch of notes sent home to your parents earnestly complaining about what a 'disruptive element' you were being to your hard-working classmates. The way we've had to put up with *you* guys. Tonio, especially. I wish a few more of your teachers would just ding you."

"Thanks."

"Of course, nowadays you're right. No teacher could get away with it. They'd be kicked out of the classroom in about five minutes. All the outraged parents'd complain about how their precious little darlings were being abused. Our parents just thought we were getting our just deserts."

Nick regards him without affect.

"You know that expression?"

"Unh-unh," he says. No interest in learning is apparent.

"What we deserved. Justice. We broke the rules, bing-bing. Punishment. Fits the crime. No big deal."

"You must've had mean parents."

"Maybe by today's standards."

"Must not've cared much," Nick huffs, "what happened to their kids."

"On the contrary. I think they cared a lot. They cared about our attitudes and behavior, too. We could never have gotten away with the stuff you kids do. The foul language... talking back. It would *never* 've occurred to me to raise a hand to my father or mother! Wouldn't even have *occurred* to me!"

"What'd've happened if you did?"

"Frankly, I haven't the foggiest."

"Think your Dad'd've punched you?"

"I don't know," Weinert says. He was Nick's age when his mother went to the hospital for her mastectomy. He, his younger brother and baby sister visited her there, pale and drowsy behind the screen. She never came home again. Afterwards his father faded into the near distance. Abstracted by grief, balding, wizened from lack of appetite – he was about as old as Weinert is now – he spent most of Weinert's adolescence brooding under a solitary lamp in the living room, only occasionally shambling off to sweeten his highball.

His Dad's mother, their grandmother, nearly eighty, cared for the household. He'd been an athlete, his Dad, in youth. A semi-pro baseball and basketball player before law school. He wore dentures to replace teeth lost breaking up a double play. He used to regale Weinert with tales of cagey cage mayhem. And when he finally perked up and remarried five years later, he zestfully reengaged his brash collegiate son in vituperative, fist-slamming dinner table arguments about politics and religion.

"Yeah," Weinert nods. "I think he probably would've. Like I... as I said, though, the circumstances just wouldn't have arisen."

Nick has made no move to regain his feet. Now that his color has waned, Weinert can see a lingering red smudge at Nick's temple.

"I hope to hell they won't arise again with us, either. Right? Think we could agree to that?"

Nick's gaze slithers away. He hitches his shoulders

and pulls a sour face. It's assent, if grudging and equivocal.

"I'm sorry about what happened," Weinert says. "Except you did bring it on."

He takes a step forward and extends his hand. "I apologize."

Nick stares down at the grass between his knees. He scratches at a dime-sized black scab on the cap of one.

"Not that an apology from you mightn't be in order too."

Nick distractedly taps his left eyebrow, winces. He looks up at Weinert and hastily resumes prying at the scab.

"C'mon, tough guy," Weinert says. "Here you go." He waggles his outstretched fingers and leans closer to make the companionate boost-up easier. Nick rolls aside and scrambles erect on his own. He dusts off the seat of his baggy purple shorts.

Weinert lets the hand fall. "'Kay," he grunts. "Guess it's time you got on home to Mommy's. She'll be mad if you're late for dinner."

"We don't eat this early."

"Whatever. Go get started on your homework."

"She's probably making something disgusting anyway. Chicken livers. Swiss chard. That's one thing about being at Mommy's house. I hate her cooking."

"She's a great cook," Weinert objects.

Nick wrinkles his nose. "What're you guys havin'?" he mutters.

Weinert shrugs. "I haven't decided yet. Hot dog stew maybe?" Suddenly he's very thirsty for the astringent, icy martini he'll sip while he dices celery and opens cans of tomato sauce.

"Wish I could eat with you."

"You will again soon enough."

"Sorry I kicked your ball."

"Oh. Hm! Well. Okay. I was probably needling you too much. Tempers get lost."

He arches an eyebrow. "Just don't ever do it again."

"Did I really hit you hard?"

"Yep. Don't remind me. Now go get the ball. That much I'd appreciate."

"Sure," Nick nods. He turns and trudges off toward the stocky old live oak whose drooping branches shade the base of the long slope up to Caroline's house. The ball rests in a crook of its exposed roots.

"Just toss it back over here," Weinert calls after him.

He walks to the bench, buckles the black rubber strap of his watch to his wrist and shoves the Swiss Army knife anchoring his keyring into his hip pocket.

Not so long ago one of the older regulars at his favorite basketball court, a guy named Don who also happens to be white and a writer, got knocked cold by another habitué named Zeke, a wiry, abrasive black guy of about thirty who treacherously punctuated a bit of routine mutual woofing with a vicious uppercut. Don said it took weeks before he could chew meat or compose a satisfactory sentence. Said he's still unable to remember the argument, or being struck. When the cobwebs cleared he filed an assault charge. Nothing seems so far to have come of it. And the pall cast by the incident on the afternoon games eventually dissipated. In fact, Weinert recently saw Don and Zeke playing against each other again with chary punctilio.

The thing is, Weinert has often stood jaw to jaw with Zeke, muscles tensed, adrenaline in flood, rabidly yapping about some alleged moving pick, over-the-back rebound or blocked shot *cum* hack.

"All ball and you know it!"

"Fuck you, cocksucker! Foul!"

"Another one of your typical cheap-ass calls!"

"Who're you calling cheap-ass? You fucking fouled me!"

"That was nothin' but ball, motherfucker!"

...Until disinterested arms wedged them apart.

One morning as he poured boiling water over the grounds in his coffee filter, Weinert fell to musing about why, with his temperament and history, he's so seldom had to cope with the challenge of an actual fight. The answer, he decided, is simply that he's big. Thin and asthmatic as a child, he's never thought of himself that way. He's definitely afraid of being hit in the face. But since he shows quick reflexes and doesn't quail, his adult height and physique have apparently served to discourage casual attack. Or insistent pursuit. Certainly nothing to complain about there.

Still, he's occasionally worried that his lack of the masculine experience of crashing a fist into somebody's physiognomy owes more to cowardice than restraint. At least it's now evident that, given the right prod, his aggressive synapses do fire. Like confirming you can still get it up after the first episode of post-divorce impotence. The wiring, anyway, is intact.

To tell the truth, he's pleased at the punch. The sensation seems to be on a kind of automatic, random mental replay. And each time the kinetic memory kicks in, he experiences a *frisson* of satisfaction. Biff, bop. Nick thumps him in the chest, he unhesitatingly uncorks the pay-back right. Tidy and efficient. No awkward, airy roundhouse. Chin tucked in... elbow high... neat loop over Nick's parry... wrist twisting... locked on impact. Crisp, clean contact where you want it, across the crest of the knuckles. Classic Golden Gloves technique.

Yeah, deployed against his kid. A spindly thirteen-year-old. A head-and-a-half shorter and a bantamweight wringing wet. Lot of threat there. Real risk of reprisal. What a testament to his valor that he finally chose to haul off on that opponent.

Took his own son, though, to land the first square blow. Because he smartly went for the body.

"Hey!" Nick is shouting across the meadow.

Weinert is already squinting at him. He nods. Nick hops, rears and slings the ball with a motion that spins him into a full three-hundred-and-sixty-degree follow-through.

The ball travels about seventy feet in the air before it bounces.

"Wow! Good heave!" Weinert calls. He strolls forward to field the approaching grounder. "Great form, too! You're a natural for the hammer-throw!"

Nick smirks. He bows his head and plods up the incline.

"See ya," Weinert calls.

Watching him go, Weinert feels an ache, a constriction deep in his chest as physical as the emanations from the bruise below his nipple.

He steps off the paved path and has to skate for balance momentarily as the rubber sole of his basketball shoe skids on a tuft of slick grass. Pain gouges his groin. Already his lower back is beginning to stiffen.

He crouches gingerly to scoop up the ball, grunts as he straightens, lumbers back to the bench with a deliberate, twisting stride that's not quite a limp but cushions the impact of his footfalls on his hips. Bending for his sunglasses he uses his knees instead of his waist – the stately, spine-favoring "bunny-dip" they used to teach Playboy Club waitresses so their boobs wouldn't spill out of their bodices.

This is what it's come to.

He slides the earpieces of the dark glasses through his hair, damp with sweat, and wiggles the hinges to adjust the pads on the bridge of his nose.

The world is suddenly dark gray, dreary. Perfect analogue to his mood. To the taste on his tongue.

He lets the ball drop and bats at it with his left hand, dribbling idly as he crosses the court toward the steps leading to the street and his car. Passing under the basket at the far end he flips up a perfunctory little bank-shot. Even that doesn't fall – it trickles off the sagging rim. The top bolts of the bracket have pulled loose. The front of the canted hoop dangles a good two inches low.

He feels an urge to leap up and snatch at it. Wrench out his frustrations, shame, disappointment. But, of course, he's too tired and sore. And, more to the point, too old. He probably couldn't reach that hoop anymore if he wanted to. As he's just found out.

Well, he does still have quick hands.

Hey, Weinert tells himself. Everything'll be all right.

He tosses up one last, careful bunny.

Only way out of a slump: Shoot your way out.

What's eating at *you?*

"Huh?" he replied, looking up from the morning's *Times*.

She handed him one of the two glasses she was carrying. "I asked what's eating at you."

"Thanks," he said. "'Eating' at me? Hm. Nothing. Why?"

She lifted an eyebrow, turned and walked to the couch. She lowered herself onto the far cushion.

He sipped through the ice cubes and set the glass aside on a stack of books piled on the table by the armchair in the corner by the fireplace where he was sitting. He watched her, frowning quizzically.

"You seem to be in a bad mood," she told him after a moment.

He knitted his brow tighter and tucked his chin into his neck, burlesquing puzzlement. "Why do you say that?"

She bent forward and plucked a *Sunset* off the scatter of magazines on the low coffee table.

"Just the way you've been acting," she said.

He sat up straighter and folded the newspaper onto his lap. "I don't get it. How have I been acting?"

"Like you're in a sour mood."

"Ah. Ha." He nodded. " *Quod erat demonstrandum* . Thing is, though, my dear, irrefutable as that circular argument may be, I am not, in actual point of fact, in a sour mood at all. I am in a *fine* mood."

"Mm."

"Really! Maybe I've just been kind of quiet since I got home."

"Maybe."

"That's my story, and I'm sticking to it," he bantered.

"Whatever."

"Hey! I'm *telling* you! I'm in a perfectly fine mood. I was tired after walking up the hill. I sat down to relax, take the load off. I just thought I'd read the paper for a few minutes."

She compressed her lips and waggled her head. "I'm not arguing. It's no skin off my nose."

"Of *course* it's skin off your nose! Otherwise why would you be bugging me about it?"

"'Bugging.' Isn't that a bit *passé*?"

"Thank you for keeping me *au courant.* In the slanguage department."

"Don't mention it."

"What I still want to know is what I was doing that projected 'bad mood?'"

She off-centered her mouth derisively. "Right."

"'*Right!*' What kind of answer is *that?* How am *I* supposed to figure out intuitively whatever it was that made you think something was 'eating at me?' *Nothing's* eating at me!"

"I'm glad to hear it."

"Are you?"

"Hey, don't jump all over *me!* Just because *you* seem to 've come home in some kind of blue funk tonight."

"But what I'm telling you is I *didn't* come home in any kind of blue funk tonight," he wailed. "Or green or fuchsia or puce or any other goddamn color, for Christ's sake! And I'm *not 'jumping all over you!'*"

"Hey."

He drew a breath to calm himself. He let the

air out loudly through his nose. "Just a little lunge," he murmured, "maybe. Grr."

Her mouth curled in a long-suffering smile. Without looking at him she picked up her drink, sipped and put the glass down. She swiped her index finger across the tip of her tongue and flipped a page of the magazine.

It was a habit of hers that had always bugged him. Annoyed him, he corrected himself. His grandmother had done it. It seemed antiquated, stodgy. And low caste somehow. Certainly unhygienic.

"Did it ever occur to you that when you lick your finger like that to turn pages you're leaving your germs all over 'em for other people?" he commented.

She gave him a sidelong glance. "What do you think I *have*?"

"Dread lurgy. Who knows?"

"It *has* occurred to me," she agreed. "Since you never seem to tire of reminding me."

"And you indefatigably pay no attention whatsoever."

"Indefatigably."

"You think there's no legitimacy to my concern."

"You could say that."

"You don't believe in the germ theory of disease."

"I don't believe anybody except you, maybe, is going to pick this up after me. And that's not very likely itself, is it?"

"One of the kids...," he proposed.

"Who would not otherwise be exposed to my germs either. And who's really into *Sunset*. Right?"

"We have guests."

"Yes, that's been known to be the case from time to time," she nodded. "Though they do not usually sit around reading our magazines. Deadly as the hospitality around here can get."

"Let's see. I'm the one who's supposed to be in the sour mood."

"I was in an *excellent* mood until you came home."

"Ah. That certainly makes me feel nice. All *hyggelig*. A real...."

"What?"

"...Compliment. *Hyggelig*. Cozy-comfy. Welcome at home."

"What's that?"

"Norwegian. Or Danish."

"Pretty esoteric."

"Really? I see it all the time these days. Suddenly. For some reason. It's always seemed to me like the *mot juste*. You've heard me use it before."

"Not that I can recall."

"It just *sounds* more warm and fuzzy than anything in English."

He pursed his lips, to achieve the full effect of the *y*. An umlauted *u*, producing a cross between hoogle-y and higgle-y.

"*Hyggelig*. Doesn't it make you want a big *hygg*?"

He blew air-kisses at her with guppy-lips and hitched his arms, elbows out, the gesture constrained and probably indecipherable because he still clutched the newspaper in his left hand.

Her mouth curled briefly, sardonically. Her interest had apparently been captured by something in the magazine.

He considered heaving himself upright out of the chair and walking over to enfold her in a hug. But from experience he knew he'd have to haul her off the couch struggling. Maybe just resistant *pro forma*, maybe not. Exquisite vigilance would be required. The tug-of-war would be as likely to trigger anger and a real hissing, kicking fight as ameliorate the atmosphere, no matter how keenly reactive he was in desisting. Or he could plop down beside her, his sharp hipbone digging into her plump flank, cooing parodically as he wormed an arm around her shoulder. Peck her on the cheek, coax her into a quick, conciliatory smooch and snuggle before she got up to finish cooking. The signals weren't propitious.

He drew a long breath and sighed it out. "So. Where are the kids?" he asked. "They gonna be home for dinner?"

"Jock's at Roger's, helping him work on his car. Steffy's got a school project. She's at her friend Michelle's and might sleep over. So it looks like it's just you and me tonight."

"Great. A romantic *tête à tête.*"

"What a prospect."

"Try to restrain your enthusiasm."

"I *would* be enthusiastic. I just have this sense of storm clouds looming."

"Well, then your sensor's busted."

She bugged her eyes skeptically.

They sat in silence for a moment.

"And how was *your* day?" he inquired brightly. He hoped the trite question and the exaggerated lilt would convey good humor.

She continued reading for a moment before looking up at him and answering, "Fine. Better than yours, apparently."

"Oh my God," he groaned. "Will you let it go? My day was utterly unremarkable! Absolutely without incident! Completely uneventful!"

"Well then. Who could ask for more? Kind of

the zenith of human fulfillment. No wonder you're so upbeat and cheerful."

"Yes, I *am* fucking upbeat and cheerful!"

"Oh, indeed. And that's precisely what I'm responding to."

"I don't know *what* the hell you're responding to."

"I'm responding to the bad vibes you've been giving off from the moment you walked into this house. *Listen* to yourself! You think it's enjoyable to be around that?"

"*Listen* to myself! *What*? What are you hearing? That I've started fucking swearing every second fucking word?"

"Okay, just stop. Right this minute. I mean it. I don't find that funny, in the least."

"Nor is it meant to be funny."

"I do not intend to spend the little bit of precious relaxation time I've got in the evenings being subjected to your... whatever. Foul-mouthed fulminations."

"'Foul-mouthed fulmi...' I like it. Nice alliteration. *Perfect* alliteration, eff and em."

"That's precisely why I asked you what was bothering you to begin with. Try to figure out what kind of unpleasantness I could anticipate."

"You could anticipate *no* unpleasantness. Because nothing was *bothering* me!"

"So you keep saying. And so I say, 'Wonderful.' You've convinced me."

He stared at her, waiting for the other shoe to drop. She studied the magazine.

He sipped at his drink.

"You mean it?" he asked finally.

"Sure. Why not?"

"All these 'bad vibes' you're supposedly

detecting?"

"I must've been mistaken. As you said."

"Whoa. *Quelle admission.*"

"I assume you retired behind the newspaper with scarcely a word," she said, looking at him, "and then I start hearing all these piteous, deep-chested sighs... and as soon as I come in and sit down and start talking to you, you begin ranting and yelling at me, 'Christ this,' 'fuck that'... hey, it's all because you're such a happy camper."

"It's my peculiar way," he nodded.

"'Peculiar' isn't the word for it."

"I'm being sarcastic," he said, as if it were necessary to explain. "The problem is, you've got those things all run together. As though they were a seamless continuum. You left out the catalyst. In the middle."

"Why should you be so tired if your day was so uneventful?"

The *non sequitur* startled him. He tilted his head and rolled his eyes, mugging Jack Benny-like to the invisible audience attendant on postmodern life. He glimpsed his lo-ball glass peripherally. Reminded, he picked it up and took another swallow.

"Maybe that's *why*," he offered.

"What are you... on Ibsen?"

"From *hyggelig*? Good guess. Actually, it's Strindberg at the moment."

"You know, I've always wondered. Did anyone ever actually see those two together?"

He smiled, a lopsided, tight-lipped, patronizing grimace. "My yahoo wife. Yes, in fact, dear. And Ibsen's older. He wrote *Peer Gynt* in 1867, twenty years before *The Father*, which is Strindberg's first play. Or mature play. And in Swedish, I might remind you. *Svensk* " He translated mentally for the practice, trying to differentiate the singsong cadences. "...*Är inte norsk och... og norsk er ikke svensk.*"

"So that accounts for three hours."

"Mm."

"What else?"

"Worked on the book, of course. Lunch with Richard at the faculty club. Usual idle chitchat. Couple of students came in, to talk about their theses.... Why am I telling you this? It was a day like all days. 'filled with those events which alter and illuminate our lives.' And I was there. More or less. Mostly less, it would appear."

"Such a cushy existence," she said. "And all you seem to get out of it is *ennui*. That's really sad."

"So... what!" he bristled. "Did the earth move for *you*? Is that what you're saying?"

"I wouldn't go that far."

"I don't need your pity. It's not sad. I've got no complaints."

"Maybe you should."

"Maybe I *should!* But I *don't!* Except when my wife starts telling me I'm giving off bad vibes."

"You were."

"*I was not!* I was giving off *no* vibes!"

"No vibes is bad vibes," she improvised.

"I was giving off *fantastic* vibes! Is what I meant to say. My *usual* vibes — joy and peacefulness and light. Good will to men, and women especially. Wives. Wit at the ready. Full of virile competence. Quiet husbandly ardor. "

"Yeah. So quiet you'd need an EKG to detect the faintest life-sign."

"Very amusing. But I'm telling you, when I

walked through this door, crabbed and meaningless as my workaday circumstances may be — and thanks to you, darling, for pointing that out to me with such withering clarity — I was happy as a fucking *clam!*"

"Gee. Clams and crabs. Together in the same sentence," she said. "The shore dinner."

"No, it's missing the fucking lobster," he growled.

"But it does have the corn on the cob. And why do these crustaceans of yours seem inevitably to be engaged in intercourse?"

He grinned in spite of himself. Immediately it turned Jack Nicholsonian. "Don't you think that somewhere *something* has to be getting some?"

She narrowed her eyes and stared at him intently for a beat. "And that means...," she challenged.

"Nothing," he immediately backed off. "Just a cheap shot."

"Not even *that* ! It's just... *point*less! If the implication is you're not getting any. As you put it so crudely."

"Well.... When was the last time...?"

"You can't even *remember*?"

"Of course I can."

He counted off mentally on his fingers. The nerve ends tingled sequentially on his right hand.

"It was Sunday morning," she prompted him. "*Sunday morning!*"

"I knew that," he acknowledged sheepishly.

"Wasn't it! And this is not frequent enough for you."

"I didn't say that."

"A man of your advanced age. And general physical...."

"Decrepitude," he gamely finished the thought for her. "And hideous aspect. And boring, one might even say spiritually barren, soul-rotting life."

"Couldn't've put it better. You should be thankful you're allowed to come within sniffing distance of a woman."

"Oooh," he leered, "that's dirty. I love it when you talk dirty."

"What you said was that somewhere some clam, some lobster, was getting more than you do."

"Actually, I don't think. "

"Or *implied* it! Obviously, that can only mean one thing. You're not getting as much as you think you should be."

"No. No. No," he soothed her. "Okay. That is, of course, I guess, the premise of the joke."

"Joke, you call it."

"Rhetorical sally. Whatever. I was merely going where the, you know, where the setup line took me. Path of least resistance. When at a loss, aim for the groin."

"Lame. Was what it was. It was beneath you. And very mean-spirited."

"I'll accept that."

She fished in her glass and worked an olive free of the ice cubes. She popped it into her mouth, closed her molars on it and took a sip. She set the drink aside, chewed for a few seconds, then said, "So. Who's this Rhetorical Sally? Is she somebody I should be worrying about?"

He rewarded her with a laugh.

"Damn. I knew I'd let that name slip one day. Same way you got wind of my affair with... *Praxis* Sally, was it?"

"No, really. Is that what's eating at you? Is that it?"

"What."

"I don't *know*! *Are* you in fact nursing some

simmering dissatisfaction with our sexual relationship?"

"No, no. You make it sound so woman's-magaziny. But I can honestly say I'm not."

"You sure there isn't some little poopsie you're yearning after? Is that the real subtext here? Some succulent, fawn-eyed little student you're mooning over? Maybe some perky blonde instructor I haven't met yet. That you'd like to be bedding on the side. Or maybe already are!"

"No! Although you do set up a couple of very appealing straw-women."

"So I guess I *ought* to be steeling myself for another bimbo eruption. Eructation."

"Ah, 'eructation.' I like that too," he nodded. "Clever twist. Although I'm not sure it actually means anything."

"You get the sense." She wrinkled her nose and wagged her head. "Really ugly, distasteful, swinish behavior."

"The bimbo burp. Also alliterative. With a certain trailer-trash internal consistency."

"You're avoiding the question."

"I don't believe there *was* a question. But in any case, I've already given the answer. No." He paused for emphasis. "No." He paused again. "A thousand times no. You have nothing to worry about along those lines. I am so far beyond anything like that it is inconceivable to me."

She lifted her glass to her lips again and drank, eyeing him fixedly over the rim.

"And I could be asking *you* the same thing, I guess, obviously," he continued. "*Should* be asking you, as a sensitive mate. Do *you* have issues about our sex life? Is there...?"

"'Issues,'" she scoffed.

He bowed sheepishly. "Excuse me. Too long inhaling the fumes. Picking all these years without protective gear in the groves of academe. "

"Yeah, well, try Berkeley High," she countered. "That's why I'm so sensitized."

"I can imagine."

"'*Iss*-ues,'" she repeated, this time with an exaggerated, sibilant British pronunciation. "Do I have *iss*-ues...? *Around*! You're supposed to say you have *iss*-ues '*around*' something. Don't you know that?"

"I forgot," he said.

"Do I have iss-ues around our... what did you call it...? 'Sex-life?'"

"So-called sex-life," he agreed. "Mm."

"Right. And there you *go* again!"

Her hand shot up from her lap. She pointed at him with a snap of the thumb and middle finger. The motion was sharp, like drawing a pistol. "That *is* what's eating at you! It *is*! *What*! *What about it*? *Spit it out!*"

"It is *not*!" he insisted. "You keep suckering me *into* these things."

"Oh, *I'm* to blame. For your snide insinuations."

"Yes."

"Esplain me!"

The mocking phrase, mimickry of a foreigner's accented, mangled grammar, was part of their private idiom. Her use of it distracted him for an instant. It was endearing. But it also piqued his curiosity, because he realized he couldn't recall the explicit source. Some old sketch. *Fawlty Towers*, maybe... the Spanish waiter...?

"Um," he said, forcing his brain back from a

rummage in the memory stacks. "You, uh... you just keep sending up these huge *target* balloons! I can't resist." He added in a trailing murmur, "I am flesh. I am weak."

"O-o-oh!" she crooned. She squinted. "O-o-ooh! You want to talk to me about *target balloons?*"

He'd said it. He submitted manfully, like one of the martyrs. He sagged back into the tall chair, shoulders splayed, as if baring his chest above the newspaper. The image of a famous painting of St. Sebastian flashed across his brain-screen. Mantegna, he thought. In the Louvre, if he remembered right. Arrows protruding from the willowy, chiaroscuro body.

"Fire away," he invited her.

"You don't see *me* compulsively firing away, though, do you?" she blurted.

He wondered if she'd been subliminally influenced by his words, which had preceded hers by only a couple of syllables. Or did their minds, after all these years, now run, as another of their shared quips had it, in parallel circles?

She'd heard the echo too. She smiled and hitched her shoulder. "Great minds...," she murmured apologetically.

"I guess you're stronger than I am," he allowed.

"Am I not flesh too?" she persisted. Again they'd spoken almost simultaneously. "Do I," she added, naturally, "not bleed?"

"Yeah, you bleed."

She grunted. "Maybe not for all that much longer."

"The jury's still out on the flesh part," he continued. "Women are made of sterner stuff. Metal... tee-ell-ee, huh? Mettle. And you are unquestionably the prototypical Iron Maiden. Well, Matron."

"I'm surprised you didn't say 'Crone.'"

"I'm merely striving for accuracy on your hymenal status. 'Matron' is in no way a demeaning term. Maybe you'd prefer 'doxy.' I've always liked that one. Has a kind of jaunty air. Boobs flying out of bodice."

"Now you're suggesting I'm a *whore*?" She goggled at him, exposing her upper teeth ominously. "Are we back to *that*? *Surely*...!"

"*No no* no no no! I think of 'doxy' as. "

"I don't care what you *think* of it as! It means a *whore*! A prostitute. Don't start wimping out on me on *definitions* now! You of all people."

"A woman of experience!" he maintained. "But it doesn't have to be... altogether out of *wedlock*, does it?"

She glared at him. "This conversation is going downhill fast. Really really fast."

"I'm *complimenting* you," he insisted.

"'Boobs flying out of bodice.'"

"Youthful and carefree. When I say you're an Iron... Doxy...."

"It's about as insulting a description as I could envision! For any woman!"

"Not at all! It combines grit and...I don't know, gaiety. Upbeatness. Sensual exuberance."

"That's the first time I can remember you accusing me of being exuberant. Or sensual."

"You have your moments."

"What about the 'Iron' part? That's the operative word here, isn't it? *Isn't* it! Just more of your code. For what's eating at you. You're saying you find me cold and hard. "

"Hey, you *are* hard. But not cold. Hard in a good way." He mugged at her.

"I suppose you'd be happier if I were willing to give you blow jobs."

"Aww! God!" he exclaimed, recoiling in astonishment and, oddly, revulsion. Which he literally experienced in his crotch. Not only did the suggestion come out of left field, it was unseemly... and remarkably unappealing in this context. Which was no context. To be sure, he would not.... He commanded himself to stop. He had no appetite for speculation on this subject, whether internally or externally, in the present circumstances.

"Isn't that....?" she persisted.

"*Hey!*" he silenced her. "Hey hey hey hey *hey*! Don't *go* there! *Please!* This is not the time, nor the place. Nor is it my *'iss*-ue!'"

"Well, *something..*!"

"No, *nothing...*!"

"Why are we *having* this argument then?"

He sighed. "Why are we having this argument?" he repeated under his breath. "How often," he said in a louder voice, "have I asked myself that question?"

He plucked his drink off the table and filled his mouth. He put the glass back and swallowed

"You know, dear" he said. "Upon reflection I have to amplify and amend my previous statement. Let the record show that in fact you *do* puncture all my balloons. Systematically and with great glee... and quite skillfully, I might add. Every time I doltishly lob one up...."

He raised his right hand languidly, palm supine, wiggling the fingers.

"...Pop! We go at each other like Punch and Judy. Like a couple of circus clowns, with long stickpins...."

He stabbed the air with his pincered thumb

and forefinger.

"Pop. Pop. Pop pop pop pop pop pop pop. Been doing it for years."

"Well, then that's truly a sorry commentary, isn't it? What kind of a marriage is that?"

He thought for a second. "Highly verbal?" he proposed. "Interesting, maybe?"

"Sounds sick to me."

"Traditional..."

"Traditional how?"

"How far back does Punch-and-Judy go?"

"Ugh. *Horribly* sick!"

"But in a good way."

"No. A bad way. The worst way."

"Healthy way, perhaps. Inevitable. Don't keep stuff locked up. It's the nature of the beast. Beast with two backs."

"I don't think so. I don't think people who love each other are supposed to be always tearing each other down."

"But we're *not*! Not in public, anyway. Or in ways that really count. Are we? It's just in private that we get off on hoisting each other on our own, on each other's... petty petards."

She drew in a long breath and exhaled through her nose. "What exactly is a petard?"

"Ah. Jeez." He found himself at a loss. "I *used* to know."

"I always think of it as like a codpiece," she said. "And I sure ain't got one of those."

"No. A petard is...." He shook his head. "Definitely something else. Hamlet? In French, *peter* is 'to fart. '"

"It *is* kind of like we sit around trading farts."

"Bomb! I remember now. A mine of sorts. That

goes *off* like a fart. Sappers put 'em under castle walls."

"'Hoist?'"

"Yeah, blown up. Hurled into the air. You know? I mean, you could hardly say someone was 'hoist' on his own codpiece, could you? It's anatomically impossible."

"Mmmm."

He could see her mulling erectile contortions.

"But you could work out a *great* bit of stage business if it were someone *else*'s petard. If that *meant* 'codpiece,'" she qualified. "One actor backs into the other's codpiece...." She lifted her chin abruptly, whistled and then made the blatting sound of low comedy with her tongue between her lips. "*Wheeep!* Pthpthpthhh."

He laughed. "Listen to you. See what a bawdy wench you are? You doxy."

"Hey, *I'm* not the one who's doing the complaining."

"*I'm not either!*"

"Oh yes you were."

"I *was not! For crying out loud!* You've been projecting completely! I never said a word."

"You don't *have* to say anything. "

"Apparently not."

"Your behavior gives you away."

He raised his eyebrows ironically.

"Don't I know you better than you know yourself?" she teased.

"Conceivably."

"So come on. Admit it. You were in a foul mood. And it's taken *me* to get you out of it."

"It took *you* to get me *into* it! I can't think of a more foolproof method, either! Accuse someone who's not in a bad mood of being *in* one, in a bad mood. Then refuse to accept denials. Pretty soon you'll have 'em groveling on the carpet, pounding their fists and foaming at the mouth, gnashing their teeth in a helpless fury."

He reached for his drink absently, but as he lifted it from the table he was suddenly aware of his cocked elbow, the cylindrical heft around which his fingers were cupped, the familiar tension in his biceps and shoulder, the slight amendment and intensification of motion that was all that would be needed to send the missile hurtling through the air. To explode against the wall or shatter a window and transform the dead air of frustration into the hurly-burly of consequences.

"...Or throwing the props around," he added.

She scowled. "A scene we've observed all too often. "

"Mistake to 've mentioned it," he muttered ruefully. "Fortunately, though, I've matured. I've attained true inner peace."

"Better hope so. Because if an episode like that ever does occur around here again, you'll be watching me and my bags vanish out the door faster'n you can say 'Presto-Change-o.' Count on it."

"Oh, believe me," he retorted, lips drawn thin against his teeth, stung by her gratuitous threat, "if I weren't a man who'd undergone a complete change-o, a man who'd finally broken through to clear, you'd've been ankle-deep in broken glass with gin trickling down the walls half an hour ago! At the least."

"Meaning what?"

"What 'what?'"

"'At the least.'"

He belatedly suspected her inference. He wasn't

certain what he'd meant. The time factor, he thought. "Meaning nothing," he said.

"Meaning you'd've *attacked* me. *Physically.*"

"Oh great," he moaned.

"Slapped me around, punched me out."

"Oh good heavens. Why in the world would you jump to that?"

"Yeah, why?"

"Hey, let's get off this track right now! I have *never* slapped you around or attacked you physically. And you know it."

"Please."

"This is something I'd forget?"

"Apparently. Or conveniently repress."

"*When* did I attack you?"

"Let's not get into that. But you did. If you recall honestly."

"I grabbed you, maybe."

"And left big purple bruises. Took weeks to heal." She idly massaged her upper left arm. "You threw me down."

"You tripped! Come on. And you bruise easily. And it was a different time. I didn't know *how* husbands were supposed to behave when they found out their wives were cheating on 'em. All I...."

"As their husbands had on *them*. For years."

"Not years. And I only did it out of love...."

"Oh!" she yelped.

"*Grabbed* you! *Grabbed* you, I mean. You refused to *talk* to me! You kept walking *away* from me!"

"You kept *stalking* me!"

"I wanted to discuss things! You were making me *crazy*!"

"You *frightened* me! I was scared of your temper.

Rightly so, as it turned out."

"Did not."

"I had no idea *what* you were going to do. Or what *I* wanted."

"Jesus," he said mournfully, "*listen* to us! You know what we sound like? The cheapest melodrama in the world. Cliché after cliché after cliché. It's disgusting."

"It's our life," she murmured.

He gazed at her. Her head was tilted pensively. She met his eyes, filled her chest with air and slowly sighed it out.

"But it does not make for the most delightful or uplifting cocktail-hour chat. Does it?" he said.

"I would have to say no."

"We agreed a long time ago to lay all that stuff to rest."

"We did. The past is prologue," she said.

"Yeah. And the present is dialogue. Bad dialogue, unfortunately, for the most part, but...."

"And the future will be... a better kind of logue. If we keep working at it."

"Epilogue."

"No, that's too obvious. And too depressing. As if everything from here on out is just an afterthought. *Dénouement*."

"Hyperlogue? What's the Greek root for 'good?' *Eu*.... Eulogue."

"Sounds like 'Yule log.'"

"Which is *hyggelig*! Any kind of log would be an improvement on this... kakalogue!"

"Damn straight!" she exclaimed.

She bounced forward on the cushion, bobbed her head emphatically, hiked her glass to him as if in toast and drained it to the ice chips in one quick gulp.

He mirrored her actions.

She snatched the magazine off her lap and slapped it down on the coffee-table pile. "Okay! *One* of us had better get cooking. Can't say this hasn't been fun. "

"*I* can say it hasn't been fun."

"Oh, you've been in a pissy mood from the get-go. Who gives a shit what you say? You were spoiling for a fight all along."

"Frankly," he said, "at this point I couldn't tell you *what* kind of mood I was in at the get-go. You've put me through two or three complete spin cycles."

"What else is a wife for?"

"Maybe we can think of something later."

"I doubt it." She cranked herself to her feet. "We may not eat until nine-thirty. I'll just warn you now."

"Anything I can do to help?"

"Aren't you generous?" she said over her shoulder. "Not at the moment. Set the table in a little while. And you'll be on your own completely tomorrow, don't forget. I've got rehearsal."

"I know," he acknowledged.

She went into the kitchen. He sat staring at the empty doorway. Dandling the empty glass in his hand. The way he would a baseball.

After a moment he bowed his head and chuckled.

He stood up, quartered the paper and laid it over the damp ring on the top book on the table. He strode toward the sound of pots clanking.

"Ain't marriage a hoot?" he called cheerily. "So, what's on the menu tonight? Besides potted spouse?"

California Standard

L arry woke up on the couch where he'd fallen asleep the night before in front of the TV set. It was Bri's voice that had slowly infiltrated his oblivion. The child was on all fours under the coffee table, sliding one of Larry's shoes around and making noises as if driving a toy car. The soft "mrrm-mrrm"s were soothing. Larry kneaded his brow and gummy eyes. He yawned, rolled on his side to blink at his son. It wasn't often that he got a chance to enjoy Bri in a subdued, completely private mood.

After a moment, Larry became aware of the open Coors on the table-top at eye level. He stretched his hand for it automatically. He didn't really want that old flat residue on his coated tongue, he realized instantaneously. The flimsy aluminum floated up empty anyway. He'd bet Bri had drained whatever had been left in the can. A tolerant, paternal smile cracked across his sandpaper jaws.

Empty or not, a sour beer aroma — and the stale smoke of cigarettes tinged with the faint pungence of the three roaches in the ashtray among the butts —permeated the gloom. The drapes were still drawn. Good thing. Larry had a headache. But that seemed to have become a permanent condition. He closed his eyes and drifted on the sound of Bri invisibly at play below him. In the kitchen, Marie was humming tunelessly to the radio.

Once he announced his wakeful presence, Larry knew, the Saturday morning tranquility of the household would slowly vanish. As if he were some swirling ridge of pressure, some "upper level disturbance" that inevitably provoked storm in itspassage. He lay inert under that certainty, pressed mournfully into the thin, lumpy cushions by its weight. In a while he'd sit up and try to play with Bri… give off some wrong vibration, suggest some forbidden turn of interest and end up with the kid squalling. In part, maybe, it was the cold Bri seemed to have had for the last six months. Greenish mucus seeped from his nostrils constantly. Bri's thin, sallow face was encased in a perpetual membrane of dried drool-and-tear-thinned snot, like isinglass. Larry was a little bit at loose ends with a two-year-old anyway. Maybe when he was old enough to talk, to play catch with….

Marie dropped a dish or something. He heard the shattering crockery, heard her curse. Three months with him at home every day, underfoot. That had to be nerve-wracking. They drank coffee together in silence well into the morning, dispiritedly watched the game shows and soap operas and trade school commercials. Use your GI bill to learn air conditioning repair. Call today. Before long he'd crack a beer. His friends were all at work, of course. Every other Wednesday he'd pick up his unemployment check, and every so often he'd drive off on a round of job-seeking. Trouble was, they'd promised he'd be put back on at the oil refinery as soon as things picked up again. And the area didn't offer a lot of other industries, unless they moved, or he commuted about two hours each way…. Not that he'd found anything.

The room suddenly erupted in squeals of strident irritation. Bri seemed to have butted his forehead into a table-leg. Larry sat up abruptly, kicked his feet to the floor and bent to soothe his son. Bri was apparently startled by the looming face, blood-shot and grizzled, and the groping paws. He shrieked. Larry scooped him up by the chest.

"Hey, partner," he murmured.

Marie came around the corner from the kitchen. "What on earth did you do to him now?" she asked sharply.

Bri flailed in Larry's grasp. "Mama, mama," he yowled.

All expectancy for the day seemed to drain from Larry's chest. Anger spurted up into the void, then collapsed like a leaden ball in his stomach. "Nothing," he muttered, as he handed Bri to Marie. From his expression, he might almost have been caught at some shameful molestation. He went into the kitchen in his stocking feet and dropped two slices of Wonder Bread into the toaster.

Vince came over at 9:30. He'd promised to help Larry clean the Toyota's carb, and he'd brought a pocketful of joints. Every so often they'd drift into the garage. Larry kept dropping tools and getting grease on himself. Somehow Saturday, which was supposed to be a relief from the humiliation and ennui of his abnormally domestic week, wasn't working out.

At noon Marie opened the kitchen door and found them leaning on the car's radiator, pulling hungrily at dirty cigarette butts.

"Finished yet?" she asked.

"Just did," Larry said. "Feel like makin' us some lunch, maybe?"

It was a bright day, but with a kind of wan brittleness to it. A hard, steady wind from the Baysliced between the low hills and pastel fuel storage tanks rising to form the rear horizon. A couple of cows grazed under electric pylons near outcroppings of rock on the distant knolls. They'd be developed soon too. The enclave of pink- and lime-colored stucco houses around them seemed to absorb the diffuse light smoldering through the veil of wind-blown dust. The spindly trees studding the tract's parched yards gave no protection from either.

"Why don't we take the boat out or something?" Marie proposed. She was still wearing her curlers. She banged a bathroom wastebasket against the inside of a galvanized garbage can. A few dry snips of hair and stiffened Kleenex wads escaped through the white pickets of the side gate and kicked down the street on the breeze. "I'm going stir-crazy in there with Bri. He could use the sun anyway."

Larry looked at Vince, whose answer was a shrug and grin.

"What about Debbie?" Marie asked.

"Debbie's buying stuff with the kids. She'll be out all day," Vince said.

While Larry took a shower, Marie put together a lunch and Vince helped. Larry could hear their droning conversation and occasional laughter over the electric razor. His temples throbbed to its buzz and he froze twice, sure he had detected angry words in the rising mutter — tiny mechanical jeers and accusations. He reached into the medicine cabinet and popped two Ritalins. He counted five left in the bottle. He emptied them into his palm and dropped them in his pocket. His image in the mirror seemed to smear, to leave blurry trails at each movement like the whites on a TV set with the contrast tuned too high. He washed the caps down with a swig from the can of Coors he'd set on top of the toilet, and combed his long, damp hair with his fingers.

They got a ticket on the way to the marina. A gust of crosswind made Larry swerve and bite the freeway shoulder. The puff of dust drew the unwelcome attention. He was doing seventy, and Marie had been suggesting he slow down. The CHP black-and-white sirened them over from three dips back, where it had been lurking unseen. God knew what that was going to cost. With Vince holding and Larry already spaced— he swilled the incriminating remains of the beer he had pinched in his crotch when the cop was out of sight — Larry had to rein his reactions sternly. Luckily his eyes were masked behind aviator sunglasses well smudged with Bri's fingerprints.

They passed the cop's scrutiny. Bri, bucking and screaming against the restraints of his kiddie seat in back, probably helped accelerate the transaction. Larry, in a fury of frustration and self-pity, could have moaned. He slammed his fist against the rim of the steering wheel as he pulled back into the slow lane. The cords in his neck stood out twitching.

"Gimme another goddamn beer!" he snarled. "And don't you say squat back there, you hear?"

He'd calmed considerably when they pulled into the marina, though. The yellow plastic sheet they used for a boat cover was crusted with salt. Brackish rainwater had accumulated in the hollow over the cockpit. Most of it ran out across the seats when they tried to gentle it up and overboard. The varnish on all the horizontal brightwork was peeling. The cockpit mahogany was rimed with a gritty film of salt in spite of the cover.

Larry unlocked the cabin hatch and found the floorboards awash in bilge water. It had been several months since they'd come down to the boat. In fact, he'd been nervous as they'd crossed the gangplank to the dock-gate — suffering from a belated worry they might find the little sloop chained to its slip and one of those cardboard harbormaster's notices fastened to the mast, announcing for all to see that he had neglected, been unable, to pay his berth rental. Christ, what a scene Marie would've thrown then! But he was only four months behind. She didn't know. So far, all it meant was an interest penalty. He was still safe for a while... probably... before they tried to auction the thing off for fees owing.

He ducked into the low cabin and pumped the bilges while Marie laced Bri into his tiny, mildewed International Orange life-jacket.

"Poor little *Stormfalk*," Marie lamented. "We've just got to take better care of her."

She paced the slip, frowning at the boat's blistered white hull paint, bleeding rust, leaky cabin-top seams. "This is criminal! This is a disgrace! You know? Dad'd just be *sick* if he ever saw it. Look at all that growth on the bottom!" Slimy vegetable trailers undulated along the waterline. "If you aren't going to look for a job, Lar, I wish you'd at least come down here and put a couple of coats of varnish on. Or caulk those seams or do something useful. While you're takin' on your daily cargo of beer and crank!"

Larry grunted defensively. "Don't see you doing anything so earth-shaking every afternoon." He'd been at her for a month to see if she couldn't maybe go back to work herself. He stowed the pump and began wrestling the outboard from its niche in the stern-space under the cockpit. He angled it up and out to Vince. Together they screwed it into the bracket on the transom.

Marie put Bri in the cabin — up forward, where the plastic flotation cushions were fairly dry. The cabin was damp, fungusy, poorly vented. She gave Bri a sandwich to keep him busy and dragged the jib bag topside. She bent the sail to the stay quickly and skillfully. Then she fed the sheets through the fairleads, nimbly knotted the ends of the ropes into figure-eights and began removing the ties that secured the mainsail to the boom. She had been sailing — mostly on this boat — since she was eight.

Larry filled the rusty tank on the outboard with gasoline. Viscous rainbow-slicks spread across the surface of the harbor from their stern when he slopped the fuel mixture overboard. The spout on the plastic jerry-can was broken, so he just had to aim for the hole as he poured.

Marie shackled the halyards to the heads of both sails. "Okay, how we doing?" she said.

Bri had begun to whimper again. She went below to restore his misplaced sandwich and to try to wipe up the mayonnaise smeared across the cushions. The gnawed top slice of bread decomposed soggily in the bilge. One of Bri's sneakers had worked off his foot and fallen into the bucket — fortunately dry — which they used for a head.

Larry and Vince strolled over to the men's restroom. Larry ate two of his five Ritalins.

They were in a downwind slip, bow first. When the men came back they untied the frayed mooring lines and walked the boat out, perpendicular to the end of the dock so that the bow faced the channel. Larry climbed into the cockpit, wound the cord around the outboard's starter rotor and yanked. It was an operation — all the while tinkering with choke and throttle — that he expected to have to repeat about six times unless he were lucky. But after a dozen tries the engine hadn't even coughed. Larry was red-faced, out of sorts, puffing.

"Here, lemme have a shot at that piece of junk," Vince offered. He elbowed Larry aside. Larry slid forward and chugged half his beer.

"Why not get yourself a real engine instead of this Tinker-toy?" Vince scoffed. He was always making fun of their little six-horsepower pusher, practically original equipment with the boat, now twenty-two years old. Marie's father had bought *Stormfalk* from the Swede who'd had it built. Vince was only an occasional sailing companion. He was making payments on his own ski-boat — a flat, shallow-hulled fiberglass platform for a 265-horsepower engine, all chrome and flaring exhaust pipes, like alpenhorns. He preferred to trailer that to the mountains on weekends.

"Crap! Spark's not firing," Vince declared. Sweating, he unscrewed the plug and shook his head over the corroded, carbon-laden tip. Then he hurled the offending plug into the black harbor water.

"Hey!" Larry objected.

"Shot completely," Vince said. "Got another one?"

"What d'you think?" Larry grumbled.

"Wanna go somewhere and try to pick one up?"

"It's beginning to get awful late," Marie protested.

Larry swirled the beer glumly in his can. "Jeez, it worked okay last time."

"You could take one outta the car, temporary," Vince suggested.

"Let's just sail out!" Marie urged. "Look, we've got plenty of wind! You couldn't ask for a more perfect day!"

"Yeah, hell. Not worth the waste of time and effort," Larry agreed. He flipped foam in a dismissive wave at the outboard. "This bastard! Ought to drop the son of a bitch overboard too, huh?"

To tell the truth, he had always felt as scornful as Vince of the anemic foreign assemblage of obsolete metric parts. The boat beside them in their double slip was a flossy fiberglass-and-teak job with a husky inboard Diesel. In general, this was not a marina in which salty old wooden hulls were appreciated. Power boats predominated, and the sailboats tended upward in opulence from their neighbors' gadget-laden, stainless-steel-fitted twenty-four-footer. *Stormfalk* – lap-strakes, tar-seamed planking, green-patinaed brass — was the definite nadir of the pecking order. At least among this caste of *nouveau* mariners. Not that Larry felt any different.

"Maybe I'll get us a nice Johnson or something," Larry mused. Forgetting for a second that he couldn't even pay the slip fee.

They had seldom gotten underway using sails alone. Since they were docked downwind, it was far easier just to putt-putt out and set the sails once they had some maneuvering room in the main harbor, or were safely beyond the breakwater.

Until two years ago when Marie's father had given them the boat as a third anniversary present, Larry had never set foot in a sailboat. He'd sneered at them. Chichi toys for snobby posers. And for all Marie's deferential instruction, he was still not entirely comfortable in it. But he'd never let on to that. He had spent four years in the Navy, after all, as a boiler-tender third class on a fleet oiler. One drunken night in Hong Kong — age eighteen — he'd had a fouled USN anchor and the motto "Death Before Dishonor" tattooed on the muscle of his right forearm. So blue water was in his veins.

Larry put down the beer and trudged forward to hoist the jib and main while Vince stowed the motor. There was a crisp westerly breeze. The jib flapped out sharply as Larry wound the halyard fast around the cleat on the mast. He began hauling the mainsail up. Unfortunately, he'd forgotten to release the boom from the short length of wire — the boom-lift — that supported it when not in use. The mainsail bellied taut immediately as he heaved. The boat heeled sharply — the big triangular sail unable to spill its air since the boom was restrained from swinging freely — and dipped beneath the protective rubber bumper lip lining the concrete dock.

"Jesus…!" Larry cried. He had pitched sideways out of his down-haul hunker when the sail filled, and since he was hanging on to the halyard already, had cranked the sail on up to the top of the mast as he fell back. A chunk of toe-rail disintegrated into splinters, gobbled off by the sharp underside of the dock.

"The boom-lift!" Marie shouted, leaping up from her seat in the cockpit. The abrupt sideways cant of the boat knocked her off her feet. She fell against Vince, scrambled upright and stumbled to reach the boom-lift shackle. "Let go! Lower the sail!" she instructed Larry

He had tried to release the halyard as soon as he'd recovered his balance and realized what was happening. But the track in which the mainsail rose along the mast had gotten rusty or gummy with neglect. The little plastic sliders sewn into the sail were stuck. It wouldn't drop. Bobbing on the ripples of the harbor, *Stormfalk*'s rail was undergoing a constant nibbling from the dock-bottom.

Larry abandoned the dangling halyard and started scrabbling at the sail itself, trying to drag it down by the armful.

Marie released the shackle.

The boom scythed outward with a clap of billowing Dacron and a creak of tortured hinge. Vince, naive spectator on the starboard cockpit seat, was almost decapitated. The swinging boom caught Larry in the stomach and jackknifed him backwards into the shrouds. He grabbed one just before he toppled between them and overboard onto the dock. The brass eye on the point of the boom gouged a shallow furrow into the taffrail of the cabin cruiser berthed next to them on the other side of the narrow dock. And then for some reason the mainsail tumbled down.

"God," Larry muttered, squinting ruefully at the scar they had inflicted on the cruiser. He fingered the raw wound tenderly and wolfed down his jitters with cigarette smoke. But, he thought, there was no reason to volunteer anything, admit responsibility — unless confronted, which seemed unlikely. He darted guilty glances up and down their section of the marina. Luckily no one appeared to have noticed anything out of the ordinary. Marie had dashed below to console Bri, who had banged his head when tumbled. Then she came up and sighed beside Larry over the rasps their own side paint and rail had suffered. That started a brief exchange about whose fault it was. Vince's presence seemed to cool them.

"Okay," Larry said, sardonically. "Ready to do it for real this time?" He snatched a can of 3-in-1 oil from the bin under the cockpit seat and squirted some into the track. Then he raised the main once more.

The wind was pushing them against the end of the dock. It came from almost due west, across the breakwater and intervening fingers of the marina, at a forty-five-degree angle to the narrow channel they had to negotiate. Larry took his skipper's station at the tiller and sent Vince out on the dock to shove them off. Marie assumed a tense, subordinate supervision. Vince tossed the lines aboard, gave the bow a hearty push outward into the channel, grabbed a shroud and swung himself onto the deck. Larry sheeted the jib tight and angled the tiller to his right.

Stormfalk lunged forward, instantaneously responsive. Except that the wind in the forward sail was too much for the rudder to compensate. Gathering headway fast, they surged directly toward the stern of the neighboring sloop.

"Watch it," Vince warned.

"Put your rudder over!" Marie snapped.

"It is!"

"Slack that jib!" Marie added, lunging for the cam cleat together with Larry.

"It is!"

Vince, tangled in the flailing sheet, was trying to squirm under the jib.

"Fend us off, Vince!" Marie yelled. "Fend us...!"

Vince had managed to clamber forward in time to absorb most of the impact with his out-flung arms. Punching at the other boat's backstay, its transom corner, anything convenient, he deflected *Stormfalk's* momentum enough to carry her bow out and past the vulnerable rudder. The target rocked and twisted in its moorings as they clattered past, but was undented. The fluttering jib slapped crazily. As Vince kicked a sneakered foot against the dock and sent their bow smartly left, Larry leaned from the cockpit and gave a last defensive nudge to the sloop's stern.

"Christ," he sighed as they curled past it. He snubbed the jib sheet taut and wound slack out of the mainsheet on its winch.

"Mind your tiller, honey!" Marie warned. "No, no…!"

Larry had neglected to shift the rudder to check their swinging bow. At the moment he made fast the jib, he was heading diagonally into midchannel — as he intended, but still turning toward the wind, still drifting left. He had cleated the sheet too far in. The back of the sail, instead of its front, filled with the fresh breeze. As soon as the sail cupped the wind they heeled and boiled ahead, accelerating in a tight left-handed circle that was driving them directly across the narrow arm of water toward the boats berthed opposite.

"Let go that jib!" Marie cried. "Shift the rudder, shift the rudder!"

Before Larry could react she had bounded off her seat and slammed the tiller all the way left, out of his grasp. He was diving to his right for the jib sheet, and wrenched it loose from the quick-release teeth of the cleat.

But *Stormfalk* was a sturdy boat. More than two tons of steam-bent oak, Douglas fir, mahogany, lead ballast and cast-iron keel weighted her classical figure. Once carrying headway, she was hard to stop. And the inlet was much too confined for leisurely corrective maneuvers.

"We're gonna crash!" Larry moaned. "Here we go again!" He vaulted out of the cockpit and scrambled forward.

With an agonizing inevitability, helpless under forces of wind and inertia that could not, once applied, be easily undone, they hissed through the water, sails flopping, and rammed nose-first into a stately Chris-Craft. Vince waggled his legs off the bow and succeeded in blunting the collision to a degree. Larry arrived an instant too late to contribute his muscle. Marie had shoved the rudder around again, seeing that there was no hope of avoiding some kind of ignominious landing, but had been unable to squeeze them into the cramped void between the two boats in the double berth.

PLUCKY DUCKY II read the chromed letters on the cruiser's transom. *Stormfalk* shuddered and reared as she struck. Her heavy brass nose-chock punched a foot-long vertical furrow in the cruiser's stern, editing its name to *PL KY DUCKY II.*

Larry grabbed a stainless-steel rail post and held the two boats apart.

"Just sheet those sails in, Marie, let's cut this crap, get the hell out of here!" Larry snarled. His face was splotched with an angry, irregular flush. "Ready? When I back-wind the jib...."

Marie nodded grimly. She sat forward, one hand on the tiller, the other clamped to the cockpit coaming. Vince, at Larry's feet, was groaning and cursing and kneading his left ankle. The owner of a robin's-egg blue sloop tied up across the dock from the cruiser had popped his head out of his cabin-hatch like a gopher from its hole at their approach. Several bystanders were dashing toward them to offer assistance, attracted by the shouts and clattering sails and obviously erratic cross-channel yaw.

The sloop-owner had hopped off his boat and now stood on the edge of the dock, gesturing at Larry.

"Toss me your bow-line! Gimme your line!"

Larry shook his head. " 'S okay. We don't need any help. Watch it!" He snatched up the clew of the jib, hooked his body between the shrouds and stretched the sail across the wind.

"Here!" the man insisted. He wore mirror-surfaced sunglasses and a fancy yellow flotation jacket. He made a stubborn swipe at their jibstay and snagged it, dangling far out over the water, hanging by his right arm from the cruiser's inboard taffrail corner. As he glanced down, a frown twisted his mouth agape as he caught sight, from that acute angle, of the outlines of the missing letters in the cruiser's name, the dented stern and cracked paint where seam compound had been warped loose by the impact-stress on the planking. If she'd been going any faster, *Stormfalk* would surely have holed the cruiser's transom.

"Look, you did some damage!" the guy said.

"We'll leave a note when we get back, talk to 'em later," Larry growled. "Let go! We're goin' out!" He had relinquished his grip on the cruiser's railpost. Under the force of the wind in the jib, the bow strained to fall away. The guy had to release their stay or find himself being tugged dangerously horizontal over yawning harbor. He let go.

"Thanks." Larry grinned evilly. "See ya."

"Not if I see you people first, skipper," the man replied. He raised his voice, calling after them. "I know who you are! I'll be sure to let Griswold know too, don't worry!" He jerked his thumb at the cruiser.

Larry opened his palm in a smug wave. "'Preciate it, friend," he called. His fingers had been knitted into a fist. He d been within an ace of hammering it down on the guy's wrist.

They threaded the channel and tacked out through the marina harbor without further difficulty. Larry, humming a chantey of obscenities, busied himself coiling down lines. Marie steered. Vince rose and limped back to the cockpit.

"God, you guys sail by ear, huh!" he cracked.

Marie managed a pained smile. Vince rotated his ankle experimentally. "Bent the mother some kind of funny way when we hit that Chris-Craft. Speaking of which… what about that?"

Marie shrugged. "Ask him. Commanding officer, if I remember."

When Larry came back to the cockpit Marie rose wordlessly and offered him the tiller. Bri was mewling in full throat below. As Larry edged past her he snarled into her ear: "You ever do that again, what you did back there, and I'll punch your teeth down your throat. I mean it. Fair warning."

Marie stared.

"You know what I'm talkin' about. Takin' the tiller out of my hand that way. I knew what I was doin'."

Marie set her jaws. Fury kindled behind her eyes. She vanished through the hatch as if plummeting through a trap door.

Vince squinted at the breakwater, trying to look as if he hadn't heard.

Larry hunched on the lee of the thwart and brooded over their shame. In fact, he had constantly observed similar trains of mishap in the marina, when even fairly experienced sailors suffered lapses of judgment in tight quarters. Nevertheless, a certain embarrassment inevitably attended. Given his foul mood already, he was in no shape to be philosophical. He was angry — at himself, at Marie, at Vince for being there to witness.

He finished his Coors as they sliced past the high red marker on the north end of the breakwater. They took the first spray over the bow, and he turtled his neck into his shoulders. But his wince as the sharp needles of Bay brine dashed against his cheeks softened into a grudging grin. There was an exhilaration about this stuff, sailing, beating into the sparkling swells of the open Bay, seeing oneself as a member of that fortunate elite—"boatowner—that was intensified here.

To the west, the low coastal mountains were mottled with black-green oak and fir and even redwood. The palette itself was richer there. A few expansive houses nestled in clearings on wooded promontories. By contrast, the sere headlands he looked back on over his shoulder were a pallid, grassy monochrome — knobby bluffs cropped by the constant wind and the long vanished herds of Don Castro and his Anglo successors. Now these bare folds were stippled with gasoline storage cylinders, refinery stacks and sprawling fragments of North Bay slurb. A couple of tankers lay at their deepwater pumping piers. Off the starboard bow a silver bridge curved across the strait, arching between curiously bare and lonely little islands — weatherworn red rock whitewashed by bird droppings. Dazzling sails and creamy powerboat wakes caught the sun all around them. Hundreds of tiny white triangles clustered in the lee of a lush island across the Bay to port. The sky was cloudless except for one uncharacteristic cumulus puff scudding above the peak of the island.

Larry threw his beer can over the side. "Hey, Marie," he called into the cabin. "Gimme a beer."

There was no reply. Bri was still crying.

"Hey!"

"Get it yourself."

He looked at Vince.

"What d'you mean!" he bristled. "You're down there. I can't just drop everything, y' know. Gimme a fucking beer!" He paused. "Please? Make you feel any better?"

"I'm changing Bri right this second. You'll have to wait."

Larry flashed a wry smile of tolerance at Vince, who shrugged his husbandly commiseration. Then, after a second, Vince rose, winced as he put weight on his ankle, craned over the forward seat of the cockpit and fished up a six-pack from inside the cabin. He wrenched a can out of its plastic noose, handed it to Larry and took one himself.

"Wanna smoke a joint?" he asked.

"Sure," Larry said.

Marie came up and rejoined them. "I kind of tucked Bri in down there," she addressed Vince. "I hope he'll take a nap."

"That'd be a miracle," muttered Larry.

Marie glared at him. She got herself a beer and

227

they ate their sandwiches. She accepted a few draws on the joint.

After a while the tensions in the cockpit seemed to ease. Bri's howls became less frequent, and eventually a prolonged silence suggested he might actually have dozed off. They cruised south on a tong reach — all the way past the island's southeastern point. A panorama of city spires, wharves, bridges spread before them. Through a gap in the headlands under an orange span far away off their starboard beam, they could see the open sea. They came about. They tacked north, the island's shoreline cliffs on their port quarter, and the three of them sat side by side with their heads thrown back, basking in the hot sunlight reflected down on their faces by the tall white mainsail overhead. They polished off two six-packs and started on a third, plus another joint. Vince went forward to the lee shrouds and urinated over the side. Larry followed in a bit, hauling himself along clumsily. Masked by the main, he tossed down two more Ritalins. Marie crept quietly into the cabin—so Bri wouldn't be disturbed—and peed into the bucket. The sizzle was audible. Vince kept his head turned but Larry, further aft, stared at her.

He was seeing things now as if from a great interior distance. His inflamed eyes seemed to have receded deep into his skull behind a thick, gelatinous film through which he peered with dull intentness. He caught a glimpse of her pubic hair. A slight sexual charge had entered the atmosphere. Larry, Marie, Vince and Debbie were constant camping and boating companions, so a certain frankness about bodily functions had become inescapable. But at base they maintained a rigid conventionality. The sight of Debbie in her bikini — swelling breasts, wide hips, soft abdomen and sufficient hint of nipple under wet spandex to stoke the imagination —always set Larry on edge. Marie was taller, bonier, certainly less compliant in Irish temperament. To Vince those novelties were just as intriguing. Dark, mercuric Larry and fairer, phlegmatic Vince exerted their own diagonal appeals. But there was almost no risk that any of them would ever yield to the occasional dim fantasies.

Bri woke up as soon as Marie rattled the bucket. She dumped it over the side, dipped it into the wake to rinse it, put it back, gave Bri a cracker and brought him topside to sit on her lap. Hitched to the boat by a lifeline shackled to a ring on his kapok vest, he began squirming. After a while Marie surrendered to the child's struggles and let him wriggle free. At once Bri accidentally stamped the cracker into crumbs on the sole of the cockpit and tangled himself up in bights of the lifeline. That started him yowling again.

"Can't we stifle that kid?" Larry muttered.

"Don't talk that way!" Marie chided. She unwound Bri. "Be good boy," she admonished. "Nice Bri. Bri want cookie?"

The child stuffed the offered Oreo into his cheeks and clambered across Vince's knees toward his father.

Larry leaned forward and leered paternally into the paste of mucous and crumbs that defined his son's face. Trying to make contact, he pointed toward the receding island. "See, pretty?" he simpered in falsetto. Gulls wheeled off the beam. "See birdies? Pretty birdies?"

Bri punched out a fist at the beer can Larry was

holding loosely between his knees. Bri loved beer. His grab caught Larry off guard and tipped the can. Pungent Coors gurgled out over Larry's Levi bottoms and wool sweat socks.

"Jesus Christ!" Larry yelped. He hopped up as the frigid liquid soaked through instantly to the skin.

Bri's fingers were locked securely into the poptop hole. He yanked again. More beer slopped out on Larry's feet.

"B'i wa' bee-bee!" the child insisted. "Da-da bee-bee." At two years two months, he only issued demands.

Marie snatched him away before Larry could slap out.

"Bee-bee! Bee-bee!" Bri shrieked. He drummed his heels in ire on Marie's lap.

"Damn it to hell!" Larry' moaned. "Look at what he did."

He wrung his pants bottoms sorrowfully, ineffectively. There was nothing to do for the clammy socks. "Let's put him down below again, if he's gonna act like that, for Christ's sakes. Little bastard."

Marie's face hardened. She shook her head. "He needs sun.

"Keep him away from me," Larry grumbled. He drained what was left in the can, threw it over the side and cracked a new one.

A thin sound penetrated the soft whish of wind and wake. It was repeated — a voice.

Larry peered up in surprise. He jerked the tiller toward his hip, and they fell off with a snappy heel. A light blue sailboat came into view on the port bow. It had slipped up out of nowhere, almost dead ahead, maybe a little to starboard and heading for them nearly bow-on when Larry first spotted it and reacted.

It was less than a hundred yards away.

"Hey!"

That was what they'd heard, all right. Now the approaching boat suddenly came about smartly into the wind, parallel to their heading. Its name, *Bluechip,* was painted in a tasteful script on the transom. A figure in yellow was hailing them, waving an arm for attention. The words drifted across to them clearly.

"Quit littering the Bay! Jerk! Keep your garbage aboard that scow!"

Larry shaded his eyes against the glare, incredulous. Those glasses, the yellow jacket, light blue sloop…!

A woman and another man stared at them from the cockpit. Curiosity and amusement, smugness and contempt seemed somehow all packaged together in the trio's handsome, haughty faces, their casual feet-up-elbows-back repose, their correct, expensive nautical clothing. They were holding plastic wine-goblets.

The rebuke was tiny and strained by the time it penetrated Larry's overloaded consciousness. The inside of his head felt as if it were stuffed with a wad of carpet-padding — some densely woven, furry lining that plugged his inner ears but at least contained the echoes and re-echoes of thought, conversation, sensation long enough for him to get around to processing them. He was dealing with the world on a several-second time delay. If a little exaggerated right now, it was not a condition unfamiliar to him lately. And somehow the galvanic responses of muscles and emotions seemed not to be particularly affected.

"Might try sailing with your eyes open, too!" the guy shouted. "I was on a starboard tack!"

Larry blinked at Vince and Marie. They sat frowning at the other boat. Things were beginning to darken around the edges of his vision.

"I gave you the fuckin' right of way!" Larry bellowed.

The guy didn't respond audibly, but his companions twitched with laughter. The guy bent forward to his sheets. The blue boat slowly began to show them its name, drift abeam, curl left into the wind in lazy resumption of its previous southwesterly course.

Larry shoved his own tiller into the stops.

"Watch it!" he snarled at Vince and Marie as he fumbled around them. He trimmed sails as he brought *Stormfalk's* nose up fast into the wind. There was no gainsaying her handling characteristics. Even with a foul bottom she came to weather eagerly. When the jib luffed Larry flicked the sheet off the starboard winch, at the same time cleating down the main. He wanted to point just left of the wind. The boom abruptly pivoted overhead, slicing from right to left as the mainsail suddenly filled with breeze from the new direction. There was a shuddering clunk as the boom was snubbed up on its stern traveler. They heeled steeply to port. Larry took a fast turn around the portside winch and heaved. Gray-green water churned below him, at his elbow, the toe-rail almost awash. The winch bearings whined and the taut headsail too sucked them forward, now with a bellyful of breeze.

When the deck fell away, Vince and Marie had thrust their feet against the downslope cockpit seat to brace themselves. They hunched into their collars as the hurtling bow bit into a wave and flung spray back at them. Marie twisted her shoulders to shield Bri. The breeze had freshened as the afternoon had worn on. There were whitecaps here and there.

Marie grimaced over the cabin-top. "What... uh... what're you doin', Larry?" she asked.

He didn't reply. He hiked quickly around the tiller to the high side of the cockpit and perched on the coaming. He glowered fixedly at the blue sloop off their starboard bow. It was still coming around in a broad, unhurried turn.

"Larry...."

Yellowjacket and his sailing friends were all facing forward now — sipping their Chablis, relaxed and jocular, studying the picturesque cliffs along the island's northern point. The flood tide surged and lapped against a tumble of rocks glistening offshore. Sometimes seals lay there. A blunt-bowed sightseeing ferry thrummed out toward them through the strait between the island and the wooded peninsula to the north. Further inside, boats weaved thickly around the cove and the state beach on the island's northern shore.

"You planning to go over to the cove?" Marie said. "Because if you are...." His sullen silence had put a cutting edge into her voice. "...I wish you wouldn't." She'd had a sudden suspicion that Larry thought the nervy creep in the other boat might be headed for the cove, and that Larry was brewing up in his mind some awful unpleasantness. "It'll be a half-hour at least, just to get there," she reasoned with him. "And it's past four already. Let's head ba-*ack*!"

She yelped as a sheet of spray interrupted her. It plastered her cropped brown hair flat against the weather side of her skull. Her ear protruded from the soggy curls like some waxy fungus growth, and a viscid bead of saltwater clung to the bottom of her pinched red nose.

"Oh! God!" she spluttered. She wrung her face with a cupped hand. "This is a *terrible* course! Lar? We'll get *soaked!* Bri'll catch his *death!*" She ruffled the child's limp hair. The dousing had startled him into momentary quiet. They took another wave. Water swirled aft, bubbling along the deck. The howling wind carried most of the spray past them to port.

Larry, for God's sake, come about!" Marie shouted. She glanced forward. They were overtaking the blue sloop rapidly. "Hey! You better give that guy more room!" She peered at Larry with concern, squinted back at the sloop. "He's still coming left, Lar. D'you realize that? He's turning into you! Come right!"

Larry showed his teeth above the rim of his beer can. "He's upwind, and we're both on a starboard tack. Now he's gotta keep clear of *me!*"

"No! You're overtaking!" she cried.

Larry's grin broadened. Damn right he was! He'd maneuvered more crisply, got the jump on them. Having delivered their reprimands, having shown themselves clearly and then ostensibly opened the distance by a slow turn away to an opposite heading, Yellowjacket had presumed his safety. But Larry had cut inside the turn and led it beautifully. Now, no matter what Marie yammered, the blue sloop was crossing his bow. They'd have to bear off before him. Nor was Yellowjacket, for all his arrogance, such a great shakes as a yachtsman himself. He remained carelessly oblivious to their soundless sprint up his port quarter. Probably now was the time.

"Sea room!" Larry crowed.

His voice, of course, was whipped astern

234

instantly. The air was thick with the wind in sailcloth and rigging. Every chromed detail of *Bluechip's* hardware stood out clearly now. Tipped toward them, she could be surveyed almost in aerial plan. The very stitching in the gaudy flotation jackets of the three people in the big, high-sided cockpit could be discerned — the laces of the leather deck-shoes the male passenger had crossed before him on the seat, the wind-ruffled, razor-layered backs of their well-barbered heads.

"Sea room!" Larry chortled louder.

Marie sat stiff with disbelief. Her eyes, widening in terror, were riveted on the looming sloop. No more than thirty or forty yards away now, twenty-five, twenty….

The woman — who had been lolling on the lee side of *Bluechip's* cockpit – suddenly decided to scramble upslope to windward. As she about-faced to settle on the starboard cushions she caught sight of them. Her lipsticked mouth gawped open. Her arm jerked up.

Yellowjacket twisted on his seat. The expression that washed across his fly-eyed features was everything Larry could have hoped for.

They struck just aft of midships. Forward of *Bluechip's* cockpit. The fiberglass sloop reeled away as *Stormfalk's* bow plunged deep into her tender hull. *Bluechip* was driven sideways through the water by the force of the blow. Yellowjacket had made a last desperate, *in extremis* effort to turn away, which slowed him even more. And Larry had cannily swung his rudder hard aport at the instant before collision. Because they were both still heeled, *Stormfalk* drove on cleanly through the impact like a sharp knife incising a chunk off a roast. Her sturdy oaken stem amputated a section almost three feet long and a foot deep out of the blue sloop's deck and hull. And while the undercurve scimitared through the fiberglass at the waterline, *Stormfalk*'s brass bow-chock was ripping through *Bluechip*'s teaked cabin bulwark. A gleaming winch was sheared away. A porthole vanished in a burst of splintered glass.

Bluechip's boom, carried to port, lanced against *Stormfalk*'s cabin as they lurched together. It shivered and missed impaling Larry by inches. A hunk of mahogany molding disappeared, but otherwise *Stormfalk* had inflicted the collision at perhaps the strongest point of her entire anatomy. She had suffered little more than a few sprung hull planks and a massive erasure of her bow paint.

"Holy...fucking... Christ," Vince breathed. It had all happened so fast — and yet, paradoxically, as if in slow motion, and in an almost unearthly silence. The silence of sail. Now that he had broken it, Vince filled his lungs with air and swung around on his knee to peer across the water.

Marie was ashen faced. Things were going on in her throat, but words hadn't yet formed. She gaped, aghast, at Larry, then glanced beyond him at the receding sloop.

Larry held his head up, chin jutted forward, lips curled at the corners. He squinted into the wind. "What . . . *what!*" Marie stammered in a husky whisper. "What've you *done?*"

Larry just grinned. With lordly deliberateness, he turned his head to enjoy the scene: the bastards slowly sinking.

"What in the hell? *What in the hell!*" Marie's voice

236

shrilled upscale in cyclonic disturbance.

"Shut up," Larry said.

Marie was momentarily incapacitated, apoplectic.

"Jesus, Lar," Vince murmured. "We... gonna help 'em out or anything? We okay?"

Larry's heart was thumping in his thorax and he was somehow aware that his nerves and glands were seething in perfectly normal adrenal response. But mentally he was tingling to an exquisite calm — a numbness, actually, a detachment almost complete, founded on the liberating enormity of the outrage in which he had just indulged. It left him fortressed inside his alcohol-dulled judgment and amphetamine-stoked rancor, utterly inaccessible except at his own whim.

They had recovered headway. When *Bluechip* was perhaps fifty yards back on their quarter, Larry ducked his head and brought them about to a port reach. They circled for the stricken sloop.

But it had also tacked around with difficulty to a northerly heading. *Bluechip's* wound had been sustained well above the waterline when on an even keel, and although she had gulped down a healthy swallow of bay at the moment her hull was slashed open, Yellowjacket had had the presence of mind to come as quickly as possible to starboard. Heeled away from the westerly wind, *Bluechip's* yawning puncture tilted high and dry.

Maybe because of the water she had taken, possibly because of the jangling shock undergone by her occupants, the sloop seemed logy. She wallowed in the swells, shimmied on her course. *Stormfalk* slid abeam with ease. Larry drifted in closer as they slithered by.

"What was that," he hallooed cheerily, "about sailin' with your eyes open?"

Yellowjacket looked pale at the gills. But his rage proved tonic. He shook his fist and out-decibeled the wind.

"You goddamn... stupid... incompetent... fucking son of a *bitch*!" he screamed. "I'll sue the fucking *balls* off you for this! You fucking... goddamned ... fucking *imbecile*! I'll have your *ass*! You motherfucker! You just wait! Get the hell away from me! Stand clear!"

The other two sleek yachtspersons aboard were no longer visible. But a bright blue sleeping bag and then a plaid air-mattress and then a plug of something orange — a wool blanket perhaps — began to protrude from the jagged crater in her hull. So those other two must be down there below, Larry surmised, madly stuffing anything handy into the potentially fatal leak. Standard damage control – he'd been through that drill in bootcamp in Great Lakes.

"Sure you don't need any assistance?" Larry crooned. "Actually, you're supposed to stuff the hole from the *outside*. So the water pressure keeps the plug pushed in. Think you're so fucking smart! You don't know jack*shit*! *Do* you, asshole?"

He levered the tiller hard to port.

"How about a tow, maybe?" he taunted. "I'll come alongside!"

There was no time for Yellowjacket to evade or even react. *Stormfalk's* brass bow-chock careened toward the fat of the blue sloop's bow and wrenched off another eight-inch triangular slab of fiberglass sheathing, like a shark eviscerating a side-stroking swimmer.

Larry wanted, if possible, to bounce off the other

boat rather than wedge them together inextricably. He reversed the rudder just before the concussion. *Stormfalk*'s superior weight rattled the fine-boned glass sloop as if it were a rat in the teeth of a terrier. *Bluechip*'s shrouds twanged, snatched vindictively at *Stormfalk*'s rigging in passage. But the wood-hulled vessel bludgeoned free.

Marie came off her seat screeching, convulsively dropping Bri to the cockpit floor between her legs as she hurled herself toward Larry and the tiller.

He calmly locked his knee and drove the heel of his upthrust sneaker into the pit of her abdomen.

Marie's grunt was a hoarse baritone, torn from her diaphragm with the resonance of a man's. She doubled over his blocking leg, recoiled backwards, raked Vince's ear with her fingernail as she flailed for balance.

Vince had come up off his seat in defense. Marie folded heavily on her pelvis in the narrow space at the bottom of the cockpit, on top of his feet. Her head cracked against the mainsheet winch as she took Bri down beneath her with her shoulder. The child sat against the corner, legs pinned, wailing in startlement.

Vince plucked a foot free. Then, with a wince, the other. He climbed onto the seat and hunkered above Marie. He wagged his head at Larry with an expression as vacant as a carp's — as if Larry and all that had happened were elements in some particularly chaotic hallucination.

Larry noted the luffing jib. He wiggled the tiller to find the exact course for their set of sail. *Stormfalk* felt sound. He glanced down into the cabin for signs of leakage, rising bilge water. Saw none. He frowned back over his shoulder at *Bluechip*. She was still plowing along, heeled to starboard, grievously disfigured but with her two lacerations borne fairly safely above wave level. Her pocked bow did occasionally burrow into a whitecap. The male passenger was scrambling forward. Probably to drop the jib, Larry guessed.

"Larry… listen," Vince said. That was all.

Larry cranked the tiller over and swung them across the blue sloop's bow. He needed to trim the sails.

"Okay, okay," he said. "We're goin' back that way now." He extended his arm toward the huge green landmark gas tank at the base of the treeless hills to northeast. Just beyond lay their home marina. "Get outta my way."

He brushed Vince aside and loosened the jib sheet in the starboard cam-cleat. Marie still lay gasping, chest heaving, face raddled, on the cockpit sole. He stretched across her wordlessly and fed out mainsheet. He was on guard to field any sneak kick or punch with his thigh or elbow

They ran east.

Marie struggled up into a sitting position on the wet cockpit floor, rubbed the knot swelling behind her ear and started whimpering. Soon she was blubbering. She hugged Bri to her breast and rocked him.

Larry killed his beer — almost the whole can — in a single long guzzle. He flipped the dead soldier over his shoulder.

"Get up offa there. Get outta my way," he growled at Marie. He made a curt shooing motion and reached toward the main winch behind her.

She sniveled at him, her eyes smoldering with malice behind the tears.

"Sit over there and make it quick!" Larry commanded.

She angled herself to her feet resentfully and perched with Bri on the seat at which Larry's index finger was leveled.

"Comin' about," Larry warned Vince through his teeth. It was, he realized with a flash of anger, an unnecessary statement with the wind astern.

He kicked *Stormfalk* into a tight turn to windward. When they were scudding before it, the breeze had seemed to subside, the proper aftermath hush to descend on them. There was little sensation of speed. The flood tide ran up gently behind them, lifting and cupping their stern with an even caress as it licked beneath and past. But now, as they beat closer to the wind's westerly eye, the lee rail began to cant away. The rigging hummed in a rising pitch, the bow wake sizzled and spume spat at them as they surged again toward the teeth of the weather.

Yellowjacket had taken in his jib to reduce his way. He wanted to ride up and over the cresting waves, not bulldog through them with his porous bow. Probably he intended to limp along as far as possible on that slow northerly reach, then run the short dogleg into the marina on a nice horizontal plane. With any luck he'd make it home successfully.

Larry had designs on that luck.

He'd looped far enough away to build a good returning head of steam, he figured. Now, with *Bluechip* broad on his port bow, maybe a quarter of a mile off, he steadied up and concentrated on holding her there. Right between the first two

shrouds. "Steady bearing, decreasing range" —
he'd learned that in the Navy too, from the
quartermasters. It was the iron-clad formula for
collision.

"Larry... oh, my God!" Marie cried.

"Jesus. Lar!" echoed Vince.

Both his wife and friend grimaced out in
anticipatory horror and empathy at the maimed sloop
he had in his crosshairs.

"Light me a joint, man!" Larry ordered.

Vince goggled at him. "Hey. Hey, Lar? Buddy? No
shit! You outta your tree? You can't do this, if you're
thinkin' what.... I mean, for Christ's sakes! Let up on
the poor bastards!"

Larry chuckled. "Light me a fuckin' joint, I think I
asked."

"No, man, no!" Vince tossed a twisted glance over
his shoulder at the rapidly diminishing interval. "Bear
off! What about us? We'll damn well sink!"

Marie screamed and scrambled to the attack. She
clawed at Vince's arm to clamber around him. But
Vince too had launched himself off his backside. He
dived for Larry and cracked him across the side of the
face with his forearm. At the same time he tried to
smother Larry in an immobilizing embrace.

Larry ducked, a trifle sluggishly, which was why
his cheek absorbed the forearm shiver. But he
humped his back under Vince's octopus-lunge.

Vince grappled for a better hold and kicked his
right foot at Larry's fist on the tiller. It spun out of
Larry's grasp.

Larry bulled his shoulder into Vince's chest and
worked to drive him back into body-punching
range — forward in the acutely inclined cockpit.
He jabbed with his right fist blindly and struck

Vince on the ham. Larry had leverage, and he grunted as be wrested Vince's weight up, up, straining to muscle him over the coaming.

Stormfalk had pinched left into the wind in response to Vince's kick at the helm. She went into irons, sails flopping slack, and suddenly took the breeze again. Now it was over the starboard bow. The boom shifted, freight-trained across the cockpit like an incoming mortar shell.

A centimeter before it slammed to the end of its tether, it demolished the bone in Vince's nose.

They heeled. Vince had gone limp over Larry's burrowing shoulder. Easy as slinging down laundry, Larry tipped him overboard.

In fact, he almost went himself. But he had a handhold, and he shoved his knee against the seatback at the last instant to prevent himself from somersaulting across the coaming. Marie cowered three feet away from him.

"You wanna go for a swim too, you bitch?" he panted.

"You're crazy," she said. She stared at him as wide-eyed and wary as if he were a coiled snake. He made a sudden move toward her and she screamed, drew up her knee against the blow. But he was only reaching for the jib cleat.

She drew a breath. "Vince," she said. "For God's sake… Vince! We gotta pick him up!" She peered deep into Larry's rheumy, red-misted eyes. "Right? Right away!"

Larry snickered. He'd brought them under control again — but decided simply to circle on around to port. He squinted at the blue sloop.

Marie bounced erect and shaded her eyes. Bri was tucked over her hip. The fast movements had fascinated and pacified him. Marie panned anxiously back along the fading slick of their curved wake, searching for some sign of Vince — a bobbing head, a mound of blue nylon flotsam in the foamy chop. She chewed her lip. "He got hit by the boom, you know, Larry! Just before…. He might be out cold! He could drown if we don't find him quick!"

"Bastard," Larry muttered. "S'posed to be my fuckin' friend. Jumps me. The hell could I do?"

"There!" Marie flexed her knees in exultant relief and waved her outstretched arm. "Vince!" she screamed. "Vince!"

Larry glared sourly in the direction she was pointing. After a moment he distinguished a pale solidity among the broken swells.

"Are you all right?" Marie shouted. "Hang on!"

Vince lifted an arm limply in acknowledgment. The lower part of his face seemed blurred. Smeared, Larry realized, with dilute blood from his nose. The plunge into frigid Bay had revived him, though.

Larry rose on one knee and cupped his mouth. "Hang in there, ol' buddy!" he yelled. "It's only about three miles to shore. I got faith in you. You can make it, I betcha!"

Marie blinked away momentarily from Vince.

Larry's cheeks were crinkled in nasty mirth. "We'll send the Coast Guard out after you if we get there first!" He held up three fingers. Then folded one and crossed the others. "Scout's honor!"

They'd worn around half-circle.

"Jibe-o!" Larry sang.

Marie stared at him and sagged into her seat just in time to duck under the guillotining boom. "Larry!" she sobbed. "Have you gone insane? What're you,

244

what're you…?"

"Can it, cunt!"

He trimmed sail.

"Matter of fact," he announced suddenly, "I think you *would* do better takin' a bath! You can hold your fuckin' boyfriend's head up!"

He pounced off the thwart, punched for her chest, grabbed two fistfuls of waterproof parka and sweater beneath and hauled her up bodily off the seat. Bri plopped free under her startled arm. Larry wrestled her across the cockpit and they both fell on their hips against the lee coaming. She struggled to free herself, shrieking and pleading and cursing him in a desperate self-defense that unleashed every verbal and physical hostility she had ever harbored. She tore at his face with her fingernails and slashed open the corner of his left eyelid. Blood streamed down his cheek. She drummed her toes at his shins and scissored her knees in frantic bicycle-attack on his genitals. He hacked at her forearms with his own, trying to block her swarming slaps. Finally he cocked his right fist and drove his knuckles into her face, full on the mouth. The reverberations through teeth and bone traveled the length of both their bodies. She was stunned long enough for him to jam his left wrist into her crotch and worm it between her thighs. He heaved.

Bri's little life-vest buffered him against most of the spills he took when sailing, but it tended to exacerbate his clumsiness. When Marie dropped him he pitched forward off the seat and struck his forehead on the cockpit sole. He was already so enmeshed in his lifeline that he'd used up all the slack. Now he dangled from the cleat in the upsidedown position in which he'd landed, one sneakered foot kicking uselessly in the air, the other trussed up tight. He howled in fright.

Marie had gone into the water like a topsy-turvy beetle. The image of her frenzied, despairing cannonball had burned itself into Larry's mental emulsion — a comfort as he fingered the acrid slit in his left eyelid.

She popped up astern almost immediately. She was still close enough for him to enjoy her bedraggled coughs and gasps. She pummeled the wake in reflex clumsiness. He leered at her and then spun away to his knee, to appraise the ground *Bluechip* had gained by virtue of the mutiny.

Only after a few seconds of strategy-plotting did he absorb the urgency in Bri's tremolo and become aware of the kid's predicament.

"Jesus," he muttered. He jumped for the cleat and plucked the knot loose. Bri collapsed in a limber-backed somersault to sprawl shrieking in the tangles of his lifeline.

Larry eyed his son uncertainly. He was poised between sympathy and the last parting strands of his tenuous patience. For three and a half hours, it seemed... no, for the past God knows how many excruciating months... he had been listening to this same implacable, unreasoning, ill-humored cacophony. Only the intensity and cause varied, never the shrill, nerve-rasping frequency. It rang in his ears night and day. He scarcely even noticed it anymore. He just droned through his life on continual edge, his skull pealing to Bri's incessant squeals.

It took him a few minutes to spot Marie again. She was a good swimmer, and she'd struck out for Vince. The two of them were only a couple of pools' lengths apart when Larry luffed up to them. Their heads rose and fell with the surging, wind-roiled tide. It would help coax them toward the northeastern shore. He'd opened the hinged section of the port cockpit seat as he'd come about. Now he dragged out two moldy, sodden Navy-surplus life jackets stowed there.

Vince's hair streamed in bangs down his forehead. The whites of his eyes shone glassily beneath, like a panicked animal's. He was treading water, upright but low, chin submerged. He looked exhausted. His nose had stopped bleeding. In fact, there was no color at all in his face and he stared up at Larry without gesture or appeal, just an imploring watchfulness.

"Don't say I never did anything for you, pal," Larry called. He flung one of the life jackets sidearm out toward Vince. "I even sent Marie along to keep you company. Isn't that thoughtful? She'll be along any minute. The both of you can sing songs to each other."

Marie had been swimming a strong crawl until *Stormfalk* hove toward her. She shifted to a dogpaddle and grimaced up at Larry with cautious expectancy.

"How you doin', babe?" he inquired pleasantly.

She considered for a second, then gulped, "Help us out. Larry. For God's sake. Don't leave us here."

He smiled. "Got a present for you." He spun the other orange life jacket over the stern. It splashed her in the face.

"Oh yeah, another thing." he added. "I almost forgot."

He reached down and cupped Bri tenderly under the armpits. He hoisted the child chest-high, on display. Bri responded by arching his back, pumping his feet, bucking and punching out blindly with balled fists, gnashing his teeth and screaming between paralytic spasms of breathlessness — a perfect demonstration of the tantrum he'd been performing ever since Larry had released him. Larry bunched up the loose line trailing off the life-vest.

"Your son," he declared, wrinkling his nose, "misses you. And I think you two deserve each other."

He hurled Bri backwards into the air.

The child went rigid, described a gentle, twisting arc and plummeted feet-first out of sight. Marie had gasped and lunged as if to catch him.

Bri reappeared immediately at arm's length from her. The child was buoyed face-up — as advertised when they'd bought the life-vest. But he'd swallowed enough Bay to choke the tantrum out of him for a few seconds.

L arry overhauled the blue sloop within the space of a half a can of Coors. As Yellowjacket made a futile effort to protect his starboard side, Larry dogged him with the superior ease of a Zero dispatching a crippled Mustang.

On the first two passes Yellowjacket fell off to leeward at the last instant, but Larry turned into him anyway. Both times *Stormfalk* peeled fresh divots out of *Bluechip'* s flimsy port quarter. Through the ugly gaps in her hull, Larry could see drapery and teak-railed bunks and gimbaled lamps on the bulkhead paneling and a gallery counter with a silvery water spigot — all in half-lit disarray. There was something abject about the sight, nauseating — like a glimpse of a corpse's intestines through the autopsy incisions. Larry had fetched their boat hook topside, a long slender wooden pole with a halberd-like metal fitting on the tip. He wielded it at each impact to assure that *Stormfalk*'s battering bow wouldn't hang up in the blue sloop's guts. His vicious spear-thrusts at their cabin and cockpit coaming kept Yellowjacket and crew at bay. They cringed behind the seats or cowered into the hatch when this blood-streaked madman bore down on them. Even Yellowjacket had ceased his shouts and curses — terrified or reconciled into muteness.

After Larry's second run the passenger scurried out to the mast to hoist the jib. But *Bluechip*'s added speed only upped the rate at which she was taking water. Her bow — grotesquely herniated by the garish blobs of stuffing protruding from the hole — groveled in the seas and shook them off with a dwindling willingness. Now Larry thundered up on her from the starboard quarter. Any way she turned, *Bluechip* would lose.

Stormfalk's husky stem bashed in her starboard ribcage amidships.

Bluechip seemed to sigh, to quiver with release as her skeleton was stove and her soul seeped out. She sagged on *Stormfalk*'s bow like a *picador*'s gored horse on the bull's horn.

Larry parted them with a savage jab of his boat hook.

"Hope you enjoyed your day on the Bay, Mr. Stockbroker, sir!" he sneered. He brandished the boat hook menacingly.

He circled them until the indefatigably weather-vaning little aluminum tell-tale on the mast-tip washed under. He'd never seen a boat sink before, except in the movies. It was interesting just how fast she went.

A convulsive panic overcame the woman when the swells actually frothed into the cockpit. The men had to wrestle her out with them. They all three clustered around a life-ring and watched their wet sails gradually soak out of sight. They bleated at Larry for help for a surprisingly long time.

He sailed north. A couple of boats had apparently observed the sinking. They poked nearer curiously, out of the strait. In the residue of adrenaline he'd been oozing, he considered ramming them too. The idea of going amok, just heading on over to the cove and taking out as many as possible of these genteel, snooty bastards with their cushy job security and stock options and weekend fucking yachting togs and wicker hampers and impeccably rigged tax write-offs... the idea appealed to him. But exhaustion suddenly neutralized his malevolence.

He cracked another beer. He ate half a stale baloney sandwich he found in the cabin unwrapped. A good deal of bilge water was sloshing around down there, but he was too tired to pump.

He sailed aimlessly, drowsing in and out of intense bouts of emotion: rage, remorse, glee, anguish....

He wished he'd salvaged Vince's joints at least. He ate his last Ritalin.

He noticed a white helicopter with a red Coast Guard slash buzzing and hovering like a dragonfly far astern. It circled, banked, tilted, squatted low over the water, tilted forward, squatted again. The thwap-thwap was faintly audible pulsing louder and fainter with the wind velocity. He smoked a cigarette and watched the chopper until it flew off. The sun was settling into the coastal ridge. Flashes of gold answered off windows on the eastern slopes.

The wind was beginning to bite. He curled his freezing toes and tucked his feet under him.

He drank another beer, shuddering with each sip. His teeth were chattering. He kept his hands inside his pockets, hunched into his shoulders, guided the tiller with the crook of his arm. He'd sailed under the silver bridge and well up into the next broad bight of the Bay. The sky was turning purple. The shoreline here was almost completely rural, desolate. The wind seemed to have shifted to the north. There were no other boats out at all that he could see. He tried not to think. Maybe he could anchor for the night. He didn't like it in here, though. There was something spooky. And he'd never actually used the little Danforth anchor nested in its mildewed coils of line way up under the bow in the chains. He tried not to think. He came about and sailed south.

Just before dark he started to cry.

The world was black, but dusted everywhere with icy points of light. He realized he'd lapsed into a kind of tinny unconsciousness in what seemed the eyeblink between dusk and night. He was shivering uncontrollably. His torn lid burned with the salt crust of his tears. It scared him to think he'd been dozing out here. Near at hand, high off the water, a green beacon pulsed. A bit further away a red one answered at a shorter interval. Lighted channel towers. He was in mid-Bay, almost. After a moment he began to sort out his bearings. He was just about due west of the marina. His head pounded. His stomach was a shriveled, acid ache. The wind filled his ears.

With a whimper of resignation, despair, he surrendered to the relentless tug of consequence. He turned for home.

T he *S.S. California Standard,* bound for Richmond Long Wharf out of Estero Bay, with a draft of 32 feet and a cargo of 120,200 barrels of San Joaquin Valley Heavy Crude, had just reported Southampton Shoal Channel Light Number "2" on her starboard beam when the first mate gasped and plucked at the master's sleeve.

"I took it from the pilot, ordered six short blasts, right full rudder and all back full," Captain Erik O. Eklund, 56, testified before the Coast Guard Marine Board of Investigation. "But he wasn't carrying lights and he never even came about or made any action to avoid us. It was like… well, I guess even with the whistles and all… I mean, I guess he must've been asleep or something."

Eklund was cleared of negligence, although his evasive maneuver *in extremis* was ruled the cause of the grounding. The tanker was refloated in two days.

Spillage from the rupture in Number Three forward tank, starboard, was estimated at less than 50,000 gallons.

The oil-soaked body was discovered on the mudflats four days later by a bird rescue team.

David Ollier Weber graduated from the University of Cincinnati with a degree in philosophy (Phi Beta Kappa). He has been a Woodrow Wilson Fellow in English literature at Columbia University; an apprentice seaman aboard the Norwegian tramp steamer *MS Tancred* (he had the wheel watch between Scylla and Charybdis); a copyboy for the New York *Times;* operations officer and navigator aboard the U.S. Seventh Fleet destroyer USS HIGBEE (DD-806); a general assignment reporter for the *Daily Review* in Hayward, California; public relations representative for the Port of Oakland; editor of the employee magazine of Pacific Gas & Electric Company; and a free-lance journalist specializing in healthcare, science and medicine. He has owned classic wooden sailboats, Siberian huskies, standard poodles, cats and chickens; felled redwood trees on California's Mendocino coast and built a house from the lumber; roasted his own coffee; and remarried his ex-wife. For many years he suffered from a serious basketball addiction; post- hip replacements, he confines his exertions to fly fishing and growing olives for oil on the western slope of the Sierra Nevada. He is a father of four and grandfather of six, all boys. His wife is an Episcopal priest,

www.ingramcontent.com/pod-product-compliance
Lightning Source LLC
Chambersburg PA
CBHW060422180626
46817CB00007B/2618